The Olympian

John Baxter Taylor Jr
(Courtesy of the University of Pennsylvania Archive)

The Olympian

An American Triumph

A Novel by
Craig T. Williams

Philadelphia, 2010

PUBLISHED BY
Vintage World
700 East Main St., 2nd Fl

Norristown, Pa 19401

610.633.2968

www.vintageworld.net

ISBN: 978-0-5955094-3-0 softcover

ISBN: 978-05956170-4-3 e-book

ISBN: 978-14502610-5-0 hardcover

To Andrea Cristina Williams

&

Alexa Sophia Williams

There is in this world no such force as the force of a person determined to rise. The human soul cannot be permanently chained. — W. E. B. DuBois

Contents

The Olympian: An American Triumph

1

Truth

April 1905
University of Pennsylvania
Philadelphia

I took a deep breath before opening the door to the dean's office. His secretary glanced up, then back down at her paper as if the door had opened by itself and I was not standing there.

After several moments of silence, she finally said, "Yes?" in a martyr's sigh.

"I'm here to see Dean Adams," I said.

"Do you have an appointment?" She never allowed her eyes to touch mine.

"Well, no, but it's an urgent matter."

She sighed. "What could be so urgent that you've entered the office of the dean without an appointment?"

"I'm John Taylor. Professor Ryan sent me here for a conference with Dean Adams. He said the dean would be expecting me."

"Well, you should have said that first thing, Mr. Taylor. Dean Adams has been waiting for you."

In another time and place the strange conversation would have made me laugh. But this was not the time or place for laughter.

"I suppose he is," I said with as much sarcasm as I dared allow, "may I enter?"

"Certainly." She dismissed me with a wave of her hand and turned back to her work.

I entered the inner office to find Dean Adams seated behind his desk, his chair turned away from the door so he could gaze out the window. The light of the morning sun fell across the sill and gleamed on his balding head.

He heard me enter but did not turn from the window. "Yes?"

"Dean Adams, I'm John Taylor, and I have been sent here to discuss a pressing matter with you."

"It appears you have violated our honor code, Taylor," he said roughly, leaning closer to the window. He was paying more attention to the potted plant in the sill than to the man losing his senses just behind him.

"I have done no such thing." I pulled a chair away from his desk and sat down before my legs gave out.

He turned slightly in my direction. "Well, then, how do you suppose you and one of your classmates wrote the same opening for a term paper?"

What? I wanted to laugh. "That's not possible," I said aloud.

He made a sound that might have been a chuckle. "Are you saying you and Charles Cook worked on your papers independently and yet share the same opening statement?"

Charles Cook? The Charles Cook I knew would never write a congratulatory essay about a colored boxer. The idea was absurd.

A Novel by Craig T. Williams

"No, sir. I am saying I wrote my own paper ... all of it. Every word. Jack Johnson is one of *my* heroes. Can you imagine that he's also one of Charles Cook's?"

He disregarded this and continued as if I had not uttered a sound.

"The University of Pennsylvania takes its honor code very seriously." He turned fully to me at last, leaning forward in his chair. It creaked, and even *that* sound seemed accusing.

"Yes, sir, I understand," I murmured. "I take it just as seriously, I assure you."

He sat back, his chair tilting toward the window—and away from me. His pale gaze was steady and cold. "We will conduct an investigation into this matter."

I felt a swift surge of relief. Good, then the truth would be revealed.

"We can begin with you taking responsibility, giving Charles Cook and your good professor an apology."

The words seemed to float in the air before my face. What sort of investigation began with an assumption of guilt and an apology?

"I will do no such thing," I said.

His eyes widened. "You do understand you can be expelled for this violation?"

"Sir, with all due respect, if I were guilty, I *would* take that very seriously. But I assure you, I am innocent of these charges. I have never cheated in my life. You can't be telling me that Charles Cook wrote a paper about the boxer, Jack Johnson."

He lifted some papers from his desk and studied them as if the resolution of the matter were contained on those sheets. He shook his head from side to side, the papers whispering accusingly between his fingers. "Charles Cook wrote a paper about boxing, the first page of which I have here. It is all but identical to yours." He paused to look up at me. "An apology is required."

Defeat rose up to burn my throat. I pushed it back down—I could not give in to this. "I will not apologize. Have you read his entire paper?"

"I have read enough to know that the openings are too similar to have been written independently."

"And you assume I was the one who cheated."

When he said nothing in return, I rose from my chair and stood there for a moment, looking down at him in disbelief, wrestling to keep my anger on simmer. When I didn't leave, he spoke again, without looking at me.

"This matter is under investigation ... and you are suspended until further review."

"But sir!" I protested.

"You will receive a request for a committee meeting in the mail," he said dismissively, returning his attention to another stack of papers on his desk.

"Please hear me out!"

His gaze leapt from his desk to collide with mine so forcefully that I instinctively backed away. "Exit the door by which you entered," he said stiffly, "or I will have you removed."

"Yes, sir," I whispered.

A Novel by Craig T. Williams

I walked out past the secretary, who suddenly seemed to notice me. She shook her head as if she, too, had judged me and found me guilty. This time I paid her no mind and strode from the dean's office with as much dignity as I could muster.

The impact of the day's events had affected my body. My shoulders slumped, as I trembled with outrage and disappointment. I had done everything in my power to live an uncommon life. I had used my athletic skills to make my place in the world and had spent late nights studying and preparing for class so that my exceptional work would at least be regarded as "good." To have my hopes and dreams snatched away by a man such as Charles Cook—a man who already had the world at his feet—was beyond comprehension.

Where did I go from here? How did I explain to my parents that I had been accused of cheating? How did I look my dear Mary Agnes in the eye and tell her that the man she respected and loved had been labeled "dishonorable?" What would I say to my coach and teammates?

What could a man say when the virtue he had lived his life by was erased in a single day?

I mustered all the power in my body to make my way out of the administrative building without displaying my anger and despair. The faces of the other students were a blur to me; all I could see clearly was the flag waving in the wind over Franklin Field. I moved toward that familiar ground as if pulled by a magnet. I had to run. Running was my saving grace, a not-so-ordinary talent I possessed. There was a freedom in movement against the wind that could not be put into words. This was my sacred ritual and rite of passage.

Passing through a sea of students, I made my way across campus. As the track's ranks of bleachers came into view, my legs began to move on their own. I sprinted the rest of the way, weaving in and out of foot traffic and dodging the bustle of harried students, until I stood on the track at Franklin Field. There I finally stopped and allowed the magnitude of this unforeseen calamity to roll over me.

Thanking the good Lord that the field was empty at this hour, I dropped my duffel and ran, my street shoes' leather soles loud on the track's gritty surface.

I had experienced many victories on this track. In those moments I seemed to go beyond time and the limitations of an ordinary man. They were tiny windows I was privileged to peer through, but they afforded sweeping views of extraordinary scenes. And I knew I was extraordinary, too, or at least that my talent was. My coach at Central High had called me the Black Eagle, and though I'd never seen one in flight, I had a deep feeling that this bird and I had much in common.

I had an eight-foot, six-inch stride. Coach said that was the "longest stride known to man." Maybe so. What it meant to me was that my legs carried me with a certain grace, like the wings of that black eagle. We had that in common.

We both *flew.* More than that—we both understood flight and, I had thought, freedom.

I ran with abandon, pursuing freedom with every step. As I pressed myself to speeds only the eagle and I knew, the air made an amazing sound. It hissed with resentment because I challenged it. It whistled in pain because my body cut it like a knife. My legs pumped, my heart pulsed, my feet hammered the track—steady, rhythmic, insistent—like the constant hum of a Scott Joplin rag that you just don't want to end. I told myself that the water filling my eyes was from the wind.

No matter how fast I ran, I could not win the race against my thoughts. I could not escape this situation into which I had been thrust. I ran knowing that when I went home later, I would break my parents' hearts with a single word: *resignation*. The very word was a cage that put to lie the sense of freedom that running gave me. I was not free. Not really. Not when guilt could be assigned to me because of the color of my skin.

Oh, certainly I had the freedom to choose between fighting the injustice—thus bringing the accusation of cheating into the open—and simply going quietly away. And I had chosen. I had made the decision: I would voluntarily resign as a student of the University of Pennsylvania, preserving the life my parents had built at the cost of every dream they had ever dreamed on my behalf.

As galling as that was, I would not allow my family's future and fortunes to sit on the chopping block waiting for those in the "higher" court to either uphold a lie or override it with the truth. I'd seen how the lines had fallen—my professor and my dean had decided that Charles Cook was the truth and I was the lie. They had agreed between them that truth, like beauty, was in the eye of the beholder.

The Gospel of John says, "Then you shall know the truth

and the truth will set you free." I had always believed that. Now I found that the Good Book did not say what happened when the truth could not be known. I had discovered that this day for myself. This day I was trapped inside a lie, its bars rising out of the ground to cage the eagle and stop its flight.

I staggered to a stop. Even in running there was no release from this cage. I picked up my duffel and started for home.

2

Glory Days

May 23, 1902
Central High School
Final Track Meet

It was a peculiar thing, I reflected as I tied on my track shoes, that one event should be able to inspire both joy and longing, excitement and dread, satisfaction and discontent. But that was the nature of seasonal sports: preparation for the meets went on almost as long as the track season itself, then suddenly, it was over and you found yourself running your last race of the school year.

The *biggest* race of the school year.

I glanced up into the stands that ran down the long axis of the track oval, looking for Mama and Daddy. I found them easily in the sea of mostly white faces and waved. They waved back—Mama beaming as if I'd already won my event, Daddy typically stoic. It was a sunny, brisk day and they were dressed as if for church. Daddy wore his trademark bow tie.

I did my stretches along the sidelines, watching teammates run their races. I cheered when they won, shook my head in disappointment when they didn't, and gave high praise for effort either way when they came off the track.

Then it was my turn, my event: the quarter mile. I drew a position in the middle of the track. Good—this was the catbird's seat, as far as I was concerned. I could watch the field from here and, if things went my way, I could even influence the pacing of the race.

The starter called, "Marks! Set!" His cry of "Drive!" was lost in the percussion of the cap pistol he fired into the crisp air.

I leapt out to a quick start, inviting my competitors to try to keep up with me. They accepted the invitation. I kept the lead for a measure of strides and then slowly relinquished it. I hung with the pack for a moment, and then slipped farther back, riding right behind the leaders—two tall white boys, one from Central Manual High, the other from Benjamin Franklin.

I pushed them, let them hear me there, right on their heels—let them feel me breathing down their necks. I dropped back farther, counting the strides, ticking off the yards of the run ... waiting.

When we reached the final turn, I gave myself the whip and leapt forward. Not inched, leapt. Suddenly that skinny Negro boy they thought they'd left in the dust was licking at their heels again. Now he was pressing them. Now he was passing them. Now they urged themselves forward ... and had nothing left to give.

I could hear Coach Pitton's voice above the rush of air, the thunder of feet, and the roar of my own breath: "Fly, Black Eagle! Fly!"

Fly? I knew how to do that. I lengthened my stride and flew free of the other runners, clearing them by a stride, by two, by three, by nearly six strides by the time I broke the finish tape to the roar of applause and the lively waving of

A Novel by Craig T. Williams

crimson and gold hats and kerchiefs.

My teammates rallied around me, slapping my sweating back. They stepped back as Coach Pitton approached, hand out and smiling. He took my hand in his and shook it up and down and slapped my shoulder.

"*Good* race, John! Good race! You're the best quarter-miler in the city, my boy. Congratulations!" He turned his smile on the rest of the team. "The numbers aren't tallied yet, fellas, but I believe Central High may have just won the day." He patted me on the shoulder and then moved off through the flock of athletes milling on the sidelines.

One of my teammates, Duncan—a pale, freckled kid with a shock of carrot-colored hair—stepped up and pumped my hand like crazy. "That was great, Johnny!" he told me. "You saved us, is what you did! Didn't I tell you?" He turned to the handful of kids around us. "Didn't I say that Johnny Taylor'd come through, no matter what?"

Another boy, whose name was James, grinned at me. He wasn't on the track team, but he was a friend of Duncan's, so I guess you could say I knew him secondhand. "Yeah, you told us, Duncan. As if there was ever any doubt." He popped me on the upper arm with his fist. "Good goin', Johnny."

I grinned back, feeling a warm glow of camaraderie flush over me, heart to head to limbs.

"Hey," said James, glancing at Duncan and giving him a friendly elbow to the ribs. "We still going to Bassetts for ice cream?"

"Heck, yeah! What better way to celebrate, right? Double chocolate, here I come!" Duncan grinned at me again, and I opened my mouth to ask if they'd wait till I'd spoken to my parents to get permission to go.

The words, thank the Lord, never got said.

"Well, see you in class Monday, Johnny," Duncan said, and he and James rolled off, chatting and laughing with a train of other kids in their wake.

I stood and watched, puzzled, the flush of warmth I'd felt deserting me, leaving me feeling … singular. I shook myself. For a moment I had forgotten: we were of a kind on the track, but once we stepped off the oval, I was colored and they were white. It was funny, too, because I knew that Duncan often took ribbing (and worse) for his brilliant red hair and his slight Irish brogue.

Still, they'd given me my due. I *had* come through. I allowed that thought to cheer me until Mama and Daddy came to find me along the sidelines. I went to them glowing with pride—a pride I saw reflected in my mother's eyes. Her face was trophy-bright as she clasped her hands over her heart and said, "Oh, Johnny, that was *wonderful.*" The last word rode out on an ecstatic sigh.

I grinned at her and then looked to Daddy. His eyes sparkled and the corners of his mouth turned up. He put his hand out toward me and I moved to take it just as something hit me in the middle of the back—something small, hard and damp.

I turned to see an overripe plum lying behind me on the ground. Raucous laughter drew my eyes to where a couple of boys from Benjamin Franklin High stood in a tight knot of mutual courage. As my eyes met theirs, they turned and moved away, dancing like scarecrows in their track uniforms.

A Novel by Craig T. Williams

"Way to go, Jim Crow! Hey, Blackie!" they called and dissolved into idiot laughter, their dance deteriorating into a staggering shamble. "This is a white man's sport! Why don't y'all go back to the jungle and swing through the trees?"

They were gamboling like the monkeys at the zoo now, and I felt the red rush up from my heart to burn all the way to the tips of my ears. All I could think was that my mama was seeing this—hearing this.

"Yeah?" I fired back before I could think better of it. "Well, if it's a white man's sport, how come a colored man beat *y'all*?"

Their faces flushed splendidly. "Yeah, well ..." one of them said, and then he caught sight of their coach looking a bit infuriated a few yards away. They shut up and stomped off.

I turned back to my parents, grinning fiercely, and was caught in their gazes like a fly in honey. Well, at least my mama's gaze was honey. *I'm proud*, it said. And, *I'm afraid*.

Daddy's gaze had no sweetness. It was all fury.

"It's all right," I said. "I'm used to-"

"Why'd you have to sass those boys?" Daddy asked, his voice hushed. "You're the captain of your team, son. Why'd you cork off like that?"

"Me, cork off?" I asked, confused. "They started it. I didn't do anything to them but win the race."

He just looked at me—eyes glittering.

He's *afraid*, I realized. "It's okay, Daddy, really. It's just stupid name-calling. They were mad at having lost."

"I didn't see them throwing rotten fruit at the other boys

who beat them," my father observed. "I didn't hear them calling anyone else 'Blackie.'"

I shrugged. "I said it's okay."

"No, damn it. No, it's not okay."

"John!" Mama said as she cut sharp eyes to my father. "Your tongue!"

Daddy ignored her—something he *never* did. "You don't draw that kind of attention to yourself, you hear? Shinin' is one thing—you don't need to call attention to it. You cain't fight them on their turf. And you don't go getting all smart-mouth with them. Not for any reason. All you did just now was give them one more reason to hate you. You put your-self above them, Junior. You put yourself above them, and they will never forget it."

He glanced about as if to be sure none of "them" had heard us and then jerked his head in the direction of our buggy. "Gather up your things, John. Let's go home."

There were no words on the way home. Daddy was still angry, Mama quiet and withdrawn, so I just sat in back and thought about what had happened—how my win had somehow been turned into a loss.

Put myself above them? Well, of course I had. That was what winning was about, wasn't it? You crossed the finish line first and for a time—moments, days, weeks, even months—you were the fastest, the holder of the record, the best. You were a champion.

My father had always been a bit "cautious" about my competitive career, but there was always this underlying glow of pride. Today, however, it was absent. Until this moment, I had thought of winning as something to be celebrated. But looking at Daddy's grim face I suspected there would be no celebrating this victory.

At home, Daddy, pulled up in front of the house, looped the reins around the brake and helped Mama from the buggy. "Put the horse up and feed him," he told me coolly. "And clean the tack while you're at it. Don't come in until it shines, you hear me?"

I heard. I got up in the front seat and clucked old Bean into a walk, guiding him through the alley and around to the carriage house. I backed the buggy in next to Daddy's catering wagon, then went through the process of unharnessing our horse and putting up his tack. I know Daddy meant this to punish me, but taking care of Bean—even polishing his tack—was no hardship on me. I loved that old horse—loved all animals, truth to tell, but especially horses, and of all horses, I loved old Bean the best.

He wasn't that old, really. But he'd been around as long as I could remember, so I thought of him that way. I'd curried him, tacked him up, rubbed down his legs when they were sore, seen to his achy belly and his cuts and bruises ever since I could remember. In grateful appreciation for my pampering, he listened to me. Bean and I were best buddies. Now, I put him in his little box stall, poured oats into his bucket, tossed hay into his rack and began to brush him. As I brushed him, I told him all about the meet today, how I'd come from behind to win my match, how my coach and teammates had praised me ... then gone on about their business without me.

The Olympian: An American Triumph

He snorted at that and turned his big head around and nudged me as if to say, "We'll I'm not going about my business without you, J. T. Not me."

"Thank you, kindly," I told him as I brushed and brushed his glossy hide. "But I promise you, Bean. One day, I'm going to *have* that ice cream."

I didn't have ice cream that night, but I did get cake. When I finally came in from my chores—tired, but satisfied, I found that Mama had baked me a beautiful chocolate cake. In our dining room, in the privacy of our family we did celebrate the team's victory—and my personal victory—and even Daddy smiled, whether at me or at the cake, I wasn't sure.

★★★★

November 22, 1902
Central High's Dedication
Philadelphia

It is not every day that the president of the United States speaks at a high school, but today President Theodore Roosevelt had come to do just that at Central High. He was to preside over the dedication of the school's new, modern marvel of a building, and as an alumnus of some small celebrity, I had been invited to attend. I had moved on to Brown Preparatory School after my graduation from Central and had already begun to make a name for myself there as part of the track team.

A Novel by Craig T. Williams

The front row seats were taken up by a host of important folks: senators, the governor, the mayor, teachers, and scientists—almost everybody who was *somebody* in the city of Philadelphia. Alumni from years ago had even traveled here to be a part of this day. We were seated with those alumni in the second row, just right of center, with me sandwiched between Mama and Daddy, Mama clutching my hand and squeezing it almost numb.

There was an expectant hush as President Nicholar Maquire took center stage, said a few words that I doubt one soul there remembered the next day, and introduced the speaker. President Roosevelt took the platform, wearing a slight smile. A pleasant enough man, he stood about my height, though he was much thicker. I studied his every movement and vocal inflection as he congratulated the football team on their win. They had beaten our biggest rival, Central Manual Training School, 28-0 the day before, making today's celebration even sweeter.

It was one of those moments that catches hold of something in your mind, and you know in the moment it's happening that you will never let the memory of it go. I wanted to keep my own personal memory of this man—the first president to invite a Negro to the White House—and for dinner, no less. Most white folks had turned on "Teddy" the previous year when he'd invited Booker T. Washington to sit at his table. Some freed Negroes took it as a sign that equality was surely imminent, and although a few didn't take well to Booker T.'s words on Negro forbearance and patience in his book *Up From Slavery,* we all saw the significance of his

The Olympian: An American Triumph

White House invitation.

I glanced at Daddy to catch his eye. He was beaming up at President Roosevelt as if he'd been the guest in that dining room on Pennsylvania Avenue himself.

President Roosevelt took a long look around the cavernous room. His eyes lit on me for a a few seconds and stayed. For a moment I imagined that he had come all the way from the White House to speak personally to John Baxter Taylor, Jr.; that being the case, it was only right to give him my undivided attention. I met his eyes.

He smiled, raised that fine, firm chin, and spoke to the assembled crowd. He spoke on his upbringing, and how he had been sickly as a child and suffered from terrible asthma.

"My mother and father worried about my health daily," he said. "They feared I would die reaching for my next breath, but I refused to give in. I am a hunter. I determined to find my breath, create my way, and live my life as a man of strength. It is why I so admire the athlete," he added, bringing his gaze to me again.

I understand.

The last words he spoke to us (to *me*) were these: "As you go forth in life, remember this: it is not the critic who counts; not the man who points out how the strong man stumbles or where the doer of deeds could have done better. The credit belongs to the man who is actually in the arena, whose face is marred by dust and sweat and blood, who strives valiantly, who errs and comes up short again and again—because there is no effort without error or shortcoming—but who knows the great enthusiasms, the great devotions, who spends himself for a worthy cause; who, at the best, knows, in the end, the triumph of high achievement, and who, at the worst, if he fails, at least he fails while daring greatly, so that his place shall never be with those cold and timid souls who knew neither victory nor defeat."

There was a moment of silence followed by such applause that you might have thought the Lord himself had stepped up on the stage and delivered that speech. We all came to our feet in great passion.

The words *daring greatly* tasted like they'd spilled out of a honeycomb and poured themselves into my body. If the Black Eagle did take flight and failed, at least he failed while daring greatly. From that day forward, I had a deep affection for President "Teddy" Roosevelt and his words. The critics didn't matter—just as he said.

I realized, in a moment of illumination, that Mr. Roosevelt reminded me of Coach Pitton—a fierce man with a gigantic spirit, who often gave his running teams words like Mr. Roosevelt's. They were words that lifted you to your feet, and then lifted you to flight. When Coach Pitton called me Black Eagle, when he'd call out, "Take flight, Black Eagle! Take flight!" that was the best coaching advice I ever got. After that, I knew what to do: *fly*. That's what eagles do best.

I will dare greatly, I decided, smiling so big my cheeks hurt, clapping so hard my hands stung, and I shall live my life as no ordinary man, bound by a game of chance, but as a man who lives life greatly.

★★★★

The Olympian: An American Triumph

March 1903
Brown Preparatory School
Yale Interscholastic Quarter-Mile Race

"You Taylor?"

I turned to see who was speaking to me and found myself looking at a lanky fellow from Boston. Behind him, our two fellow competitors watched wide-eyed as if his speaking to me was somehow dangerous.

"I am," I said, not quite smiling. Let him interpret my expression as he wished.

He held my gaze and struck an intimidating pose—chin up, hands on his hips. "Thought you should know," he said, holding position, "I came here to take the win."

"I'll keep that in mind," I replied without intending to sound sarcastic, though it couldn't help but come out that way.

He made a face that told me he'd like to say more, and then moved away from me toward the track. Speed respects speed, I thought. I'd let my legs do the bragging. I was at the peak of my performance and eager to face off with the greatest in their category in the quarter-mile race. There was a draw to determine our placement on the track. I received a good position in the center of the group—my favorite place.

As we were called to take our positions, I walked with studied ease onto the track beside my three fair opponents. They offered heavy stares. I imagined that it was not because of the color of my skin, but because of the size of my reputation in the quarter mile. I'd already won the Princeton Interscholastic event and our relay team was undefeated, and I had every confidence we'd remain that way at the end of the day. That confidence wasn't just in my own ability, but in the combined talent of the relay team—the names Beson, Mulligan, McGuckin, and Taylor were synonymous with winning.

The race began with a shouted, "Marks, set, drive!"

The pistol fired and I leapt from my position as if flames had been lit beneath my feet. So did my boastful competitor. It almost seemed like an unfair race to the other two athletes running with us; before we'd gone a hundred yards, they were so far behind us, they were choking on the dust we had kicked up.

The runner from Boston was more than impressive, and was doing much to keep his word and "take the win." At 220 yards we were neck and neck, our arms and legs pumping madly. We were two well-oiled human machines exerting personal will against the will of the wind. I could hear him breathing heavily, and I knew he could hear me.

As we came around the final corner into the home stretch, it appeared that the Boston boy with the big mouth would do as he promised, but the appearance was only illusion. He had an eight-yard lead—a gap that would widen even farther if I slipped and lost focus.

But I wouldn't slip, and I knew it. *My* race was just beginning.

I had set the pace dramatically from the outset and had wittingly pushed him out ahead of me just far enough to engage his ire; once in the lead he would do what he could to stay there. So, I pushed him and kept pushing him until he teetered between determination and exhaustion. I could tell by the change in the angle of his body and the height of his knees as he rounded that last turn—I had run him into the ground.

I edged out.

Faster.

Faster.

And yet faster.

I saw his head tilt slightly and knew he could hear me sweeping up behind him like the dark of night.

He panted. No, he moaned. Then he cried out in exertion as he tried to maintain his lead.

I knew what he was telling himself with each footfall: *Hold on. Maintain. Hold on.*

The distance between us was waning. I was eating it up with every step. Then there was no distance between us, and we ran side by side, might by might, force by force, for less than a second before I hit full stride and blazed past him as though he were standing still.

The crowd leapt to its feet in wild applause that cascaded across the field. I broke the finish tape and not only took the race but set a new national record with a winning time of 50 3/5 seconds, the fastest high school or prep time in the nation that year.

It was sweet.

It was simple.

It was destiny.

A Novel by Craig T. Williams

And the next day, the headlines spoke for themselves:

TAYLOR, STAR OF A GREAT TEAM,
BROWN PREPARATORY SCHOOL!
TAYLOR LEADS BROWN PREPARATORY TO
VICTORY AT YALE INTER-SCHOLASTICS!
SETTING NEW RECORD IN 50 3/5 SECONDS.
TAYLOR, BEST PREP SCHOOL QUARTER MILER
IN THE ENTIRE COUNTRY!

Of all the write-ups in the paper that year, the last headline was by far my favorite. It was featured in our Negro paper, the *Philadelphia Tribune*. It was meaningful for me, and not just because there was a write-up about me, but because another man who had just made history was in the same issue:

JACK JOHNSON BECOMES COLORED
HEAVYWEIGHT CHAMPION!

I was close in age to Jack Johnson, but there was a vast difference in the way we were living. There were two photos of Jack in the *Tribune* article. In one picture he stood, all confidence, in a sea of white folks, wearing a finely tailored suit, a broad smile flashing gold teeth, and a great pride and strength you just don't see every day, especially on the broad shoulders of a Negro man.

The second photo showed Jack standing in a boxing ring looking like a giant with a gentle Southern smile. He had the shape of a man that could beat you to the ground and the expression of a man who would then extend his hand to pull you up as if to say, "This is what I do—don't take it personally."

The article read, "Negro boxer, Jack Johnson, standing 6 feet, 200 pounds, defeated 6 foot 3 inch, 203 pound 'Denver' Ed Martin after twenty rounds and captured the title of Colored Heavyweight Champion of the World!

"Johnson, born in Galveston, Texas to former slaves Henry and Tina 'Tiny' Johnson, became a professional boxer just six years ago and now earns up to $1,000 per fight. Asked about his win, the 'Galveston Giant' laughed lightly and said, 'Winning is my focus and my sights is set on Jeffries to take the U.S. heavyweight title from him.'"

I read the article over and over again in the quiet of the bathroom, where I could read uninterrupted for bits of time. I had a great respect for Jack Johnson. He was his own man, living life on his own terms. Jack had outright *said* that he intended to be *the* champion of the world by taking on Jim Jeffries, the white heavyweight champion. It amazed me. I wondered if this fight would ever take place. No colored had ever fought for the championship against a white boxer.

Daddy thought Jack Johnson was a "bit much" and was "setting himself up nicely for a lynching." But I saw it differently. The way I saw it, Jack Johnson was saying, "Look at me. Tall, proud, big, and a MAN living his own dream."

He showed me that a colored man didn't have to cower, didn't have to live down and shuffle from side to side as if a real thought never came into his head. Jack Johnson had fought his way into his own paradise, and I had every intention of running all the way to mine.

A Novel by Craig T. Williams

★★★★

June 2, 1903
Brown Prep School Athletic Awards Ceremony
Philadelphia

There are places and times when the color of a man's skin takes a backseat to what that man has done. Colors blur when a race is being run, and a team, school or a club is being represented well.

So it was that I took a front row seat at the 1902–1903 season-ending awards ceremony in the gymnasium at Brown Prep. I could tell by the unkind stares from some of my fellow students that they probably didn't take too kindly to me having a better view than they had. They offered no verbal protest, but a man's thoughts can often be seen behind his eyes.

"Don't let it get to ya, J. T."

I turned my attention to the athlete sitting next to me—Mel Sheppard, a fellow I'd come to think of as a friend, in spite of the very clear difference in the color of our skin. Mel was a distance runner—the best at distances of 880 yards and more, I thought, though he could run a crack relay stage, too. I was mighty pleased to call myself his teammate.

"They're just jealous," Mel said, scratching behind one of his oversized ears. He grinned to emphasize the point, stretching the freckles over his high, narrow cheekbones. "They couldn't keep up with us if they tied our legs together. Which is why we're sittin' up here and they're..." He turned his head and waggled his fingers at the scowlers several rows behind us.

I darted my eyes in that direction, but didn't look too long. I remembered what Daddy said: it was okay to shine ... but not put myself above them. Fine. I'd let Mel do that. As for me, I sat there in the front row grinning ear to ear— one of just ten Negroes in the whole audience. I knew at least four other people with brown skin in the same room, and that was only because they were related to me—father John Baxter, mother Sarah, sister Hattie, and my cousin William, who had been raised as my brother.

This was not only a proud moment for Brown Prep, but a pride filler for the Taylor family. John and Sarah's boy was being recognized, and every time I turned my eyes in their direction, I saw them light up like the morning star.

Mama's face was round and beaming. There was something old and sacred locked behind her bright eyes as she sat next to Daddy. She looked rather romantic with her upswept hair and elaborate, wide-brimmed hat. She wore the most stunning pink hobble skirt with a slit in the back. Stylish, that was Mama. She was what I thought women were supposed to be in these progressive times: gentle in spirit and quiet of nature, but a force not to be crossed even on your best day. Sarah Taylor tolerated no foolishness in her household, and her children knew it and respected that fact with unquestioning reverence.

I was in awe of Mama's beauty. She was a petite woman with golden bright skin and light brown tresses. Her hair had a beautiful texture and framed her heart-shaped face with glorious waves. I loved to look at it—at her. In her youth, Mama said, people called her *redbone* and teased her because of her light skin. She could blend into almost any crowd of people, in any situation. Though she stood only five feet, two inches in height, she was a powerful woman. If Mama fixed her mind on something, it was as good as done.

Don't misunderstand—Mama was a gentle spirit and quiet of nature, a God-fearing, salt-of-the-earth woman. But she was also a force to be reckoned with. In that way, I guess you could say she was two people in one. Which one you met—the gentle rain or the blazing fire—depended on you.

Mama never went to college, but she did encourage her children to read and to present speeches many a night. *Encourage* is putting it nicely. Back in those days it felt more like punishment, but now, with me looking to attend a university and William in college, Hattie already married off, and my brother Clinton working as a chef, it looked like Mama's "punishment" had served us all well.

My brother Clinton was eleven years older than I and had left the house when I was a youngster, which left me, Hattie, and William to sit, obedient, as Mama and Daddy gave their lectures on life.

"You'll walk where we couldn't," Mama would say with emotion in her voice. "And do what we couldn't. Your father and me had one foot in slavery, one foot in freedom."

Hattie, William, and I would sit stiff as boards when Mama started speaking on slavery. What could we say? We didn't know slavery, we only knew of it. We were free, so the best we could do was shut up and listen, which is really all she wanted us to do in the first place.

"You are the hopes and dreams," Mama would say, looking deeply into each pair of young eyes, "of every slave that never heard the words *you're free*."

How does a little kid, born free, take in all of this and *make* it make sense? Guess you take it in a little at a time, hold on to it, let it roll around and sit in your belly for a while. Then someday when you least expect it, it comes back to you in the form of a gut feeling. Then you know what to do with it all.

Daddy was altogether different from Mama. He was tall, handsome, and rugged, with a face that seemed to be etched of stone ... till he smiled. When he smiled, he melted from the inside out with warmth. And you did, too, because you couldn't help but heat up under that kind of righteous loving.

Born into slavery in the South, but free by the age of four, Daddy carried a heavy shadow that hovered around him as a keepsake from his ancestors. He reminded himself nearly every day that his children were free, because he couldn't forget that *he* had been born a slave. Freedom, and the urgent need to protect it, was the air we breathed in our household. Daddy's philosophical nature was sprinkled everywhere like sauce and seasoning on food.

A Negro without an education is little more than a slave.
Hold firm to a solid trade.
Invest in your tomorrow.
Take care of the pennies and the dollars take care of themselves.
Build your own house and buy your own land.
Learn how to grow your own food.

A Novel by Craig T. Williams

Be your own man.

Daddy was always prepared with ready-made speeches by the man he admired most, Booker T. Washington. Daddy loved Booker T. so greatly that sometimes I thought he would lay down his very life for him. Daddy was endlessly preaching Washington's philosophy on "the dignity of a man's hard work." He'd mouth Booker T.'s words like a preacher quoting scripture.

"There was no part of my life that was wasted on play," said Daddy, sounding just like Booker T. Washington himself. "In living memory, almost every day has been taken up by some kind of labor."

"Is that how you want us to be, Daddy?" William would ask with wide-eyed innocence.

After coming to live with us as a toddler when his father—my daddy's younger brother—and his mother were killed in a house fire, William had only known my father as "Daddy." He lived for Daddy's approval and soaked up Daddy's wisdom like a sponge.

"Hard work is all I ask of you boys," Daddy would say. "And that you get some sort of plan for yourselves."

Daddy's watchword was *self-reliance*. He had his own catering business and earned his living by the industry of his hands, laboring sixteen hours a day to take care of us. Mama was a seamstress in her spare time, which wasn't much with taking care of a family. Though not an educated man, Daddy was a self-taught businessman, whose quality of work and integrity of name earned him a fine reputation in the city as a respected caterer. He was also known for being a sharp dresser, and every day of the week you could find Daddy wearing his long, slim trousers, pegged narrow at the bottom to contrast with his broad, padded shoulders.

They were a charming pair, Mama and Daddy, and crazy in love. They wanted nothing more than to see their children embark on a journey worthy of emancipation. They viewed us as gifts from heaven and had welcomed each child with loads of love.

They'd been thirty years old when they had Clinton. Six years later their beautiful baby girl, Hattie, entered their world. When William was orphaned, Mama and Daddy took him in without hesitation. Then much to my parents' surprise, I was born five years after Hattie, which made me the "miracle child" since my mother turned forty-one two days before my birth on November 3, 1883. I was a tiny baby, but deemed "a fighter" by the midwife. As a gift to Daddy, and as a tribute to his fighting spirit, Mama decided to name me after him.

Mama and Daddy had done everything within human power—short of sending a telegram to the good Lord himself—to give us all we needed to get where we were going in life. That, in part, is how I came to be a student first at Philadelphia Central High School, one of the most prestigious high schools of academic excellence in the country, and then at Brown Preparatory.

So there I sat, one of only a few Negroes in the school, and the only one on the track and field team. I had been given a noble distinction and the opportunity to compete as one of the best in the country. Today I was to be rewarded for my "athletic talent in outstanding contribution to Brown's track and field team"—that's what the papers said—and for my service as the captain of the track team and my achievement as the interscholastic quarter-mile champion.

None of that had come easy.

Mel nudged me and whispered, "Congratulations, Johnny-boy."

"You, too, Mel."

"Can I tell you something?"

He didn't wait for me to say "yay" or "nay," but just went on, smooth as can be. "When you first came to Brown, I didn't expect a whole lot from you. Figured you were a fluke. But you sure as hell proved me wrong."

"Why, thank you, Mr. Sheppard," I said, grinning.

He shook his head. "If you'd told me a year ago that I'd be eating a darkie's dust on the track and liking it, I'd've called you crazy. Guess you're the exception that proves the rule, eh, Johnny-boy?"

It had never bothered me that he called me "Johnny-boy" until that moment. Suddenly it bothered me a lot. *The exception that proves the rule?* I looked him squarely in the eye and kept my face composed. "But I's not the exception," I said, glad my daddy couldn't hear me speakin' dialect. "We's *all* that good." I grinned broadly and he, deciding I was joking with him, laughed —if a little uneasily.

Uneasy myself, I glanced back in the audience and found my mother's face. I needed that face, those eyes, that smile—needed to connect with someone who valued me—not my speed or my winning ways, but *me.* Mama gestured at me to face front as the ceremony got under way with speeches and special mentions and all that. Then they began handing out the awards.

I couldn't help but glance back to catch the smile in her young-ancient eyes as the dean of the school called my name, his voice booming with authority: "John Baxter Taylor, Jr., for his winning performances at the Princeton Interscholastic, the Yale Interscholastic meets, and anchoring our relay team to an undefeated season including the Penn Relays Prep School Championship."

I rose to receive my award, legs trembling, knees knocking against each other. I can only imagine what I looked like, all wobbly and hesitating.

Is that him? People would wonder. The champion runner? Kid can barely walk.

I raised my chin, pulled myself up straight, and moved to shake hands with Dean Evans. My eyes lit on the medal he held in his left hand and did not wish to leave it. It was golden; I was golden.

"Taylor," the dean said, "you have made this school proud. Your service as the backbone of our track and field team has been the key to our success all the way to the championships. You're a credit to your ... to your team, young man."

For a moment, I thought he'd been going to say "a credit to your race," but then he was shaking my hand and I was lifted off the ground by the thunder of applause. It was like an invisible wave—the excitement of the audience roiling the air. I could ride that wave forever if they'd just let me stand here on this stage that long. Had I tried, Dean Evans would have probably applied a boot to my backside to help me regain memory and movement. I chuckled at the image as I floated back to my seat, filled with the pride of being my own man. That's all Daddy ever wanted for me.

I wished I could take this feeling—this very one, this very moment—stick it in the pocket of my trousers, and hold on to it for a thousand dark nights and counting. I would try to do that, I determined. Whenever my path seemed dark or dim, I'd reach into my pocket and bring out this moment, glorious and gleaming, and be content.

3

Celebration

In my hands, I held the open door to a new life. It was the door to another set of rules that I could live by—my own. It came in the form of a letter. It was from the University of Pennsylvania's Wharton School of Finance.

I had been *accepted*.

I was filled with joy, realizing how proud my parents would be when I showed them my letter that night. By dusk that evening, the roar in my belly could be heard a mile or two away. The acceptance letter to Wharton and the excitement of this life-changing moment were a bit too much to handle on an empty stomach.

I sat at the dining room table in our twin row house on Woodland Avenue, hungry for a good meal and excited beyond belief. Tonight we were having Daddy's famous crab cakes with fried potatoes, and Mama's green beans and apple pie. The only thing missing was Hattie's butter cake. I missed my sister's smile and her melt-in-your mouth treat, but I was also happy that she had found love and married James Barber. Luckily, they resided in Philadelphia, and with a bit of notice I could have cake and milk anytime with my "other" family.

Our supper was a team effort, and with Scott Joplin's "Maple Leaf Rag" playing through the house, it was also a festive one. There was nothing like it—Mama in the kitchen wearing a homey apron that made her food look all the more inviting, Daddy on the other side of her, an equal contributor to most of our meals.

Sometimes, Daddy wore the apron more than Mama, which we kids always got a kick out of. It was rare, indeed, to find a man in the kitchen doing everything from seasoning meat to scrubbing pots. Our Daddy was no ordinary man.

I never will forget the special supper that preceded our move to Philadelphia from Washington, D.C. I was seven years old when Daddy called us inside with the big news, the seriousness of the occasion carved deep into his forehead. He sat me, William, and Hattie down beside Mama, and looked at us with a penetrating gaze.

"We're leaving D.C. and moving to Philadelphia. I'm gonna start a family business."

Silence fell over us as we shot quick glances at one another.

Family business? I thought and William asked, "Does that mean we have to drop out of school?"

Daddy cleared his throat. "There are fine schools in Philadelphia," he said, "and we'll have a nice place to live, right near the college there. You'll see Negroes in Philadelphia running their own businesses and going to those big universities, getting a fine education. I've dreamed about this all my life," he added, "and now we all gonna live it."

Daddy's serious look dissolved and left him beaming with hope. Still there was silence. Nobody knew what to say. How do you look a change that big in the face—no matter how good it sounds—and not be a little scared? Washington was the only place I'd ever known.

"Sound good to you, men?" asked Daddy.

Daddy never called us *boys*. He hated the word with a passion. Said he'd heard it all his life, and that it made "giant men small."

"You was born a man and you'll die a man," he told us nearly every day.

At a loss for words, William and I simply nodded.

"Baby girl, how d'you feel 'bout that?" Daddy said to a smiling Hattie.

"Wherever the good Lord takes us is fine with me, Daddy," she said softly.

We glanced over at Mama, who was glowing from the inside out. She smiled at my Daddy and he burst into a grin just looking at her bright face.

As I reflected on the moment later, I could call that look by its proper name, *pride*. Mama was s of Daddy in that moment. This was bigger than a Negro dream—it was an American dream. Owning a business was something a Negro could scarcely imagine. Just making a living was dream enough. Now a freed man, his wife, and his family were going to step into the American dream and live in a way their mothers and fathers could see only as they slept.

Two weeks later we left Washington, D.C., and arrived at 3223 Woodland Avenue in Philadelphia. Mama found work right away as a seamstress—mostly dressing the professors from the University of Pennsylvania, since the campus was just a few blocks away—and Daddy went to work at one of the restaurants as a waiter so he could learn the "right way" to get started in business.

Daddy didn't believe in doing something over again. He always told us, "Once you start something, you finish it. Make you a plan; then you have a way to go."

Daddy did it his way. It took two years of hard work before he finally opened the doors of Taylor Catering Company. It started with small gatherings, but soon talk of the "best crab cakes in town" spread throughout Philadelphia. When the *Christian Recorder* published an article on Daddy that included a picture of him standing over a plate of steaming food, almost everybody from the African Episcopal Church came out for "The Taste of the North, the Love of the South."

Daddy loved seafood—eating, cooking, and catching it. He always said if he could make his own heaven, it would be on a boat with a "fishing rod in my hands, white clouds over a blue sky, and the glory of the Lord shining on me."

"William! John! Set the table!" Daddy's booming voice disrupted my thoughts, bringing my recollections to an end.

William and I traded "love taps" on the back of the head as we raced toward the kitchen.

"Quit that foolishness and tend to the table," Mama warned.

We straightened up right away; like I said, Mama was a gentle rain *and* a blazing fire.

Between the crab cakes, green beans, potatoes, and apple pie, I didn't know which way to go at the table.

"Pass me one of everything!" I said.

Daddy and Mama both laughed.

"You sure are greedy," said William.

"A growing man needs a full belly!"

Supper was a peaceful time in the Taylor household. We didn't have big, heavy conversations at the dining table. Daddy would say, "Heavy news on top of a man's dinner plate ain't good for the belly." So we always kept it light and easy at the table.

I was about to break tradition. My big news was building up in me to the point that I thought I would burst. Everybody paused as I reached into my vest pocket and pulled out my letter, like a magician pulling a rabbit out of his hat. Then I cleared my throat and read its contents aloud.

"'John Baxter Taylor, Jr.,'" I began proudly, "'you have been officially accepted into the University of Pennsylvania's Wharton School of Finance …'"

Before I could continue, a great breath of air was sucked out of somebody's lungs. I wasn't sure if it was Mama's, Daddy's, or William's, because all three of them looked as if they had just seen a ghost. Mama was the first to get enough air back into her body to respond. She screamed, covered her mouth, and pulled back from the table. Daddy sat still and motionless, and William looked dumbfounded.

"I am the dream," I said to Daddy, before turning my

eyes to Mama. "Mama, the one that you insisted on!"

Daddy leapt from his seat and snatched me up to the tips of my toes. Mama joined in the embrace and William did what he did best—showed his great love by rapping me on the back of the head one time for good measure.

"Oh, this calls for a mighty celebration!" Mama said, clapping her hands.

4

Nobody's Hero

September 1903
University of Pennsylvania, Philadelphia

I rode destiny until the day I set foot on the University of Pennsylvania campus. Then it would seem, at least for a time, that destiny would ride me.

Though UPenn was just up the road from the Taylor house, it seemed a world away. Founded by Benjamin Franklin in 1749, the university offered every student practical as well as classical instruction in real-world pursuits. To enter this institution as the free son of a former slave was a symbol of the great advancement of the American Negro. In the words of Franklin himself, "energy and persistence conquer all things."

The campus could swallow a man whole if he wasn't careful. Situated right in the middle of the city, the buildings on the campus were larger than life—certainly larger than me. Hundreds of faces passed me, and I them, and we all made eye contact, but none of us saw *ourselves* in each other. They saw me as I saw them, as true strangers. At UPenn, I was nobody's hero.

There was a part of me—a big part of me—that wanted to run back home to safety and lie at my mother's feet like a child and say, "Mama, they're just too big and me too small." But who was I to stand atop Mama's and Daddy's dreams and crush them just because I was afraid? I still had lofty ideas and grand visions for myself, but as I walked upon this chilly ground, littered with dead leaves, I was hard pressed to find one good reason to carry me to my first class. Yet I was *here,* and that should be reason enough.

As I made my way up the broad walk to College Hall, I was forced to stop in awe of the beauty and craftsmanship of this fine work of art. College Hall was one of the most elegant structures I had ever laid eyes on. An enchanting structure of mellow brick and stone with two beautiful towers and tall, arched windows, it made me smile for the first time since I'd arrived on campus.

Now, there's a man who knows how to work with his hands, I thought, in admiration of the craftsmanship. It was a masterpiece.

As I navigated the corridors in College Hall, I was surprised to find myself exchanging glances with another man who looked like me. I sighed with deep relief; brown skin had never looked so fine. It was a humble exchange between us, for we both simply nodded, and then he quickly disappeared behind a closing door. Everything was said in a glance. Sometimes a man speaks his loudest when he does not speak at all.

As I rounded a corner, I saw a group of young white

students huddled together, laughing. There were four of them, and they wore clothing that identified them as athletes. Track men, no doubt. I could smell the blood of other runners from a quarter mile away.

These huddled students appeared to be close kindred of Demon Mischief—gawking at girls and taunting the more studious-looking boys. I found that interesting. Was that how they established the pecking order—by their appearance?

As I turned my attention away from them, I caught theirs, and they all turned to stare, which made me fidget. The tallest of the four detached himself from the group and stepped to the fore, silently proclaiming himself the leader. He was also the blondest and the fairest of skin. He had the bluest eyes, and the broadest smile, which looked sinister when he smiled real big—at least to me.

Now I could not turn away, because they were addressing me with their matching glares. What would I say— "How do you do? I'm John."

To my utter surprise, that was exactly what I did say. They laughed, and I wished I could roll the words back into my mouth and hide them under my tongue.

The leader emerged from the group and made his way to me. I stood in the middle of the hall, looking brand new, whereas he looked like he had been here a thousand years. He walked around me, then came full circle and stood in front of me puffed up with arrogance.

"How do you do?" I asked again. I was unsure of what else to do, but unable—or perhaps unwilling—to back away from this absurd encounter.

A Novel by Craig T. Williams

He examined me from head to toe, his inspection so thorough he must have memorized every detail of my attire.

What does a man say in this situation? And how does he remove himself from unpleasantness without putting his manhood on the line? I was no coward, but I was no fool either.

My new acquaintance didn't seem too pleased with such a simple, unimpressed response to his intense gaze. He leaned in close as though he were finally going to speak—so close I could smell his presence. I did not respond, just looked at him, because I was beginning to think that perhaps he was mad. Not angry mad, but missing a good part of his mind. He just stood there and smiled. That smile was not meant to be friendly.

If my daddy were there, he might have called this young man a loon. I wouldn't call him that, because I could tell by this silent, hostile reception that it would not get me far on my very first day of school.

"Charles Cook!" A voice thundered from the corner.

I didn't care where it came from, only that it broke the thick tension in the air. He was the man from College Hall. I could see now that he was an older man. He came to where we were standing. His skin was lighter than mine, but not by much. He was not a student or a teacher. Judging by the green uniform he now wore, and the full bucket of water he pulled alongside of him, reason suggested he was a janitor.

"You bein' the cause of trouble here, Charles?" he asked Charles Cook, meeting him eye to eye.

"No trouble at all," said Charles with a smile of delicious

deception. "I was just welcoming a new student."

The janitor did not lay friendly eyes on Charles. In fact, they were filled with displeasure, enough of it that Charles excused himself without further commotion.

"They call me Pomp," the janitor said to me with a warm smile. He appeared to be in his fifties or sixties, his fine wavy hair and neat mustache dusted with the mark of time. His face was long, with a high forehead and a determined chin. There was a scar just above his brow, but it did not detract from the impression that *this* face was made for smiling.

"John," I said, extending a hand.

"Don't pay them no mind," Pomp said, shaking my hand. "Ignant *and* rich ain't a pleasing combination."

I laughed. It sounded like something my daddy would say.

"First day?"

"Yes, sir … it is." I felt pride for the first time since I'd stepped onto the campus.

"'Bout time." There was fire behind the words.

"Huh?"

"Glad you're here, son," he said with another big, friendly smile.

"Thank you, sir. Just trying to find my way."

"You ain't got to worry about that, son," he said. "I been here a long time, and there's one guarantee I can give you."

"Sir?"

"If you don't find the way," he said with a grin, "the way will surely find *you*." And with that he turned and walked away.

"Thanks!" I shouted after him.

He just threw his hand up in the air and chuckled. "See you tomorrow, son."

"But ..." I said, stumbling over words, almost panicked. "How ... how ... will you know where I am?"

"I know *everything*," he said. "That's what makes me *Pomp*." He disappeared around the corner just as he had earlier.

I smiled. I surely wanted to find him the next day. To my surprise, my first friend on campus was not a fellow student or a fellow teammate. Instead, it was a janitor who made his wages by sweeping the floors of one of the most brilliant institutions in the world.

Life sure was funny. Just when you thought you understood it, it changed.

★★★★

September 1903
University of Pennsylvania
The Bowl Fight

I was filled with excitement as I made my way toward Franklin Field on the University of Pennsylvania campus. I had purposely dressed in my suit and hat so that I could be one of the spectators and not taken as a participant in the big event—a university tradition known as the Bowl Fight. So many students flocked to the field that I looked out over a sea of hats as I walked toward the scene of the battle.

The Olympian: An American Triumph

School history said that the conferring of a ceremonial trophy—a literal bowl—had begun as a fun way for the sophomore class to "honor" the lowest freshman third honor student for his achievements, the lowest of the academic standouts of the first term when there were three per year about thirty years past. But according to Pomp, that "good fun" had lasted only a couple of years before it became an intense struggle of man against man to gain control of the bowl by whatever means necessary. At some point any freshman crack picked by the freshman would do and the sophomores would do their best to put the freshman in the bowl while the freshman, in turn, tried to protect their classmate and break that bowl. Great fun no doubt.

It was odd, I know, to have a fascination with seeing my fellow students grabbing hair, throwing punches, and tossing one another about like rubbish. But I had to admit, the stories sounded so enticing that whether I was the only Negro in the stands or not, I had go *see.* It sounded like the Battle Royals that black colored boys were rounded up for and forced to fight to the last, except these boys were fighting willingly for their own entertainment. I was not foolish enough to throw myself into the circle of participants lest the color of my skin make me an easy mark for the many punches that would be thrown. No, it was best to join the hundreds of spectators and watch from the sidelines.

There was no formal seating arrangement, and folks found a place to watch the fight as best as they could—atop the grandstands, on the dirt or grass, against the fence. I sat quietly off to the side and watched as the fight began. No

A Novel by Craig T. Williams

one paid me any mind until that Cook fella showed up.

Charles Cook, representing the sophomores, walked onto the field holding a cherry wood bowl. He held the bowl away from his chest and turned around with it so that all could see it. The bowl was about two feet in diameter and had the emblems of all the fraternities painted around the inner rim. Though I had blended into the crowd without disturbance, Charles spotted me and reared his head back a bit as if in surprise.

I hoped this wasn't a mistake.

In a humiliating answer to my concern, Charles turned toward the largest throng of onlookers, jumped about, throwing his arms and legs in the air, and began to sing in a loud voice, "Come, listen, all you gals and boys, I'm just from Tuckyhoe; I'm going to sing a little song, My name's Jim Crow."

My face began to tingle as what felt like the whole crowd responded with great zeal and sang the chorus of "Jump Jim Crow." Many folks jumped up and began doing the dance as if they had practiced it in their sitting rooms for just this moment. I could only bite my lip and watch in horror. I was stung with the realization that this mocking dance had become popular not only in America, but throughout the world. I had been disturbed by the sense of being invisible here at UPenn, but now I would have welcomed invisibility.

Charles turned back to me then and, seeing the uneasiness on my face, burst into laughter. The crowd, which was really only a handful of sophomores, laughed with him.

I looked around for a friendly face and found none. Not even Pomp had come to view this spectacle. I shook off my unease and put on a disinterested face. They'd have to do a lot more than sing "Jump Jim Crow" to rattle me.

Charles smirked and turned back to the crowd. To my relief he continued with the celebration. "On behalf of the sophomore class, we present this bowl to Rollin C. Borthe, for his outstanding accomplishments," he said loudly.

The unfortunate Rollin walked out onto the field with a smile upon his face. He accepted the bowl from Charles and waved it in the air as the crowd cheered.

Now, this was how the first Bowl Fight had ended—nice and peaceful and with great celebration. But this was not the case on this night. Charles snatched the bowl back, and the rules of engagement were clear: anything goes.

"Sophomores!" Charles roared, as if he were a general leading men to war.

In response, the sophomores rushed onto the field with fists in the air, leaping at one another to crash chest against chest.

My eyes widened.

Charles turned in my direction. "Going to join your freshmen?" he taunted.

"Uh … no."

He laughed loudly. People turned their attention to us, glancing from Charles's face to mine. "Will you not fight with your class, John? Or are you yellow?" he said, inching closer to me. I didn't know what to say.

He found my silence amusing. "Well, real men fight. So

run along, runner!" he said, with hatred in his eyes. Then he turned from me and went back to his teammates as if our interaction had never occurred.

Again, I wanted to melt into the scenery and fade away.

Rollin let out his own cry for freshmen and my classmates rushed the field. As they flowed, screaming with excitement toward the inner circle, I retreated. It was clear that I didn't belong here. I began the journey home with a soul-deep feeling that my family would be very disappointed in me. Not because I had backed away from confrontation, but because I had let Charles Cook get to me.

As I made my way home, I held a strong resentment for Charles and everything he stood for—the belief that he was better because he was wealthy and white and that those attributes gave him the right to tease and humiliate whomever he chose. Though my family was not poor, we never used money as an excuse to act better than anyone else or to make any man feel inferior.

As Mama and Daddy always said, "The good Lord is with us all, and we must treat everyone like we know it, whether they see their own good or not."

My home training reminded me to try to see the Lord's hand on Charles, but my mind could not respect him as a man.

5

Stammered

I always found peace along the banks of the Schuylkill River. More than a hundred miles long, the river seemed to demonstrate the greatest freedom of all, running a mighty course that was entirely contained within the borders of Pennsylvania. Every time I walked along the water's edge, I imagined that in the same manner, I, too, could be at once mighty and self-contained.

Because the river was within walking distance of both campus and home, I often came to the Schuylkill to contemplate things I had yet to figure out. It seemed at times that there were much bigger lessons to be learned than Daddy or any establishment of higher learning could teach. At the river, I could put aside all my concerns, because it was here that I came to be a friend of nature. I loved the sheer reliability of nature. I knew that the flowers were going to bloom in spring and that leaves were going to turn to rust in fall and die in winter. I knew air was going to blow cold in December and warm in June.

I sat on a bench near the bank of the river and gazed at the glistening ripples. The sun was just beginning to set, blending beautiful shades of pink, orange, and red on the bellies of the clouds and casting a breathtaking reflection upon the water. I sighed in appreciation of the stillness and beauty of the moment.

"Excuse me," a soft voice said, interrupting my thoughts.

I stood and turned.

"I think you dropped this." A beautiful woman with a mesmerizing smile stood just behind me with her hand extended in my direction. In her hand was a trouser sock, which I knew at a glance belonged to me. It must have fallen out of my bag as I walked along the river.

Embarrassed to have my personal belongings held up for public viewing, I quickly accepted its return. "Thank you," I mumbled.

She smiled again, and it struck me that she was one of the prettiest young ladies I had ever seen. Her big brown eyes drew me to her, along with those curling lashes, caramel skin, and gleaming black hair. She was so pretty I thought she had to be a figment of my imagination. She was wearing a green skirt and white blouse with a green sweater over the top. Her clothing was average, but somehow she managed to make it seem the height of fashion.

For the life of me, I could not find my next word. So instead, I began to stammer, "I … I … I …"

"Dropped it by mistake," she finished, gazing at my sock.

The Olympian: An American Triumph

"Yes." I'm hardly the kind of man who fears women, but I felt a kind of fear in her company that I'd never known. Her smile entranced me, and I was afraid that I looked like a bumbling idiot. Still, I maintained my smile, showing nearly every tooth in my mouth.

"Mary Agnes Montier," she said. She extended her hand again, this time for me to shake.

"Oh, yes." I finally snapped out of my daze. I should have introduced myself first, but my tongue was tied in knots. "John Taylor, Jr., pleased to make your acquaintance."

She smiled again and I crumbled a little more. "You have the other one?" she asked, referring to my lost sock.

"Yes."

What was I saying? I had no idea. The other sock might have been in the river for all I knew. I was so nervous I didn't know what to do with myself. I was starting to fidget while trying to force myself to stand still. I feared that if I did not get control of myself this minute, I was going to start looking *foolish.*

"Do you come here often?" I asked.

"As often as I can. It's so very peaceful." She closed her eyes as if tasting that peacefulness.

I couldn't stop looking at her. Her radiance was burning holes in my eyes. She had gone off to another world, daydreaming; I took the moment to notice that she was carrying a tablet of some sort and a thick book. I glimpsed the title, *A Tale of Two Cities.*

"Are you a student?"

She slowly opened her eyes. It was as if she were looking at me for the first time. She held my gaze so long, it would have been rude of me to blink. Then without any warning, she simply let me go and looked out over the river.

"Are you a student?" I repeated.   "I see you're reading a pretty hefty book there." I just had to know *something* about her—anything at all would do.

"No, I just love to read. I work on Hickory Lane in Fairmount Park. I'm a nanny for the Porter family. Do you know the Porters?"

"No," I said, thinking it was a peculiar question. Fairmount Park was a prestigious North Philadelphia community, and Hickory Lane was known for its well-to-dos. I imagined the Porters were prominent people in society. "Should I know them?"

"They own a big restaurant close to downtown. Porter's Steak Restaurant. I'll be going now," she said casually as she started to move away.

"No!" I blurted.

She stopped and looked at me curiously.

"I … I … I …," I started stuttering all over again.

She laughed, though not unkindly. "Do you have some sort of speech difficulty?"

"No. I just wanted to know …"

Silence … and more silence because I could not fit my mind around the words I wanted to say. My ability to communicate had deserted me. This had never happened before.

"I just wanted to know if I will see you again."

She looked at me and raised one eyebrow.

"Here, I mean … at the river."

She did not answer at first, just looked at me while my heart beat out of my chest.

"If you *will* see me again?" she questioned. "Or if you *can* see me again? There is quite a difference between the two."

"If I *can* see you again."

"Would you like to see me again?"

"Very much so."

"Will you tell me one thing about yourself, John Taylor, Jr., that I don't already know?" she asked. "Since I know nothing about you, I imagine you'd have a lot to put into words."

I searched my head for something meaningful to say. It was hard to tell *one* thing, when the truth was I wanted to tell her *everything*. But that wouldn't have been a practical way to approach our very first conversation. I decided to try to impress her.

"I'm a student at the Wharton School of Finance."

She was silent and without expression; I didn't know if she was impressed or unimpressed. Maybe she didn't like finance.

I said, "I am an athlete, a runner," and still she was silent. Maybe she didn't like runners either. "My daddy makes the best crab cakes in all of Philadelphia."

Still there was no response. Maybe she hated crab cakes. I was sinking fast, losing her every second that I remained a stammering idiot.

Don't stammer, John. Don't stammer.

"Apple pie is my favorite dessert in the whole world," I said with a big grin. It was my last try at winning a prize today, even if it was just one more pretty smile. And finally, she did smile. I was greatly relieved.

"My favorite pie is cherry," she told me.

I felt a burden lift off my shoulders. Apple and cherry pie seemed a respectable foundation upon which to build a friendship.

"It was a pleasure meeting you, Mr. John Taylor, Jr.," she said as she turned and began to walk away in the direction of Fairmount Park.

"Can you tell me one thing about yourself, Mary Agnes Montier?" I called after her.

She turned again and gave me one last smile with a wink. "I just did."

And with that she turned back around and kept on walking.

★★★★

One Week Later
Schuylkill River

Just like magic, I found her again, a week to the day. The weather was warm for this time of the year and she was sitting under a tree inscribing notes into a thin notebook with that thick book, *A Tale of Two Cities*, beneath it. My heart dropped several beats the moment I laid eyes upon her. Lord Almighty, she truly was the most beautiful woman I had ever seen.

"Mary Agnes?" I called out to her.

She was just as surprised to see me, and looked equally pleased as she rose from her seat on the ground and offered me an inviting smile.

"Mr. Taylor," she said.

"I am most surprised to see you ... pleasantly surprised, of course."

"Yes," she said with a nod. "I am most surprised to see you as well ... pleasantly, of course."

"Is this where you spend your leisure moments?"

"Perhaps."

"And whose company do you keep in your leisure moments?" I further prodded. "If you don't mind me asking."

"Is that your not so elegant way of asking me if I am spoken for?"

Was I that obvious? Embarrassment silenced me.

"I spend most of my leisure moments with Phillis Wheatley," she said as we began walking along the river's edge.

"So, I take it you're a poet, too," I said, nodding at the notebook and small bound volume she was carrying.

"Yes, I am, and I am impressed that you know who Phillis Wheatley is."

"Kidnapped and sold into slavery at the age of seven," I said, intent on showing off my knowledge. "She was one of the greatest poets of our times. Everybody knows that."

"Not *everybody*." She drew out the word for emphasis. "Did you know she learned English, Greek, *and* Latin, even though she never had any formal education?"

"That I did not know," I admitted.

"She died in complete poverty. That's *not* going to be

my story." There was passion in that statement.

"What *is* going to be your story?"

She smiled, and her eyes widened and got real dreamy looking. "I'm going to be important one day ... I'm going to be remembered. Like Angelina and Sarah Grimke."

"I don't know much about them. Who were they?" I couldn't remember *every* accomplished woman who had ever lived.

"They were the first women in the United States to argue for the abolition of slavery," said Mary Agnes, "*and* their father was a slave owner himself. Imagine that."

"Interesting."

"Indeed it is. His own children speaking out against what he had done. They insisted on equality for coloreds and for women. The Grimkes didn't care what other people thought about them, John. Don't you think that's brave?"

"Yes, I do."

"Do you care what people think about you, John Taylor?" she asked.

"More than I care to admit at times." The honesty of the words leaving my lips astounded me. I was at ease with Mary Agnes. I found the ability to be free, to be myself—the way I was on the field. I exhaled with relief and looked at this interesting woman with great appreciation.

"Acceptance, or lack thereof, by others does not define who and what you actually are," she said with conviction.

"Let me guess: Phillis Wheatley?"

"Nope," she said with a trill of laughter. "Mary Agnes Montier."

"I would like to see you again." I blurted the words before I could catch myself. "I'd like to take you some place *real* special."

"Well, John Taylor," she said, "you best find your way to Powelton and Curie in Greenville ... to the prettiest little row house on the road, and see Mr. and Mrs. Montier about that."

"I will!"

She laughed, then turned around and started walking back to the tree I had found her sitting under, without me.

"I'll see you soon!" I called after her.

"That depends entirely on you," was her final word on the matter. "Entirely on *you*."

6

The Inquisition

Early October 1903

I don't know which pulled me from my sleep, the smell of Mama's cooking or the sounds of the horse carriages making their way up the road. I was right in the middle of one of the best dreams of my life. Mary Agnes and I were at the river and she was reading Charles Dickens as I lay with my head resting against a tree, listening to the rise and fall of her melodic voice.

To cap the moment, I smelled bacon frying—paradise.

The dream was peaceful until the yelling of a carriage driver ripped me from sleep and tossed me back into the world, a world in which I had not seen Mary Agnes in days. I got up and peered out my window, careful not to wake William. Not that I minded waking my brother from his dreams, but I was in the mood to let my thoughts wander without interruption.

The driver was standing next to a carriage with a broken wheel, and turning a nice shade of crimson. I returned to my bed to enjoy a few moments of solitude. Just as I got settled the driver banged his thumb with a mallet and let out a horrible howl. With all the commotion, or maybe the fragrance of bacon, William tossed and turned my way, one eye opening to sum me up.

"What are doing there, Johnny?" William questioned. "Didn't Daddy tell you if you keep touching that thing you will go completely blind?"

"Did I wake you? Well, let's see how awake you are. You think you can make it out of the room faster than I can catch you?" I leaned toward him.

William's gaze locked on my face, trying to read my intention. I refused to let the smile form on my lips. William slipped one foot out of the bed as if he thought he was invisible. We locked eyes, both knowing that a wrestling match, Taylor versus Taylor, was about to begin.

"Morning, Ma!" William yelled.

What kind of girl move was that?

We tussled and tossed, making fun until Mama shuffled by and hollered, "Cut all that foolishness out! Breakfast is on. How many times do I have to remind you," she added, "that Miss Harriet likes her quiet."

By Miss Harriet she meant "Moses" Harriet Tubman, who some folks claimed stayed in this very house after she escaped slavery. Mama seemed to believe that Miss Harriet had in some fashion become the spirit of our home, and wanted her soul to find rest in our little row house.

No matter how many times we reminded Mama that there was no official record of Moses passing on or of her ever staying in this house, Mama would just shush us and say, "Never you mind whether she's here or up there with the Lord. Wherever you go, a good piece of you stays behind, so you all mind yourself in Miss Harriet's room 'cause she wants it still in there."

William and I stopped the noise and gave Miss Harriet and Mama some peace.

Mama went on by the doorway of our room, and William and I stood there gritting at each other until we laughed as quietly as we could.

"Come here. Sit down a bit, William," I said.

"Now you know Mama said..." he whined.

"I'm not wrestling you. I want to discuss something important."

William's eyes widened as he sat down on the bed.

"Well, ain't nobody died or nothing like that," I said jokingly.

William had much more experience with the females, and I was anxious to hear his wisdom. Not that I didn't admire the beauty and intelligence of a pretty young lady, but I'd always kept my focus on the track. My life, until I met Mary Agnes Montier, was filled with studying, running, and looking out for Charles Cook. Now I had great interest in adding something new to my list of activities and I didn't want to botch it up.

"Well, what do you look all serious for, if you don't have bad news? Come on, spit it out," he pressed. "I'm hungry."

"Listen, William, I, uh, I ..."

"I, uh, I?" he mimicked. "Now you can't talk. Say your piece, brother."

"There's no way you're that hungry. Stay focused." I rolled my eyes back in my head and sat down next to him on the bed.

"Why are you stuttering so?" he asked.

"I don't see how this is humorous," I said. "Listen, I have a … an intention to court a nice young lady, and I want your advice."

Now his eyes got very wide. "Well, it's about time you took your head out of the sand and looked around you a bit."

I popped him in the head with my pillow. "Come on, William. I need your opinion. I have to go make my intentions known this afternoon."

"Just who is this young woman that's made my brother stop and take notice?"

"This is a man-to-man conversation—why do you have to poke fun? Her name is Mary Agnes."

"Mary Agnes… What's her family name?"

"Mary Agnes Montier."

"Where's the family live?"

"William, you are not writing a piece for the *Inquirer*," I said, pushing him in the shoulder.

"Well, Mama and Daddy are going to ask those questions. Why shouldn't I?"

"They live in Greenville."

Greenville was a section of West Philadelphia filled with the homes and businesses of stable families that had lived in the city for generations.

"Okay, they got some history," William said, "and you

do, too. You walk in there hat in hand, be friendly and sincere, and tell an anecdote or two. Tell them about your daddy settling his family in Philadelphia, chasing after a dream. And then ... you ask them if they've ever tasted the best crab cakes in town."

"Come on, now. We can't go in there boasting."

William looked at me, head tilted to the side. "What do you mean *we*?"

"There's nothing wrong with two brothers going for a nice stroll."

"There is if one's yellow."

"All right, all right. This is different and she's ... she's like Mama. She's a spitfire—witty and sharp. And she smells so good. I'm at a loss for words whenever she comes near me. I forget what to say and can barely think the right thoughts. I do believe she makes me ... flustered."

"Are you going to be the man in this courtship?" laughed William, pushing me almost off the bed.

"I'm just saying..."

Mary Agnes Montier had made an impression in my mind and heart, one I had tucked away like my news clippings. I had every intention of making the best impression so her parents would be proud and pleased to allow their daughter to accompany me someplace very special indeed— the Philadelphia Zoo. I don't know where the thought came from, but it had popped into my head that Mary Agnes would love to see all the exotic animals at the zoo. Besides, being around animals always brought me a certain peace. Aside from running, being near an animal was my greatest joy, and I was certain I'd be able to keep my wits and my humor around them so Mary Agnes wouldn't think I was some kind of stammering clown.

I dismissed my brother with a wave of my hand. "Never you mind, William. I know all I need to know. I'm John Baxter Taylor, Jr., son of John Taylor, respected businessman, and Sarah Thomas Taylor, one of the finest seamstresses in Philadelphia."

"That's what I'm telling you. Know who you are, and that will make all the impression you need. You," he said, pointing to me and standing, "are no ordinary fellow."

Then William did something unusual. He leaned in close and whispered, "I'm proud to know you and honored to call you 'brother.'" Then the singular moment passed and his smile returned. "Now let's eat, Sport."

With that, William turned and walked out of the bedroom.

★★★★

I crossed the bridge in my Sunday best—a black suit and matching hat. I wanted to show the Montiers—especially Mr. Montier—that their daughter had captured the eye of a man who was on his way in the world. Maybe I should be strutting alongside the road to prove my point, but there is a time and a place for everything, and this was *not* the time or the place for a humble man to puff himself down the street. It's only just the other side of the University, no need to rush. Best to stroll in slow, measured steps, eyes on the road and focused on finding the prettiest row house on the street.

By the time I arrived at the corner of Powelton and Curie, my heart was beating almost out of my chest. There are times in a man's life when he can feel change coming, and this sure felt like one of those times.

Greenville, otherwise known as "The Black Bottom," was a strong community of Negroes, made up of simple folks doing simple things. There were people sitting on the front steps of a church having an easy exchange of words. I saw children jumping rope and playing jacks off to the side. Men pitched horseshoes in a park while commerce was conducted in the middle of the road.

The houses were practically identical, but one was slightly prettier. It was brick, just like its neighbors, but it had a certain kind of charm, with lace curtains and intricate floral carvings worked into the trim. It looked distinctly feminine.

"There she is," I said to myself, relieved that it had been easy to find.

I took a couple of deep breaths and began the walk up to the front door, which seemed as long as the whole journey previous. I wanted to stand there three, maybe four minutes, and take a couple more deep breaths so I could muster the courage to knock. But before I could even make it to the first breath, the door swung open and a tall, light brown colored man wearing a vest, a large pair of pants, and a most unfriendly expression was standing in the doorway, towering over me. Now, I was close to six feet, and in comparison, he was *much* taller.

I must be at the wrong house, I thought. Could this man be related to Mary Agnes Montier?

"Sir," I said with a respectful nod and a tip of my hat, "I ... I ... was looking for Mr. and Mrs. Montier's, but I do believe I may be at the wrong address."

"What address are you looking for, son?" he asked with a deep voice that poured from him with no hint of good-humor.

"I ... I ...," I stumbled and bumbled, "don't have an exact address."

"So you just go up to folks' doors knocking with no exact address?"

"No, sir, not usually."

His left brow rose, and his mouth twisted to one side. "What is the nature of your business?" he asked, eyeing me top to bottom. I hoped he was admiring my suit, not questioning my mental faculties.

"An inquiry, sir," I said.

"What kind of inquiry?"

"Well, sir," I said, dropping my gaze. "It is of a personal nature. If you could just point me in the direction of the Montiers', I would be ..." but before I could spill out the words, he pointed a single finger toward his own chest.

"Mr. Montier?" I asked, my voice squeaking.

He did not speak in reply, just nodded.

Oh, boy, I thought. *This isn't going to be easy at all.*

"I'm John Taylor, Jr., Sir." I said, extending my hand for a firm handshake.

A Novel by Craig T. Williams

Mr. Montier studied me for a moment, shook my hand, then opened the door wide and said, "Do come in."

I entered with caution, lest he have a change of heart before I could get inside and state my intentions.

The inside of the house was as charming as the outside, and everything in it was delicate and perfectly placed. Encased behind glass wall, within an exquisitely crafted bookshelf, there stood a swarm of Union Army Civil War artifacts which included muskets, carbines, revolvers, a sword and medals.

"Wow!" I said, commenting on the display, "This is mighty impressive!"

Mr. Montier did not respond, but directed me to a seat in their parlor, which was just off the foyer on the right. "What is the nature of your inquiry, son?" he asked again, taking a seat directly across from me, giving me his undivided attention.

My gut was telling me that we were about to go from an inquiry to an inquisition. "Well, sir," I said, shuffling my hat from hand to hand, "the nature of my business involves your lovely daughter, Mary Agnes."

"Mary Agnes?" he asked, almost breathing fire. I could have sworn his nostrils flared.

In that moment, I didn't know whether to keep talking or bolt to the front door. "I … I … met her one day down at the Schuylkill River. She was taking a walk and I was taking a walk … and we bumped into each other and started a conversation … and, uh … uh …"

Stutter. Stammer. Stutter.

"With your permission, sir, I would like to accompany Mary Agnes to the zoo to see the animal exhibits, …Sir." The words came out in a rush.

This was one of the most awkward moments of my life. Mr. Montier sat as still as a dead frog on a log, and, following his lead, so did I.

Finally he spoke. "John …What is your name again, young man?"

"John Baxter Taylor, Jr., sir," I said with a gigantic smile. When he showed no response, it quickly faded.

"Connie!" shouted Mr. Montier, rearing back in his seat. I thought the wall trembled.

Seconds later, a mature version of Mary Agnes entered the room. This must be the delicate spirit that graced this house and brought it to life. I quickly stood and nodded as she entered the room. She was as beautiful and peaceful looking as Mary Agnes, and when she took one look at me and smiled, she had Mary's smile.

"John Baxter Taylor, Jr.," said Mr. Montier, nodding in my direction, "has come asking permission to court Mary Agnes."

Connie Montier's eyes widened with surprise and delight. "Well," she said, "this is a fine surprise."

I smiled big again, till Mr. Montier said, "No reason it should be—he isn't the first young man who's come here asking to court Mary Agnes."

My smile faded once again.

"No," said Mrs. Montier, "but he's the most handsome."

My smile returned, only to disappear when Mr. Montier

stirred and looked over at me again.

"Let's get this over with," he said, leaning back and reaching for a glass of lemonade that sat on a side table next to his chair.

The lemonade sure looked good, and I couldn't help but stare at it.

When Mrs. Montier saw me eyeing the glass, she asked, "Would you like some lemonade, son?"

"Yes, ma'am, I would."

She disappeared and quickly reappeared with a fresh cold glass, handed it to me, and took a chair beside her husband's.

"Thank you for the lemonade, ma'am," I said.

She smiled. "You're welcome, John."

"So, what exactly are your intentions toward my Mary Agnes?" asked Mr. Montier.

"I would like to take her on an outing."

"And then what?" he asked.

And then what? I didn't have a *then what*, so my eyes quickly searched the interior of my head, looking for one. "Well," I said, "and then bring her back home."

Mr. Montier's eyes widened and he turned to Mrs. Montier, who looked up at him and shrugged.

"Who are your parents?" he asked.

"John and Sarah Taylor."

"What is your father's trade?"

"My father owns his own catering business. He makes the best crab cakes in all of Philadelphia. My mother is a seamstress."

Mrs. Montier smiled.

Mr. Montier didn't.

"What is *your* trade?" he asked as his right eyebrow reached toward the ceiling.

"I am a student at the University of Pennsylvania's Wharton School of Finance."

Mrs. Montier's eyes widened and she smiled real big. Mr. Montier remained expressionless. *Translation: unimpressed.*

"Next spring I'll be on the University track team, sir," I said.

"A runner," said Mr. Montier with a raised brow.

"Yes, sir."

"Do you court many girls?"

"No, sir," I said, shaking my head. "My time is devoted to my studies and my running."

Mr. Montier said nothing. I could see where Mary Agnes got her fire. He just studied me in silence for what felt like an eternity.

"What are your intentions?" he asked again.

"Well, after the zoo …," I started.

He interrupted me by clearing his throat, hard. "What are *your* intentions toward yourself? What are you planning for your life, son?"

"I plan on going into business for myself, just like my daddy."

"Well, that sounds promising, but why should we allow you to court Mary Agnes?"

"Pardon, sir?" I asked, trying to stall for enough time to find a suitable answer.

"What makes you so special?" asked Mr. Montier.

A Novel by Craig T. Williams

"It's not that *I'm* so special, sir," I said humbly. "*She's* special."

Mrs. Montier's mouth curved upward into a permanent smile, and to my surprise, Mr. Montier finally smiled, too.

7

Friendship

The leaves had made a graceful exit. All that remained of the trees were bare branches reaching up to the sky as if asking the Lord the same question that was in human minds: *Why?* Why is it so cold that a man's teeth chatter, damming up the flow of words? Why is it so cold that people dash silently from place to warm place? The weather had changed so suddenly. The only time I was comfortable outdoors these days was when I was running. I practiced four afternoons a week with one of my classmates, Nathaniel Cartmell, who also aspired to become a member of the UPenn track and field team.

We'd discovered each other back at the beginning of the school year, drawn to the great cinder oval by our runner's blood. I'd put on my old Brown Prep track suit and running shoes and gone down to the track and there he'd been, stretching. We stood facing each other across the width of the track, looking each other up and down—me, uncertain of what sort of welcome I'd get.

"Nate Cartmell," he'd said at last.

"John Taylor," I'd responded in kind. "From Brown Prep."

"I know. You're damn fast." He swore easily. "So am I."

"That right? Then you'll be trying out for the track team, I imagine."

He nodded, then jerked his head toward the top of the track. "Planning on running this afternoon are you, J. T?"

"That I am."

"Me too."

We watched each other do nothing for a moment longer, then Nate grinned. "Then let's run."

We ran. We ran that afternoon and every other afternoon thereafter come hot, cold or indifferent weather. These days we often laughed as we ran at the way our breath sailed out on the air. Nate seemed not to care about the difference in our colors. We weren't men from disparate worlds—we were runners.

This was by far one of the coldest autumns we had spent in Philadelphia and one of the first that I wished we lived somewhere that I didn't have to pull my topcoat so tight, or push my Homburg so firmly down on my head. The wool of the hat warmed my ears, and I gave no mind to the dent in the crown and whether it was fashionable any longer. My mind was on my ears, which I'm certain looked like bright slices of tomato stuck to the sides of my head.

I laughed out loud at the thought of my fire wagon red ears, and a few students turned and looked at me as if I'd gone mad. Nothing was funny in a cold so severe you felt as though you would freeze if you didn't keep moving. Still the laugh had warmed me, and I was grateful for it. One could only be thankful that the coal miners had gotten their demands met the previous fall and were not striking this year—were it not for that, we'd have no warm places to dash to and from.

My morning classes were over and I really wanted a hot meal for lunch. There were no restaurants or lunchrooms on either side of 34th and Walnut streets that were willing to serve Negroes, and many other gathering places were off limits to those of us with brown skin, but on this day my desire for a hot meal was so strong that it gave birth to a giddy optimism: I might find acceptance in one of the college dining halls as an athlete among athletes.

I picked a dining hall that was favored by college sportsmen, entered, and felt an immediate draft of cold—not from the weather but from the students who were seated in staggered rows of tables as far as the eye could see. I guess I was just doing what I would have done at good old Central High. But this wasn't Central High. All the faces were white, which was regular enough, but all looked rather well-to-do. Or maybe they just appeared well-to-do because they had plates of hot food … and I did not.

They looked at me like an audience waiting for an announcement. Conversations stopped, except for scattered murmurs. They had been shaken from their meals, and all attention fell on me. Some stared at me dead on and others looked away in discomfort. In either case, the message was

A Novel by Craig T. Williams

clear: *Surely he's not expecting to eat in here with us.*

I took about four steps into the dining hall and met an invisible wall erected by those stares and that sudden silence.

I stopped.

There was no need to pretend anymore that I could just stroll up to the lunch counter, grab a tray, and fill an empty plate with my heart's desire. That illusion gone, I glanced around the room purposefully, as if I were looking for someone. After a seemingly thorough search, I turned around with a pleasant nod of my head as if to say, *Enjoy your hot plates. Don't mind me. I have my cold meat and hard cheese.* My heart sank as I bid farewell to the whiff of home cooking and went back out into the welcoming arms of the cold outdoors.

I made my way back across campus to College Hall. Even with the wind whipping my face and my disappointment at not having a good meal, I had to stop and take a breath when I saw the beauty and majesty of the building. It stopped me in my tracks every time I approached it. I couldn't take such craftsmanship—put into this building by a Penn man—for granted. I was always filled with awe as I made my way around the circular path and fixed my eyes on the towers and the arching windows that seemed to watch us all as we entered.

The wind suddenly whipped my head so hard it reminded me of William's "love taps." But this was no man's hand slapping me in the back of the head; this was the wind telling me to stop my gawping and get into the building before I froze. I ran up the steps and made my way through the tall, stately doors.

The Olympian: An American Triumph

I was optimistic most days, but today I felt alone, and I retreated to the place where I was in the habit of eating my lunch—the eastern tower of College Hall. I would climb the stairs to the top floor, make my way to the corner tower overlooking the forecourt, and sit in the window embrasure watching the world below me. I thought about those who enjoyed hot food, those who ate hard sandwiches, and those who would not eat at all. I was appreciative of the refuge I had found in College Hall. It was a place to get my bearings and steady myself in the world.

Today I abandoned my window perch. I placed my books and papers on the floor and stretched out beside them to enjoy my meal of cold meat and hard cheese. My first bite was interrupted by the sound of creaking stairs. Someone had discovered me.

I peered through the narrow arch that gave onto the turret. A head of wavy, speckled hair appeared above the top stair tread. A moment later I looked into the kind, wise eyes of Pomp.

"What business you got up here, son?" he asked, looking around the room.

I stretched my legs a bit and exhaled, thankful that it was just Pomp. "I just needed to find some space, Pomp. Still trying to find my way, I guess."

Pomp nodded with understanding. "You lost?"

If life had a theme question, that would be it: Was I lost? How deeply did I discuss this? How much did I expose to the friendly gaze of a stranger?

As if he could read my thoughts, Pomp flashed a smile,

sat down across from me on the floor, and cleared his throat. "Son, I's here twelve years before the first colored came through them doors." He nodded toward the front wall of the building. "I been here since I was thirteen."

I choked on my sandwich and fell into a coughing spell at the thought of Pomp being a university janitor since the age of thirteen and the only colored face for more than a decade.

He showed no interest in helping me breathe freely and continued with his story as though I had made no interruption. "My mama had three kids above me and two below me. Don't much recall my pop. He worked out of town so he wasn't there much and he died when I was nine or so, and we all had to find a way to help Mama keep the house. So I had to find me a way, just like you doing now."

I finally composed myself and looked at him. He seemed to be lost in another time.

"I swept floors and did odd jobs before Emancipation. I was right here, in front of this hall, when Lincoln set the slaves free," he said, looking upward. Tears came into his eyes. "It was something to hear ... Finally coloreds didn't have to sneak here and hide there in order to feel free. You was *born* free. You was born *free*." He smacked his hand on the floor for emphasis. "D'you know what that means?"

"Mama and Daddy tell me that all the time, especially Daddy."

Pomp shook his head so quickly I thought it might spin around on his shoulders. "Have your own view on things, son. This is your life! Your Mama and Daddy are no more than this far"—he snapped his fingers—"from slavery. *You* was born *free!*"

I had been trying to truly grasp the word *free* since I understood what it meant, and no matter how much I ran, or how much I read, or how much I tried to smile politely and be a gentleman, that was not enough to make me feel accepted all of the time. I had tasted some part of that "freedom" at Central and Brown, but that door had been slammed shut at this place. And yet there were folks like Mama and Daddy—and now Pomp—who wanted to take *free* and wrap it around me like a ribbon.

I didn't know much about the world in their day, but I knew that in this day and age, it sometimes was difficult to be yourself and still live up to expectations—your own, your family's, society's. Would Pomp—or Mama or Daddy—understand that without taking offense and saying that I didn't appreciate the progress Negroes had made, that I'd failed to understand the significance of being free? Would they understand how it felt to have one foot in freedom and the other in captivity? No longer a slave, free, but with nowhere to go.

Dream big, said Freedom. *Be anything, do anything.*

No, said Reality. *Do what's practical. Don't dream too big, because you're only going to be allowed to do so much.*

I felt Pomp's gaze as these thoughts tumbled through my head.

"Listen here, son," he said. "I know it stings, the way you get treated more often than not. But I's lived more than you and I *seen* more than you." He looked around the room once again. "You come up here to escape, but I'm gonna tell you, boy, as if you were my own son, to stand your ground. You in a special place in history, a special time for this world. A time when a free colored man can *choose* to go to a university. You can do what you want to do with your life. You don't have to be nobody's janitor. Not that I'm sorry 'bout what I've done in life," he added. "I've done right by this place and I'm loyal to it. I'm an honorary member of the class of 1858, d'you know that? I've served as assistant to two professors—worked right alongside 'em."

I sat up, listening with deep interest.

He nodded. "Yessir, I'm more than a colored pushin' a broom. And you're a whole lot more than a long-legged fellow who can run. Don't go pushing yourself into a hole that don't have to be dug. It's hard, yeah. But it gets easier every day. You got it better than your mama, your papa, or me *ever* had. So what you gonna do, son? You gonna sit up here and hide? Or you gonna make a life? I wish I could start over in your shoes." Pomp let out a small laugh. "Never you mind who talks to you and who don't. They can't live your life. They can't walk in your skin. They can't feel your pain. They can't feel what you feel when you close your eyes. So you, John Baxter Taylor, gonna have to choose your *way.*"

Pomp got to his feet, peered out the window, and said, "You just remember—you in one of the best schools in this land. And you get to choose … *You* get to say what you'll be one day. Heck, you can even be a doctor if you want. But ain't it a blessing to have the choice?"

He reached out his hand, pulling me up from the floor.

"Now you gather up this stuff and we'll have lunch in my office. I got stuff to do and can't be tending to you all afternoon. But you ain't got to eat alone today."

I picked up my things and followed Pomp to his basement "office," feeling as though I had just gotten more out of this talk than I had received all semester in my class lectures.

8

Forever

Thanksgiving Day Weekend, 1903

In the true spirit of Thanksgiving, and with the blessing of Mr. and Mrs. Montier, I was finally permitted to take Mary Agnes out on our first official outing. We were headed to the Philadelphia Zoo, and I had arranged a day and time to pick up Mary Agnes from the Montiers' in a horse and buggy provided by the senior John Baxter Taylor. Thankfully, that Almanac was right this time. That bitter cold spell had passed and the weather was even a bit warm for this time of the year.

"Son," he said to me early that morning as I prepared for my big day, "it's about time we had us a talk."

"What talk, Daddy?" I stopped shining my shoes and turned to face him.

He looked at me solemnly, but said nothing.

"Sir?" I prompted, but still he was silent.

After much deliberation, he finally spoke. "Woman talk."

"Sir?"

"Stay put," he said, holding up one finger and looking perplexed. He left my bedroom and returned moments later with Mama, who had a huge grin on her face.

Now I was the one who was perplexed. "Mama?"

Mama came into the room, laid a gentle hand on my cheek, and stroked it softly. "John, your father wants to speak to you about how to treat a woman."

"But he didn't say anything," I said.

Mama looked at Daddy and raised a single brow. "Well … I guess he's short on words today, but I want you to know the best way to treat a woman."

"Yes?" I responded eagerly.

"Treat her like *yourself*," she said plain and simple. "If you wouldn't do it to yourself, don't do it to her. If you wouldn't think it 'bout yourself, don't think it 'bout her."

I nodded in agreement. It seemed simple enough.

"And most important," said Daddy, finally chiming in, "if you wouldn't feed it to yourself, then don't take her there to eat."

They both burst into laughter while I just sat there on the bed, feeling about as lost and confused as a young man could. I guess it was the funniest show in town—me going on an outing with a girl. I caught sight of William lingering in our bedroom doorway, snickering.

"That's it?" I asked.

"That's it, son," Daddy said.

"I was waiting on something big."

Mama leaned over and kissed me on the forehead and

walked out. Daddy stood near me, still chuckling.

"That's it?" I asked again.

"Son," said Daddy, patting the top of my head the same way he used to when I was a little boy, "we know who you are, because we know who we raised you to be. Be *you*, and everything else will fall into place." He turned and left, and that was it.

By early afternoon I was on my way to Greenville so gussied up that there was no way to describe me without generously using the word *handsome.* I wore some of Daddy's Bay Rum aftershave reserved only for special occasions, a nice pair of trousers, my Homburg, topcoat, and some shiny boots. As was customary for young suitors, I stopped along the way to purchase a box of candy for Mr. and Mrs. Montier.

The second I pulled up in front of the Montiers' row house, a knot the size of a baseball curled up in my gut and my stomach began to feel queasy.

I got down off the buggy, slowly made my way up the steps to the front door, and waited for my stomach to co-operate. When things seemed to settle a bit, I prepared to knock, but before my knuckles could rap the door, Mr. Montier opened it, looking just as unfriendly as he had the first time I met him. I offered a smile as a "peace offering," and could not present him with that box of candy quickly enough. I wanted to show Mr. Montier that I had manners and was a respectable young man.

He accepted the candy with a quiet "Thank you" and ushered me into the parlor, where I sat and waited for Mary

Agnes and he sat across from me and stared.

"How are you this fine day, sir?" I asked.

"Fine."

I nodded and smiled again. Smiling was good. It helped ease my nerves. "Did you have a nice Thanksgiving, sir?" I asked.

He nodded.

Well, I thought, I can see things haven't improved much between Mr. Montier and the art of conversation.

Feeling overly warm, I began to loosen my collar while Mr. Montier's eyes followed my every move. Just then, to my great relief, Mary Agnes was escorted into the room by her mother. She was a fine and welcome sight to behold. I quickly stood and nodded as Mary Agnes took the center of the floor, looking radiant, wearing a burgundy dress that brushed the floor lightly, a shawl, and a lovely bonnet with a purse to match. She was the epitome of timeless beauty.

"Good afternoon, ma'am," I said, first speaking to her mother, who smiled in return.

With the formalities out of the way, my eyes returned to Miss Montier. "You look very lovely, Mary Agnes."

"Thank you, John," she said confidently, and I was impressed with the fact that, even with her father eyeballing us nearly to death, Mary Agnes was unshakeable. There seemed not to be a timid bone in her body. Confidence was surely her strong suit.

"Shall we go?" I asked, extending my arm.

She graciously accepted and I nodded to both parents. "Mr. and Mrs. Montier."

A Novel by Craig T. Williams

"Have a nice time," said Mrs. Montier.

Mary Agnes released my arm to kiss her mother good-bye, but she did not kiss her father, which I thought was odd.

As we headed toward the door, her father rose from his seat and grabbed his jacket and hat. Mary Agnes paused so her father could assist her with her coat and hat, and then they turned in my direction.

"We can take my horse and buggy," he said.

We?

If ever a man had to force a smile and pretend that this was the most exciting news of the day, this was one of those times. I was an athlete, not an actor, so it was hard to downplay the excruciating disappointment.

"I'll be your chaperone today." said Mr. Montier flatly.

"Yes, of course, sir!" I said, though my voice rose a bit.

Mary Agnes looked at me and smiled. Surely she must have known that this whole setup was sending shivers down my spine. Having a chaperone was a common practice early in a courtship, but I hoped that *I* wouldn't need one, especially given my reliability, respectability, and gentlemanly presentation. Obviously, I was wrong.

I thought this was my day to be a man, but apparently I was wrong about that, too. We walked by my little buggy and boarded Mr. Montier's waiting two-in-hand with its team of matched bays. Needless to say, the ride to the zoo was stiff, quiet, and very, very long.

It was a brisk fall afternoon, but the sun shone warmly as, we crossed the Girard Avenue Bridge, nearing the Philadelphia Zoo's entrance. The closer we got, the more my palms started to sweat, and I almost began to dread the thought of spending the afternoon at the zoo with Mary Agnes *and* Mr. Montier. Whatever would we talk about? It did not seem to disturb Mary Agnes in the least, because every time I glanced at her, her expression was pleasant and easy.

Mr. Montier pulled the buggy right up to the zoo's main entrance and reined the horses to a halt. He turned to Mary Agnes with a nod and said, "You two have a good time. See you back here in four hours."

"Yes, Daddy."

"Thank you, sir," I said with tremendous gratitude. A reprieve! He wasn't coming in with us after all. Now I could have Mary Agnes all to myself.

I quickly jumped down from the buggy and assisted Mary Agnes in her descent. I wanted to say, "Hurry up, hurry"—for her father might change his mind—but I didn't, because that would not have been gentlemanly. I could not wait to get inside one of my favorite places in the world—America's first-ever zoo, an enchanting place to spend the afternoon with a beautiful girl.

We walked to the wrought iron gates and I turned to Mary Agnes. "Are you ready for a day of magic?" I asked.

Mary Agnes looked at me with a shy smile. "I am always ready for spectacular moments."

My smile must have widened enough to touch both of my ears. "Great," I said, extending my arm. "Then I shall be your tour guide on this adventure."

She laughed lightly and wove her arm through mine.

A Novel by Craig T. Williams

"Now, how do you know I haven't been here before?"

"Oh dear Lord. Of course, you must have been here before," I babbled.

Mary Agnes laughed again and nudged me in the ribs. "I'm joking, John."

I exhaled. "All right, Miss Montier. Let's begin the tour by paying our fifty cents."

She nodded. "Yes, sir."

It was a pretty penny for a university student to pay, but she was worth every penny. Once inside the Garden gates, I began my tour.

"So, *have* you been here before?" I asked.

She chuckled. "No. You have."

"Why, how'd you know?" I asked playfully. "When I was young, my daddy brought me here because he knew how much I loved animals. I've always wanted to take care of them and patch up the sick ones."

"An animal doctor," she said. "Imagine that."

"What do you want to see first? The zoo has more than a thousand animals from around the world. It has forty-two acres that are beautiful even at this time of year." As the words left my mouth, I was thinking that the majestic trees and Victorian garden could not compare to the beauty I saw in Mary Agnes's face.

"I don't know … There's so much here," she said, looking into my eyes, and then far beyond them. She looked like she was dreaming again, going off someplace. I guessed poets did a lot of that.

"This zoo is the closest thing to magic that I know …

off the track. And I know just where to take you. Let's go in the direction of something with fur."

I was starting to settle into my own skin with Mary Agnes. I let my nerves go. After all, it wasn't like four hours would unfold into a lifetime or anything.

Then we were off, in our own little world, going from cage to cage, from exotic birds to rough-backed gators, to strong-smelling elephants and majestic lions. We did not hold hands, as that seemed a strong gesture for our first time out together, but we held eyes a lot, staring at each other like two small children.

After a couple of hours of walking, Mary's feet were getting tired, so we found a nice bench and had a seat. It was here that we beheld one of the most beautiful sights on the grounds—the Solitude, John Penn's colonial mansion on the banks of the Schuylkill. It was a marvel of clean, elegant simplicity—a gleaming ivory jewel amid the fall foliage.

"Did you know," Mary Agnes said, turning to me, "that the Solitude was the real-life home of John Penn, grandson of William Penn, founder of Pennsylvania?"

"Mary Agnes," I said with a laugh. "How much do you know about this zoo?"

"I said I had never *been* here, John Taylor. I didn't say I hadn't *read* about it."

I laughed and turned my eyes to the house. "Beautiful, isn't it?" I asked.

"It sure is glorious."

"You know what the Solitude reminds me of?"

A Novel by Craig T. Williams

She shook her head.

"*You,*" I said with a break in my voice, "because it's perfect."

She turned her body all the way around to face me, and my nerves kicked up again. I had never felt this way in the presence of female company.

"Why?"

"Why what?" I asked, almost afraid to look directly at her, for fear that she might see just how much I liked her.

"Why me?"

"Why not you?"

"You're a renowned athlete, a UPenn student," she said. "You've got the makings of something really big, John Baxter Taylor, Jr."

"And you don't?"

"Well ... yes ... but I'm finding my way to it," she said. "Seems like you're already there."

"I didn't realize you thought so much of me, Mary Agnes Montier," I said, surprised.

"Well," she said, pulling back a bit, "I do ... but don't let that swell your head up so big you can't fit into the buggy on the way back home."

I laughed out loud, and before I knew it, Mary Agnes had laid her head gently on my shoulder. I thought in that moment I would stop breathing, but I couldn't do that because she would surely tip over. So I sat up, ever so still, lest I disturb her hair and move her delicate frame an inch from where it rested.

I wanted her head to stay against my shoulder forever,

and if not forever, at very minimum the rest of the day.

Our first outing lasted four hours from start to finish. In another world, another place, another time, it had lasted almost *forever*.

9

The Gift

December 1903

It was the final week of the winter semester and, if at all possible, more frigid than the week before. Seasonal weather had returned with a vengeance. With the cold, the intensity of the wind seemed to increase as though it was even more determined to push people out of its way and fling them about like snowflakes. I raced the wind toward College Hall, shifting from a fast walk to a jog as I went. I was determined to win.

Footsteps fell apace with mine and a friendly voice called, "Hey, John!"

I turned to see one of my classmates. Though we shared many of the same classes, we had never been formally introduced.

"Henry Smith," he said now, and surprised me by extending a hand as he jogged along beside me.

"John Taylor." I shook his hand.

"I've heard lots about you, John," Henry said with a broad smile.

"Well," I said quietly, "hope it's all been decent."

The Olympian: An American Triumph

"Nothing but the best."

Henry and I were both new students, and in many of the same classes. He and I were close in height and weight. The only difference between us was the obvious one—the color of our respective skins. That could have been of no consequence or the biggest deal in the world, depending upon which side of a particular line you stood on.

I was not used to being noticed in such a fashion, so when, at the end of a long school day and struggling to keep my eyes open, I heard someone call my name again, I turned, expecting Henry. Instead, I saw the face of yet another white student—a stranger to me.

I paused in my journey down the corridor toward the front entrance of College Hall and waited for him to catch up to me.

"John," he said again, sounding as though he had been running for miles to catch me.

"Yes?"

"My name is Arthur. Arthur Quinn." The name seemed familiar. "Nate Cartmell put me on to you. He said you'd want to know about the celebration being planned for Pomp."

"Celebration? What are you planning?"

"Well, you know how special Pomp is to the university."

"Yes, indeed I do."

"Some of us have gotten together to give him a proper retirement by way of holding a Jubilee," he said, rubbing his hands together for warmth.

I smiled broadly. "I'm certainly interested. Pomp has

been so helpful to me. I don't know what I'd do without his presence here. What can I do to help?"

"Well, the Jubilee is scheduled for next year and we're putting it on the entertainment calendar now. I'm the treasurer of the planning committee, and I would appreciate the support of the Philadelphia community in arranging a special surprise for Pomp."

"Say no more," I said. "What do you need?"

"Can you go around and talk to his friends and relations? Let them know about the fund-raiser? He's a respected medical healer in the Seventh Ward, you know. We thought it would be a wonderful surprise to make them part of his celebration. Sort of bringing everybody together under one roof."

"Of course, Mr. Quinn," I responded eagerly.

"Call me Arthur." He held out his hand and we shook. Then he went on, spilling his words with such excitement that I thought he would burst. "Pomp lives in the Seventh Ward, over on Lombard Street, and we would love for his folks to know how honored he is here. You know the class of 1858 and just about everybody around Penn looks up to Pomp." "You don't have to do an advertisement for Pomp, Arthur. As soon as you said it was a celebration for him, I was willing to assist in whatever way I could."

"Great … just great. This is going to be *dandy,*" Arthur gushed. "Thank you for being so supportive." He laid his hand gently on my shoulder.

"No, thank *you* for honoring the man. It means a lot," I said. Little did he know I was thanking him for reminding me that the world holds both good and bad, strangers and friends, noise and silence, often at the same time.

He smiled. "I'll get the information for you and we'll meet up next year. Have a Merry Christmas and a Happy New Year!"

"You as well, Arthur," I said as we parted ways.

Every day life is filled with surprises. Though I had seen the faces of students light up when Pomp acknowledged them by name, I'd had no idea just how much UPenn was willing to support him. It saddened me a bit that Pomp would be retiring next year, but I was pleased to be able to assist him in retiring in style. Mostly, I was glad that he was still here when I arrived.

I walked out of the building, smiling at the beauty of the human spirit. Seemed as though just when you begin to see life one way, something shifts and you get a whole new perspective, which may or may not change who you are, but certainly changes how you see things. Isn't it funny how you can be celebrated and ignored at the same place? How a man can have the lowest position and be regarded in the highest possible light at the same time? Well, the Bible says it, I guess: *The last shall be first and the first, last.*

"Could that be a smile on your face?" said a familiar voice.

I sure was popular today, I thought, turning my head in the direction of the warm voice. Pomp stood at the bottom of the steps with parcels in his hands.

"Well, hey there, Pomp. I was just…" I stopped myself just before letting the cat out of the bag.

Pomp looked at me waiting for me to finish.

"…just about to head to your office."

"Well, well," he said. "You're looking a bit more lively than you did the other day. That's the spirit!"

"I'll be all right, Pomp."

"Son, you remind me of a fine young man who served here at the university one year. He went out and did a study of my ward at one time, and I am a great admirer of his." He took a package from the top of his little stack and held it out to me. "I want to give you this."

"A gift?"

"Something to help you see things clear. Make the right choices."

"I surely appreciate you thinking of me, Pomp," I said. "I … I didn't really think to …"

Pomp interrupted my stammering attempt at apology. "This ain't about exchanging gifts, son. I got everything I need anyways. This school is everything I have, always has been, and you a part of that. So I have to do my best to make you feel you're a member of this family and help you to continue the tradition of greatness that this university has created. Now, you read this book over the break and we'll talk about it when you return." Pomp turned and began walking away.

"Yes, sir," I called after him. "Thank you, sir."

He tossed his hand in a careless wave. "Think nothing of it, son."

I stood there feeling a gratitude I could barely explain or contain. Pomp had singled me out for a gift. I was certain he had not taken the time to do this for any other student. The thought of Pomp saving his money and taking the time to purchase this for me meant the world to me.

The wind whipped up College Hall drive, cutting right through me, but I didn't mind. I stood right there and opened my gift. *The Souls of Black Folk* by W. E. B. DuBois, read the cover. I opened it to the flyleaf where there was a photograph of the author. I swelled with pride, seeing Dr. DuBois's brown face. I flipped to a page and instantly related with his words:

It is a peculiar sensation, this double-consciousness, this sense of always looking at one's self through the eyes of others, of measuring one's soul by the tape of a world that looks on in amused contempt and pity. One ever feels his two-ness—an American, a Negro; two souls, two thoughts, two unreconciled strivings; two warring ideals in one dark body, whose dogged strength alone keeps it from being torn asunder.

The history of the American Negro is the history of this strife—this longing to attain self-conscious manhood, to merge his double self into a better and truer self. In this merging he wishes neither of the older selves to be lost.

"Yes," I murmured aloud. "*Yes.* Thank you!" For this had to be a gift from above.

10

"Please Pass the Chocolate"

Christmas Eve, 1903

My mind had been occupied with a single thought the day before, and that was putting the final touches on Mary Agnes's special Christmas present. I had stayed up all night, working until the wee hours of Christmas Eve, to make certain her gift was perfect. Once a decent hour arrived, I wrapped her gift delicately, gathered up her parents' present alongside it, and made my way to Greenville. It was bitter cold outside, and a beautiful blanket of white snow covered the ground, peaceful as a good night's sleep—which was more than I'd had.

My nerves acted up the moment I set foot on the Montiers' front porch. Mr. Montier would surely rip the door back before I could get anywhere near it. That part of the journey was predictable. It was as if Mary Agnes's father had a third eye that sat right on his front porch, and anytime anything heavier than a bird feather landed there, he was ready to yank the door open with a vengeance to see who it was and what they wanted. It was best to come prepared with answers, because Mr. Montier did not approve of hemming and hawing under any circumstances.

"Good morning, sir," I said with a nod and a tip of my hat, an act that nearly froze the ears right off my head.

"Mornin'," He nodded.

"I came by this morning to deliver your family's Christmas gifts," I said, handing him a box of chocolates.

"Son," he said, "you bring another box of chocolates to my house, and you're gonna have to send over a good seamstress to let out my trousers in the midsection."

Uh oh, had I given him too much chocolate?

He started to laugh. This was the first time I had ever made him laugh. Correction, it was the first time he had ever tickled himself in my presence—it was *his* joke.

"Come on in," he said, opening the door.

Inside, Mrs. Montier and Mary Agnes were seated at the breakfast table in the dining room to the left of the front door.

"John," said Mrs. Montier with a wide smile, "it's so nice to see you."

"My pleasure, ma'am," I said. "I was hoping to give Mary Agnes her Christmas gift."

"Of course."

"Hi, John," said Mary Agnes with a good-morning smile as I handed her the small, neatly wrapped package.

She opened it eagerly in front of her parents. "Oh, John," she said, holding it up to the light. "It's a framed poem."

"Interesting," said her father. "What does it say, Mary?"

A Novel by Craig T. Williams

"Yes, dear," said Mrs. Montier. "Read it out loud."

Mary Agnes looked up at me with those big brown eyes of hers and said, "I'd like John to read it."

This was not a part of the holiday program. "Sure," I said in a voice that came close to squeaking.

Mary Agnes handed me the poem and I cleared my throat three times before I was able to utter another sound. I read:

The river bends without losing its way.
The sun shines brightly, sharing its warmth.
The trees stretch magnificently, sharing their glory,
Just as you smile and share your heart with the world.
I am honored to know you,
Much prouder to be your friend.
The secrets of your spirit are not locked within.
They flow from your every word,
Every graceful step you take.
You are on the way to something big.
A proud lady
And a grand poet.
You play the part of a real life lady.
I love the way you perform.
You've touched my life in such a way
I couldn't help but acknowledge your splendor
And make an attempt at writing a poem for a poet

By writing you in my story.

The Olympian: An American Triumph

By the time I finished reading the poem, a tear had fallen from Mary Agnes's eye, and her mother's face beamed like sunshine.

Her father simply nodded and said, "Somebody, please pass me another chocolate."

11

Higher Learning

A fresh layer of snow had settled nicely into the crevices of the buildings. I thought it was truly breathtaking, but my mind could not settle on the beauty of this day. My focus was on finding Pomp. To say I had devoured *The Souls of Black Folk* would not properly describe just how much I had taken every word into my body and ingested it into my spirit. I had to find Pomp and thank him for giving me a different perspective on life.

I loved Daddy fiercely, but sometimes when he read the words of Booker T. Washington, I would get a faint wave of uneasiness, as though the words ought to resonate within me, but didn't. After reading W. E. B. DuBois's book, it felt like someone had reached into my soul, put it up to a looking glass and said, "This is who you are and this is what you believe." I suddenly saw myself in a new light. Mr. DuBois's call for one tenth of us to lead the rest rang the bell of my true feelings about who I was and who I wanted to become.

I found no fault in Mr. Washington, or in my father for holding him in such high regard. I know for certain that they were both representatives of their times, doing what they felt was best for themselves as men, and for their families. Daddy surely followed Washington's belief in building a business and becoming a property owner, and I could find no flaw in that. However, as I researched a bit more, I realized that Washington's philosophy also might lead the South, especially white folks, to believe that we Negroes no longer insisted on having equal civil rights. That we were willing to be trained to run businesses and pursue trades, while forgoing the opportunity to be formally educated. I strongly disagreed with this line of thinking, as my presence as a freshman at one of the most prestigious schools in the country clearly attested.

It also made me question Daddy's stance, which was a new line of thought for me. Daddy had always been right in my eyes, but now in search of my own manhood—my own definition for my life—I was finding that my philosophy and Daddy's were not necessarily in agreement. We appeared to be like Washington and DuBois—two men passionately committed to finding their way, to being leaders, to bringing the best out of the community, but in two different fashions—the old against the new. One was no more right than the other, but surely a man had to pick a side at some point, and my allegiance had swung toward DuBois—that I knew without hesitation.

I certainly disagreed with Washington's belief that we, as

colored people, should remove our focus from the political process, lower our sights of civil rights, and concentrate our energies on industrial education rather than the higher education of Negro youth. Yet, I did agree with the idea of assisting freemen to become business and property owners and of insisting on self-respect and thrift. I just could not agree with giving up either civil rights or participation in the political process to achieve economic success. A song had been sung in my heart when DuBois said that "Mr. Washington's program practically accepts the alleged inferiority of the Negro races."

"Amen," I said in my heart. "Amen." I had never felt as though the Lord made me inferior to anyone in this world. Slavery was a dreadful institution, and I was grateful every day that I had not been born into it. These times were an opportunity for the colored man to make his presence known in the world. We deserved high-quality education, to participate in the political process, and to be judged on our human qualities and not, absurdly, by the color of our skin.

I found in myself an awakening, a calling, to be one of the black men DuBois wrote of when he said, "those black men, if they are really men, are called upon by every consideration of patriotism and loyalty to oppose such a course by all civilized methods..."

The moment I had finished reading *The Souls of Black Folk*, I had made a commitment to myself to always be a gentleman and to stand in my truth, to represent my race as a man of honor, and to place myself on the path of greatness, always. I had not discussed my new outlook on life with

Daddy. He'd built his free world on the foundation of Booker T. Washington, and he took too much pride in his beliefs for me to bring my young self to question them. So, for now, I would discuss this with Pomp, who had seen fit to give me this gift.

Now if I could just *find* Pomp. It was a bit odd not to have seen him by now. I headed down into the basement of College Hall to his "office." I was just about to knock on the door when I heard a rustling from within.

"Pomp?"

I could hear a creaking of the cot Pomp kept in the room in case he was on campus at a late hour. There was some shuffling and the sound of feet coming toward the door. The door opened gently and Pomp stood there, looking a bit disheveled. I was taken aback by his appearance.

Pomp cleared his throat. "How you doing, son?"

"I'm fine, sir. How are you?" I asked, casting my eyes around the room. I was greatly surprised that Pomp was resting at this time of the day, and I know the surprise resounded in my voice.

"I got me a bitter cold," Pomp said, moving sideways from the door so I could enter.

"Do you need to see a doctor?" I asked, noticing the handkerchiefs scattered around the bed.

"Oh, no, no, nothing like that. Don't you worry about these old bones. I'll be just fine, come morning. Never you mind." Pomp sat on the bed looking a bit smaller than he had just weeks ago. He waved me to a hard-backed chair facing him.

"Will you be leaving early to rest at home?" I asked.

Pomp's brown eyes blazed and he declared, in the strongest voice he had summoned since I'd arrived, "Now, why would I do that? There's plenty of work here to do, and I gotta be here to make sure it's done right."

With that, the matter of rest appeared to be settled. Pomp glanced at the small book in my hands and smiled. "What you think 'bout our Professor DuBois?"

"Professor? What was he professor of?"

Pomp chuckled and coughed. "Sociology. Right here at UPenn."

"He was a professor *here*?"

Pomp shook his head. "In name only. Never taught one single class. They gave him a fancy title though— *assistant* in sociology. He could've taught, if they'd let him. He was a funny, smart fellow. Made you laugh and think at the same time. That's some talent."

I smiled with understanding. There'd been an element of that to the book.

"Anyways, far as I know, nothing much came of his being here, but he was real interested in the Philadelphia Negroes. Folks—black and white—didn't take kindly to his curiosity, but I thought it was grand that he cared what was going on with the Seventh Ward. Seems to me once you start looking into something, you on the path to fixing it. Only way to change things."

I could only nod in agreement.

Pomp's body convulsed with an intense coughing spell. I longed to get up and pat him on the back, but not wanting to insult his strength, I simply watched in dismay.

Dear Lord, I pray Pomp will be all right.

His coughing settled a bit and I leaned in toward him, nearly slipping from my chair. "I can ask my mama to make you some nice chicken soup to cure what ails you."

"Son," he said, sitting up a bit straighter, "if I have one more drop of chicken soup, I just may sprout feathers and fly."

I burst into laughter and rose from my seat. Now did not seem like the time to lead Pomp into a lengthy discussion of Washington and DuBois. I would have to save my thoughts for another time. "I wish you Godspeed to recovery, Pomp," I said, looking at him as though he were my own father.

"Don't fuss about me, son." He rose to escort me to the door.

I looked back on Pomp one more time, a feeling of uneasiness settling in my stomach.

He smiled gently. Remembering the book in my hands, I held it up and said, "Thank you kindly for this, Pomp."

Pomp nodded and closed the door.

12

Anchor

February 1904
Track and Field Pre-trials
University of Pennsylvania's Franklin Field

This was an important day for the UPenn track and field program. On this day athletes were pitted against one another to battle for a place on the team. Only the fastest, most disciplined runners would be chosen, and I had set my sights on being among them. I would finally get a chance to spread my wings. Those Wright brothers and their contraption had nothing on me.

Smoke from nearby factories cast silver clouds over the magnificence of the new Franklin Field. I loved Franklin Field as much as I loved the race itself. It was the first of its kind, a multi-use stadium that served two masters—football and track and field. Though I had run this turf before and achieved many victories here, it was my first day to enter the field as a student of UPenn, and because of that, the ground beneath my feet felt different. My heart hammered in my chest with pride and nerves as I took in giant gulps of air, long and deep.

My brown skin seemed to make the colors of my new track and field uniform glow, so I moved quickly, not wanting to draw undue attention to myself. Little hope of avoiding that: I was the only Negro heading toward Coach Robertson—head trainer of UPenn's track and field program—as he stood on the track before the new grandstands with a group of young men gathering about him.

Now, a Negro on campus was not a complete oddity in those days, but I was more than a student: I was an athlete—someone who was admired and cheered, the recipient of special recognition for my physical ability. I could *feel* the gazes on me and knew I could assume only one of them to be friendly. Indeed, my friend Nate stood just next to the coach grinning at me.

I had to be thankful for Nathaniel Cartmell's friendship. I gave thanks, as well, for the sprinkling of Negro students in the stands who were there to watch the track trials. They followed me with pride-filled eyes and watched with anticipation as I paused in front of the coach.

In a moment, the coach saw me, as did everyone else on the team. They looked straight past him to me. Following the direction of their eyes, he turned toward me a bit. There was on his face neither smile or question; he simply stood between the other runners and me like a referee at a boxing match.

"Hello, sir," I said quickly and, at his gesture, took a seat in the first row of the stands next to Nate.

Coach Robertson addressed the entire team without preamble: "The papers are calling John Taylor here the best quarter-miler in the country!"

No one said a word, but only glanced toward and through me. My skin went cold and clammy.

Nate smiled and dug me in the ribs as he leaned over and whispered into my ear, "he hasn't seen *me* run yet."

"Well," said Coach, casting a glance up into the stands behind me, "perhaps we might have a new anchor for our relay team."

It was with great dread that I followed his gaze and found the eyes of Charles Cook glaring down at me from several rows up. I knew that Charles had posted the fastest times so far in previous trials. He was considered a shoo-in for the coveted anchor position on the relay team.

"Charles," Coach Robertson said, "come on down here and let's have a little contest."

"John," Coach said, looking down toward me, "take the field. It'll be a quarter-mile, gentlemen."

Oh boy. Why did it have to start off like this?

Certain that this was no way to build a team, but unwilling to argue the point, I slowly rose from my seat with a rueful glance at Nate and moved to take my mark. Daddy had just bought me a brand new pair of running shoes. They carried me on what seemed the longest walk in history—from my seat to the starting line.

Charles caused a great ruckus coming down the stands, stomping and all. If hatred had a place in the material world, it would be sitting squarely between the two of us as we took our positions on the track.

Charles sneered at me, took his mark, and said under his

breath, "I'm not losing to you, nigger boy!"

Anger rolled up under my breastbone. That was it. Now I *had* to win. I always raced to win, but those last few words made it *personal*. Charles may have felt that he could call me whatever he liked, but that was not the case, and I would tell him so in the manner that always spoke best for me.

Coach Robertson walked slowly toward the track as though he wanted Charles and me to feel the pressure of this moment in every muscle and joint of our bodies. I leaned into my stance, prepared to take flight. Coach passed by Charles first, then me, and placed himself on the inside edge of the track. In one hand he held a small firing pistol and in the other, a pocket watch.

"Runners set!"

I took one sideways glance at the grandstand. Nate, grinning, gave me a thumbs up. In a distant corner I saw Pomp, looking a bit thinner in frame, standing in the background. He seemed keenly interested in the happenings of Franklin Field. It did my heart good to see him out and about. He'd been under the weather for so long, I'd begun to fear his "bitter cold" was something more than that.

The pistol fired and we leapt from the mark, running with the hope of victory pulling us, and pride pushing from behind. After a two-second spurt, I pulled back very slightly and let Charles catch me. His stride increased, and he passed me and pulled away. He glanced back once and then, with an arrogant smile, quickened his pace.

I took great pleasure in allowing him to think it was all over, that I would humbly take second place. I settled in behind him, just close enough that I knew he could hear the sound of my footsteps pursuing him. The moment he set his head toward the finish line, I put on a burst of speed, pulled up from behind, and flowed past him like a raging flood down a parched riverbed.

Coach Robertson dropped his arm and glanced at his pocket watch. "Time!" he shouted. "Fifty seconds!"

Just like that, I broke my own record and squashed the pride of Charlie-boy. In my head I was saying, Jack Johnson–style, "Don't take it personally. You were just due this here knockout."

My lips never moved, but I did chance to look into the blue eyes and red face of Charles Cook. Nate and a few others clapped, while the rest stared at Charles as though they were unable to believe he had been beaten so handily. Surprisingly, he remained silent, though he looked like a pot about to boil over.

I knew my new record wouldn't make the books, but for what it was worth, it was one of the best races of my life: the day I ran like the wind and left ignorance in the dust. It was my best unrecorded achievement, and from the smiles of the few supporters I had in the stands, I knew it made their day, too.

Coach Robertson gave no words of congratulation, and no special reward for my win. Like an impartial judge who had not chosen a side, he simply announced to the Penn team, "Mr. Taylor, you are our relay anchor," and strode toward the grandstands.

Charles and I followed quietly behind.

I glanced quickly in Pomp's direction in time to receive his subtle nod of approval. Though I could not let the smile form on my lips, my eyes brightened with acceptance of his congratulations, and I nodded in return.

Nate greeted me at the stands with a slap on the back. "Hey, John," he said, smiling broadly, "good race between you and Charles."

"Thanks," I replied humbly.

"You beat him fair and square. You deserve to be anchor."

"Gee … thanks,."

His acknowledgment made me feel right. Those were big words coming from a young man who did not have brown skin. I saw something very decent in Nathaniel. Very decent indeed.

13

Fatal Blow

March 1904
Track Practice
College Hall Gymnasium

In the opening meet of the season, John Baxter Taylor broke his own record in the quarter-mile race. Taylor, the first Negro athlete to grace the field as part of the Penn track and field team, carried the team to victory on his shoulders. A crowd was drawn to Franklin Field, to come and see for themselves whether there was any merit to the rumors that Taylor's speed, agility, endurance, and coordination were untouchable.

The verdict is in: Taylor is as big as his gigantic reputation.

★★★★

I lived for winning, and I viewed our first track practice as an indicator of how well I would perform this season. Running meant the world to me. When I ran, I felt as if I had a chance to live majestically, to live as a free man. I was certainly free on the field, and no one could deny that. The first day of practice would be the beginning of months of hard work during which I would condition myself to win.

Running in the gymnasium did not allow me to stride as freely as running on Franklin Field, but that was where we practiced when the field was in use for other events as it was today. I conditioned myself to focus on the results, not the surroundings. I was preparing my lungs as always, doing breathing exercises to increase my endurance when I caught sight of Charles Cook entering the gym, with Nate right behind him.

He gave his usual scowl in my direction as Henry Smith and I sat down on the bench to wait for an opportunity to run the quarter mile. Nate just rolled his eyes and crossed the gym floor to join me.

Charles climbed past us, glaring at me. He gave Nate a shove, muttering something under his breath that made Nate's face turn red.

"Shut it, Cook," Nate said.

"You shut it, gimp," said Charles.

Nate flushed again and shoved his hands deep into his pockets.

Now I was mad. Charles might pick at me. I expected it. But calling Nate childish names was just plain mean. Nate was touchy about his right hand, which was missing two fingers and part of a third. Something that happened when he was a kid. It sure didn't make him less a runner, but he hated to have people pay any attention to it.

I started to rise from my seat, but Nate and Henry both moved to stop me. "Don't let him get to you," said Nate.

A Novel by Craig T. Williams

"What'd he say to you?" I whispered as the Coach took the floor.

He shook his head. "Doesn't matter. Besides, nobody here cares what he thinks."

Coach had us running separately today so he could clock our times. We would work on improving those times before actual competitions began.

"Taylor," Coach called.

All eyes focused on me and voices fell silent. I took my position as Coach held up his hand. Just as he prepared to call out *Marks*, I caught sight of Mary Agnes sitting in the bleachers, all by herself. Our eyes met. Suddenly, my legs felt wobbly and my knees wanted to knock against each other.

"Marks. Set. Drive!" Coach shouted.

Before he could lower his hand, I was off, pushing the wind out of my way. At five feet eleven inches and 160 pounds, I guess you could say I had a runner's body. Newspapers could describe me as "one of the fastest runners in the world" all they wanted, but today my heart was not completely on running. My timing was off and, as a result, my time was off.

Mary Agnes came to see me, was all I could think about.

"Fifty-three seconds!" shouted Coach, calling the time on my race as I flew past him at the finish mark.

It looked like I'd run swiftly, it felt as if I'd run swiftly, and fifty-three seconds was nothing to turn my nose up at, but it was hardly my standard, and Coach knew it. He followed my gaze up into the stands and saw Mary Agnes.

"That's not what you're chasing this year, John," he said

with a stern voice. "Stay focused."

"Yes, sir," I said, embarrassed. The distraction of a woman could be a fatal blow to a serious athlete, and we all knew it. I suppose that's why my experience with women had been limited to almost none, but as I glanced into the stands again and rested my eyes on her beautiful smile, somehow it did not seem to matter, fatal blow or not.

14

Farewell

Friday, March 11, 1904
College Hall Chapel
University of Pennsylvania

The news about Pomp had spread across the campus like wildfire the day before. The word was that while thousands of UPenn students slept this past Saturday, Albert Monroe "Pomp" Wilson passed through sleep into death from complications of pneumonia. Life is such a fragile and fleeting thing.

I stood on the sidewalk outside College Hall Chapel, hollowed out and numb, as students from the junior and senior classes lifted Pomp's coffin into a crepe-festooned carriage. College Hall Chapel had been adorned with flowers and filled with a standing-room-only crowd of faculty, alumni, students, and folks from the community who now poured out onto the sidewalk.

There had been a hushed silence in the chapel during the eulogy. Arthur Quinn had read a glowing commemoration of Pomp's life, which he planned to place in The *Record*, Penn's undergraduate yearbook. There was still a hush in my soul as I sorted through my feelings for a man who had been so much more than a janitor. From his humble birth in Philadelphia in 1839 to his death in 1904, Pomp had spent nearly his entire life on this very campus. In that time he had helped remove the dust from men's souls, moved them to greatness, and inspired students to be and do better, and for that his life and dedication to UPenn were greatly celebrated.

"Of how many men in this world can it be truly said that their places cannot be filled?" Arthur asked at the end of his eulogy. He answered, "Pomp's place cannot."

As he spoke these words, heads nodded in unison. That made me so very proud for Pomp. One could never say that the University of Pennsylvania did not honor the memory of a faithful servant and loyal friend. Arthur had told me that *The Alumni Register* had set aside twenty-five pages in its next issue memorializing Pomp's life and times at UPenn.

Now, as we stood at curbside, the bell tolled fifty times, one stroke for each year of Pomp's service to Penn. As the last echo rang off, a collective exhalation went through the crowd and we began going our separate ways. My thoughts turned to my own relationship with Pomp. I had known he was ill. Could I have done more to help him? Pomp was stubborn, I reminded myself. In the end he passed as he lived, on his terms. I turned back to look at College Hall just in time to see a black crow fly gracefully to "my" tower and sit momentarily on the sill of my "secret window" before it rose again and disappeared into the clouds.

A melancholy smile graced my lips and my heart as I turned toward a new day.

A Novel by Craig T. Williams

★★★★

April 1904

The University of Pennsylvania didn't feel the same without Pomp. It seemed as though his presence was as necessary as the general curriculum. During the first month after his home-going, I spent more time than usual on the dirt of Franklin Field chasing his ghost, trying to achieve some sense of completion, of acceptance.

One day in April, I was meeting with Coach Robertson down on the track to discuss something that was pressing on my heart. It was a turn of events I had been following closely in recent weeks in the headlines of the local papers:

SUMMER OLYMPICS COMING JULY 1
TO ST. LOUIS, MISSOURI

The very idea of the Olympics excited me—amateur athletes were coming from *all over the world* to compete. And these were the first Olympic Games to be held in the United States. It tasted of adventure, and I dared to entertain the possibility of participating in an event that dated all the way back to ancient Greece. It was a global event—surely that meant Negroes would be competing. Why shouldn't I be one of them? Besides, Nate was going. He had suspended his schooling to go.

"You should go too, J.T.," he'd said. "We're the one-two punch." He'd feigned punches at me.

The Olympian: *An American Triumph*

No harm in asking, I thought as I began to warm up by running laps.

It was on this day that I noticed a slight difference in my body, a shift. This season's training had delivered me to a new destination, a higher level of athletic ability. My body was potent with strength, a well-conditioned machine, stronger now than it had ever been. When I jogged, I could feel the muscles in my upper legs pulse with vigor. When I sprinted, it felt as if every part of my body worked together with the harmony of a symphony orchestra. I thought of Scott Joplin when I ran—I felt like a song. From the corner of my eye, I caught a glimpse of Coach Robertson standing on the sidelines watching.

"Taylor," he called, and I directed my feet to the sound of his voice. "Whatcha got?" he asked when I reached him. Coach was like that: direct—terse, even. He didn't engage in long conversations and could typically sum up everything under the sun with one sentence, two at most.

"I've been following the stories about the Olympics coming to St. Louis this summer," I said.

He raised his brows. "Yeah?"

"Athletes are coming from all over the world, representing about twelve countries."

"Yeah," he repeated.

"Nate's going and…" I hesitated, seeing from his narrowed eyes and compressed lips that I'd said something that failed to please.

"I know Nate's going. It's why he's abandoned his studies … and his team. He should be here at Wharton and going to Europe with us this summer, not performing in that sideshow down there in Saint Lou."

I was puzzled by his attitude. Certainly, I understood how he felt about Nate leaving the team, but this was the Olympics. I spoke the words aloud. "But, Coach, this is the Olympics. This is about representing America."

Coach snorted disparagingly. "Hardly that, Taylor. Nate's going to be wearing his school colors. So will every other American athlete. And I meant what I said about it being a sideshow. The World's Fair is the main event, son. The Olympics aren't even in the 'big tent.'"

"But Nate thinks I'm at my best-"

"Which is why you should go to the international meets in Europe and England and not waste yourself on some three-ring circus. We got *real* races for you to run."

"But Nate-" I began.

"Nate is not your coach." He turned on his heel and walked off the field. "I hope you're smarter than that."

Coach Robertson was a good coach, but he was a strict man with a narrow vision. As disappointed as I was by his reaction, it left a patch of warmth in my soul that he said pretty clearly that he thought I was good enough for the Olympics, but that the Olympics weren't good enough for *me*.

As I walked off the field, following the coach, I looked off toward the grandstand entryway. There stood Mary Agnes. I was happy to see her, though from the look on her face, I could tell she was none too pleased to see me. My lack of attention to our budding courtship since Pomp's death was most likely at fault. I had been somewhat out of sorts, and it had showed in my absence.

"Hello," I said, approaching her cautiously, uncertain of her mood.

"Hello." Her gentle response lacked the warmth I had come to expect. "I was just coming to check up on you and make sure you were okay."

"I know I haven't been calling on you lately, but it's not a reflection of my intentions, Mary Agnes, I assure you–"

"Where have you been?" she asked, cutting into my apologetic babble.

"By myself," I admitted. "I lost a good friend on campus … died of pneumonia about a month ago."

Her face softened and her dark eyes filled with compassion. "John, why didn't you tell me?" She took my hand and placed hers gently over the top of it. "I thought we were … friends."

"I've just been…" I said, trying to find an answer as she stood there looking at me with those lovely eyes. Until this moment I hadn't realized how much I'd missed those eyes. "Just been…" I mumbled as she waited for me to say something, anything to justify my absence. I realized in this moment that there was no justification for it. My anguish over Pomp's death was something I could have shared with her— *should* have shared with her.

"Been what?" she asked.

"Been sad," I said, then looked away. "I didn't want you to see me like that."

"Like what?" she asked with fire in her voice.

"I'm not one to do a lot of carrying on, Mary," I offered.

"Grieving for a friend is hardly what I would call carrying on."

"I manage things in my own way, but I don't mean any harm by doing so."

"Most men do, I guess…" she said. "God forbid you ever let me see you cry."

"I'm no sissy. I don't do that," I said beneath my breath.

"Do what?"

"Cry."

She studied me for a moment, then said: "I walk with other souls in pain."

"Let me guess: that would be another Mary Agnes original."

"No, silly," she said. "That would be Oscar Wilde."

Now *that* was the Mary Agnes Montier I had come to know fondly. My smile melted into hers as she grabbed my hand and tugged me toward the river.

15

Brotherhood

Early June 1904
Birthday Party at the Montiers'

Saturday night.

Once again this felt like the very first time I had stood on the steps of the Montier home. This was a special occasion. Mary Agnes's father was celebrating the half-century mark, turning fifty years old today. It was a big milestone, and a frenzy of celebration was in the air. There was so much commotion going on inside the house with friends, family, music, and loud talk, that part of me felt like turning right back around and going back the way I had come. I took a single step backward and landed right on the soft foot of another guest, who stood behind me carrying a tureen full of collard greens. She was a rather large woman, wearing a wide-brimmed hat and a polka-dotted dress.

"Ow!" she howled, as the dish came tumbling out of her hands. I reacted with lightning speed, my outstretched hands swooping beneath the large dish.

Saved.

A Novel by Craig T. Williams

"Oh, my Jesus!" breathed the husky-voiced woman. "You saved my collard greens!!"

"I'm sorry for stepping on your foot," I said, smiling apologetically.

She gave me a good once-over. "Well, you're not light on your feet, but you are quick with your hands."

I blushed. Perhaps her description was not the most flattering for the country's fastest quarter-miler, but I could not deny that my foot probably did feel like a lead weight.

"My name is Josephine, and these here are my prize-winning collards you just rescued!"

"Evening, ma'am," I nodded, feeling more like doing a bow to make up for a rough beginning. In that moment, I turned to meet the curious and prolonged stare of Mr. Montier, who stood at the doorway taking up every inch of space between the doorposts.

"Wilton!" shouted Josephine. "Move out of the way and make some room for me and my collards!"

Wilton? I chuckled. I had never even thought to ask Mary Agnes what her father's name was. He didn't seem like the kind of person who even had a *real* name. He'd just be Mr. Montier to everyone, even his own mother.

I followed right behind Josephine, extending a handshake to Mr. Montier.

"Happy birthday, Mr. Montier."

He responded by doing what he did best—eyeballed me, nodded, and grunted all at the same time. Perhaps it was his primary goal in life to utter as few words as humanly possible.

The Olympian: An American Triumph

I was almost relieved to find wall-to-wall people, both grown folks and children, who appeared to be in more jovial spirits than our guest of honor. Everybody was well dressed and the crowd looked to be a mix of folks—from professionals to common laborers. Still, judging from their similar features, this was yet a family gathering. I felt a bit awkward, mainly because I did not know any of these people with the exception of Mary Agnes and her parents. That lasted for only a moment, however; my presence seemed to rouse the crowd, almost as if those in attendance had been waiting for me to arrive.

"John!" said Mary Agnes, stepping into the parlor from around the corner. "I've been waiting for you."

"Mary Agnes!" I said, more relieved than she could possibly imagine. I admired her soft peach dress with lace trimming on the front and a big bow in the back. "You look beautiful."

"And you as well," she said, taking note of my dress trousers, necktie, and supper jacket.

"Come," she insisted, "I want to introduce you to the family."

I followed closely behind as we made brief visits to every corner of the room. I met Grandma Elizabeth, Uncle Chet, Cousin Hiram, and, for the second time that day, Aunt Josephine.

"This is the boy that stepped on my foot and saved my collard greens!" Josephine announced to everyone in the room. They all laughed and I withered with embarrassment.

"Is Aunt Josephine your father's sister?" I whispered to

Mary Agnes.

"Yes."

"Wilton, huh?" I asked with a grin.

Mary Agnes laughed.

Just then, another large woman carrying a big yellow cake on a platter bore down on us.

"Out of the way!" she shouted. "Coming through! Coming through!"

I quickly moved out of her way, so as not to have to rescue a tumbling pastry.

"Watch out for that one!" called Josephine. "He's got lead feet but quick hands!"

"Seems a bit of a contradiction to me," injected Mr. Montier. "A superior quarter-miler should be light on his feet. Don't you think, John?"

"Yessir," I quickly agreed, hoping we could get off this topic.

"John here is an athlete … one of the best," said Mr. Montier, and I couldn't tell if that was pride or mockery in his tone.

Fleeing the neighborhood of Mary Agnes's father I noticed, in the corner of the room, a rather scholarly-looking fellow dressed in a black suit and wearing wire-rimmed glasses. He seemed to have taken notice of me at the same moment, and his eyes sparked with obvious interest. He appeared to be on the verge of stepping toward me when Mary Agnes pulled me into the kitchen to help bring food out to the table.

"I get the feeling your father isn't too fond of me sometimes," I murmured as we gathered up dishes.

"It's not personal," she said, shrugging. "He's not fond of anyone who's interested in courting his *precious* daughter."

"You think he'll ever get used to the idea?"

"Nope," she said with a smile. "Now let's go eat."

Lovely.

We entered the dining room area where an extra table and chairs had been set up in preparation for this celebration. Out of the corner of my eye, I could see the gentleman in the black suit watching me again. His gaze was direct and piercing enough to make me uncomfortable. As I watched, he leaned toward Mr. Montier and whispered something into his ear. Then they *both* looked at me.

"Who is the man in the black suit sitting next to your father?" I asked Mary Agnes as we took our seats.

She glanced across the table. "That's my daddy's cousin, Dr. Algernon Jackson."

"Oh," I said. "He keeps eyeballing at me."

"John Taylor, I think you're being a little self-conscious today," said Mary Agnes with a laugh.

"I'm fine," I replied, glancing at the clock. The hands seemed barely to have moved. This might just be the longest night in recorded history. Before dinner ended, I suspected I'd be ready to make any excuse to get out of there. I had to get up early the next morning for church, and though I was always enchanted by Mary Agnes's presence, I felt as though I were under the silent scrutiny of her family. I could tell they all had questions but were reluctant to ask.

"John Taylor?" questioned a deep voice close behind me.

I turned in my chair to see the man in the black suit standing, extending his hand to me. "Yes," I said uncertainly, surprised by his sudden appearance.

"Dr. Algernon Jackson," he said with a firm handshake. "Good to meet you."

"My pleasure, sir."

"So," he began, "you are *the* John Taylor?"

"Yes... sir," I responded, not quite sure where this was leading.

"You are a student at Wharton?"

"Yes, sir."

"And your studies go well?"

"Very well, sir."

"You are no ordinary Negro," he offered with a pat on the back.

I did not know how to respond so I fell silent. I believe a man does well to let others boast of him, lest he be seen as arrogant. In fact, the only man in the world who could pull off that kind of swagger would probably be somebody like Jack Johnson.

"I'll be in touch," said the gentleman, and he quickly took his own seat to the left of Mr. Montier.

That was odd, I thought to myself as I watched the two begin a brisk dialogue that included frequent glances at me. I was beginning to feel more and more uncomfortable by the minute.

"So, your father's cousin is a doctor," I said with a raised brow. "I'm impressed."

She smiled. "So are we. The family produced mostly

cobblers until Cousin Algernon."

Why, I wondered, would such an accomplished man as Dr. Algernon Jackson think of me as being more than ordinary? Eventually, the evening did come to an end, and I thanked Mary Agnes and her parents for the kind invitation and headed home—taking in all the air I could breathe along the way.

★★★★

The following Sunday morning
African Episcopal Church of St. Thomas

Sunday morning came early and the Taylor family rose with the sun, making our way to church for the early service. St. Thomas was the first black church in Philadelphia, and one of the first African Episcopal churches in the country. Our entire family had been confirmed there and the church was one of my favorite places. I felt strongly aligned with the words of one of the founders, Absalom Jones, whose declaration of the church intention was framed in a display case in the narthex: "To arise out of the dust and shake themselves, and throw off that servile fear, that the habit of oppression and bondage trained them up in."

Every Sunday when I entered the church, I paused to read those words to allow them to settle in real good.

The Taylor family had our favorite pew in the second row, but no matter how hard I tried to juggle our seating assignment, I was always seated directly behind Ms. Marshall, a faithful congregant who wore a big, wide-brimmed hat that took up a quarter of a pew all on its own. To make matters worse, she had this hat in every existing color. Today, the color was red.

Oh boy.

Sunday morning services for me consisted of a sermon from an unseen minister, songs from half a choir, and a hat. But on this particular Sunday, there was more than a sermon, songs, and a hat—there was also a pair of eyes. I felt as though someone were watching me.

Am I imagining things? I asked myself. Was this a continuation of last night's party? I was about to dismiss the thought entirely, until I turned around and spotted Mr. Montier's cousin, Dr. Jackson seated two rows directly behind me, in what looked like the same black suit he'd worn the night before, He looked to be with another gentleman, equally scholarly in appearance, who wore an olive-colored suit.

I had never seen Dr. Jackson at service before.

Both men were glancing at me, and I suspected their whispers were also about me. I swallowed hard and turned around, distracted for the rest of the service by the hat *and* the two men behind me.

I had no sooner stepped out into the aisle after the service than these two gentlemen were at my side, startling me and my father. By this time, my mother was already exchanging pleasantries with the lady wearing the big red hat.

"Mr. Taylor," said Dr. Jackson.

"Yes," both my father and I responded.

"Junior," said Dr. Jackson with a smile.

Well, I thought to myself, at least he's a little friendlier than he was the other night.

"Yes," I repeated.

"You must be his father," he said to my daddy, extending a hand. "I am Dr. Algernon Jackson, and this fine gentleman is Dr. Henry Minton."

I could tell these men thought they had some kind of business with us, but what could it be?

"May we have a word with you gentlemen?" Dr. Minton requested.

"Yes," we both said as Daddy cut me a sharp look. We both sat back down while the doctors remained standing in the aisle, smiling down at us.

"We are most interested in your son," Dr. Jackson said to Daddy.

"Is that so? May I ask what for?"

"We are of the belief that learned men of color should have an organization, a fraternity, in which they come together with men of like qualities that they might know the best of one another and encourage one another in their pursuits."

Learned men of color? What could they possibly want with me? "Excuse me, sirs, but how does this involve me?"

The two men exchanged a look, and then Dr. Minton said, "Membership is not based entirely on academic achievement, but on culture and good character."

"And a record of accomplishment," added Dr. Jackson.

"Which brings us to you, John Taylor, Jr."

They spoke with such quiet passion in their voices and such gentle zeal in their eyes, that it was contagious. They had done more to stir me that morning than the pastor's sermon had, though that could have been largely the fault of the big red hat.

"You are an accomplished athlete," said Dr. Minton, "and a good student. We recognize the value that someone of your quality could add to our fraternity."

"You do?"

"Indeed we do. When I was a student at Exeter Academy, I was not invited to participate in the fraternities of that time, despite my accomplishments. I recognized, even then, the importance of such a brotherhood and felt its lack."

"As did I," added Dr. Jackson. "But rather than model our fraternity on the organizations current in white society, we have gone back into the history of the ancient Greeks and studied their organizations to create the framework for our own."

"Ancient Greeks? Is that right?" Daddy asked, obviously impressed.

"Indeed," said Dr. Minton. "We have created a very special fraternity."

"We are the Sigma Pi Phi Boule," said Dr. Jackson. "*Boule* means 'council of noblemen.'"

"We are more than a public charity," said Dr. Minton, "though charity is definitely among our goals. We offer the promise of a great contribution to the lives of accomplished Negroes. We are dedicated to high ideals, fellowship, and professional opportunities for black men. The Boule is the first organization of its kind."

"And we are *very* interested in you," added Dr. Jackson.

"I am truly honored…"

"You came highly recommended by Mr. Montier," said Dr. Jackson.

… *and completely shocked*, I finished silently.

"How does all of this sound to you?" Dr. Minton asked.

"Impressive."

"All right then. We'll be in touch," said Dr. Jackson, before he and Dr. Minton shook our hands abruptly turned and disappeared through the front doors of the church.

My father and I looked at each other. I felt as if we'd been battered by a storm. And perhaps in some ways we had. This was truly the beginning of something special.

On July 17, I proudly became one of the first thirteen members of the mystic circle of Sigma Pi Phi Boule. I cherished the companionship of this group of physicians, dentists and other professionals. We met regularly on the third Friday of the month. I had not felt such an embrace of brotherly love since William had departed for Illinois the previous year. William and I were exceptionally close, and it had been difficult for me when he accepted a position as a pharmacist in the Midwest. However, I seemed to have found a group of brothers willing and able to take his place as advisers and peers.

The word *honored* could not begin to describe the emotion I felt at my induction into the Boule. In their eyes, I found acceptance. In my own, I discovered an inner knowledge that I could live up to the highest ideals of this organization. Sitting in that circle of greatness, I was proud to be one of the first selected to join the talented men of Sigma Pi Phi fraternity.

16

Shakespeare

August 1904

Mama and Daddy escorted me to the train station in a silence heavy with thought. I sat in the front seat of the buggy next to Daddy, wondering what it would be like to step out of the land of my birth, the first of my family to travel abroad. Daddy guided the buggy wordlessly, turning an almost puzzled eye in my direction every now and then. Mama sat in the rear, just behind Daddy, and I would catch her eye glancing from me to Daddy, a hint of a smile on her face.

We pulled up at the station just as the whistle began to blow, and the conductor yelled, "All aboard." We would have little time for good-byes. It was not difficult to find my traveling companions. They stood near the front of the train amid a pile of luggage with bright red *P*s emblazoned on their tags.

Mama caught my gaze and then flung her arms around my neck, pulling me down into a tight embrace. Daddy stood solid and silent beside us, his eyes filled with emotions I could not even guess at.

A Novel by Craig T. Williams

Daddy nodded in my direction, shook my hand, and said to me, "I could say I was proud of you now, but the truth is, you make us proud every day." There was an unvoiced *but* at the end of that sentence, and he seemed poised to say more, but did not.

Mama smiled in agreement with the spoken portion of Daddy's message. What, I wondered, had he left unsaid?

I hugged Daddy tightly before he could protest, kissed Mama on the cheek, and then took the dreaded walk to the back of the train, away from my fellow athletes. Coach Robertson watched as I ascended the steps into the Negroes-only car. He gave a slight tilt of his hat in my direction, and then he and the others boarded the front car. The train whistled once more and I settled into my seat just as the train lurched forward. We were on our way to New York City.

I glanced through my window and saw Mama and Daddy still rooted in the same spot, watching their "miracle child" blaze a path they had only dreamed about. Not long after, I descended into dreams myself, the chugging of the train lulling me into peaceful slumber.

The smell of the dining car filled my nostrils and I awoke just as we pulled into the New York station. My stomach grumbled, but there was no way I would succumb to the enticing smell and allow myself to be served in the rear. It disturbed me more and more to be treated as a second-class citizen. It was enough that I had to be separated from my team although we were headed for the same destination. No, I would purchase a meal along the way. For now, I settled for the dinner rolls mama had packed for me.

On our arrival in New York, we grabbed a bit of food and traveled as a group to the lower end of Manhattan Island. Our ship would not be ready for embarkation for some hours, and Coach Robertson took us on a journey to the financial district. We'd come at the invitation of one of the team's financiers, John Pierpont Morgan. We were to ring the bell on the floor of the stock exchange and announce ourselves as Mr. Morgan's guests. Our daydreams of making the newspapers were dashed on account of Mr. Morgan's chronic rosacea. No photos, but it would be something for the news boys to talk about.

My mouth nearly fell open at the sight of the U.S. Customs House. The upper stories of the massive building were supported by an elegant colonnade three stories high, and the blue granite façade boasted more windows than I'd ever seen in one building. The huge bronze doors were flanked by a pair of stone lions, each as big as a carriage. Another set of lions reposed atop pedestals at either corner. We were clearly tourists as we stood staring at the building amid the comings and goings of investors, brokers, and businessmen. None of them paid us the least bit of attention, but bustled about their business as, indeed, the entire city of New York seemed to do.

We finished our tour with the final stop for every aspiring investment banker and stockbroker: 18 Broad Street. Of course, I'd read about the New York Stock Exchange opening its new building with much fanfare to a crowd of some twenty thousand people the year before. But standing in its shadow was a humbling experience. The massive pediment atop the entry portico was supported by half a dozen fluted columns and populated by at least that many marble effigies carved in relief on its face—*Integrity Protecting the Works of Man.*

The air caught in my throat and I felt as though I had been transported to another time. A time when deciding on a career in finance had sounded grand and big. A time when being selected to the Wharton School of Finance to study the making and exchanging of money seemed the perfect way to fulfill dreams. Now, standing here, I nearly lost myself in the decision that I had made from the narrow comfort of my bedroom. Peering through the row of columns, trying to penetrate the façade of the building, I suddenly felt less definite about my choice.

I looked around solemnly at my classmates, who were overjoyed to be this close to the dream. I could not quite grasp the thought, but somehow I knew—at the deepest part of my soul—that this was not *my* dream. I was not afraid of trying, nor was I afraid of the work. I knew I could do it. I was afraid that this was simply not *it.* This was not what I wanted to do with my life. This place was devoid of the sort of nurture and healing I had grown up with. It was not for me.

To say that the course of my life shifted in just one moment may seem an overstatement, but I knew—standing in front of that fortress of commerce—that I had had a change of heart. My life would not end here. I knew that at some point I would have to stand up for my own truth. But first,

The Olympian: An American Triumph

I had to find it, name it.

I was grateful when we got away from the crowds of people and made our way to the docks. I'd thought I'd had enough awe for one day, but my mouth fell open again when we reached the pier and I saw the size of our ship. The ocean liner *Aurania* loomed like a large building afloat in the water. I was amazed that something weighing 7,000 tons could grace the peaceful waters of the Hudson River without sinking to the bottom. My knees began to wobble at the mere thought of boarding.

We entered as the Penn relay team, and then we went our separate ways yet again. I made my way to my cabin in the Negro section of steerage class, pushed my suitcase into the small closet, and sat queasily on the bed. My stomach was doing somersaults, and we had yet to leave the dock. This would be quite the journey. I stood at the port rail and breathed deeply as we began to move slowly out of the harbor. I was on my way, a Taylor man, headed to England and France.

We passed an inbound liner in the shadow of the Liberty statue. Immigrants crowded the rail, tears running down their faces, hugging each other and clasping hands in grateful prayer. She was beautiful and I felt their joy, although their arrival through Ellis Island, the "gateway to the new world, was a joyful adventure, I, however, felt a very different feeling rising up in the pit of my belly. It must be a wonderful thing to be welcomed with open arms. They were happy to be coming and I was happy to be going. Life was funny that way.

A Novel by Craig T. Williams

★★★★

England was much different from America. Everything seemed immensely older and smaller—that is everything except the government buildings and churches. Roads were narrow and heavily traveled by people speaking languages other than English. Those who did speak English uttered syllables so thick that it was hard to make out what they were saying without someone to translate it. It was the first time in my life that I felt as though I was a scripted character inserted into a Shakespearean play—*A Comedy of Errors*, perhaps.

Our first group of races took place early Saturday morning on the grounds of the famous Crystal Palace at Sydenham Hill in South London. The Crystal Palace was one of the most impressive sights I had ever seen. There was nothing in the great city of Philadelphia to compare to it. It was an 1851 masterpiece, often called an "international wonder." An iron Goliath clad in more than a million feet of glass, it glittered like a massive diamond, a million facets reflecting the light of the sun. I had always admired UPenn's beautiful buildings, but this was something altogether different. I did wonder how they kept all that glass clean.

We ran in Sydenham Park, which was also a spectacular vision to behold, with gravity-powered fountains and lush natural beauty made only slightly drabber by the season. We were competing mostly against athletes from Europe, with a few teams from some of the top schools in America. Our first race came early in the day, and when we took to the makeshift track they had constructed for the event, we discovered that the University of Pennsylvania relay team was competing against all European teams; there was not one from America in our grouping.

UPenn athletes Henry Smith, Landon Briar, Charles Cook, and myself made up the 1600 meter relay team. Once out on the track, we stood proudly upright with our chests out and heads high, intent on showing our rivals that we had sailed a wide sea to be here, and would not leave unnoticed.

The runners for the first leg took their marks in staggered order. My friend Henry would lead; Landon Briar, a very decent sprinter from Minnesota, would run second; Charles Cook was the third leg, and I would run in the anchor position—the responsibility of securing a win would fall to me. Our nerves were tightly wound, as many spectators were there to watch. Certainly eyes were on the Americans, watching to see if we were as big as our international reputation.

Coach Robertson led us onto the field with only two words of sporting advice, "Don't disappoint."

His words weighed heavy on me as the starter raised his gun and a booming voice on the loudspeaker began the meet.

"Marks. Set …"

That was all I heard. The next thing I knew Henry Smith was off and had taken an early lead on his five competitors. Henry, a strong runner with as much will as speed, held a steady lead throughout most of his 400 meter run, but by the time he handed off the baton to Landon Briar, one of the German runners had caught and passed him, putting us in second place.

Landon was able to hold at second throughout his 400 meters, and though he was a strong athlete with a decent amount of stamina, his biggest weakness as a runner was consistency. Some days he ran like a champion, but some days it seemed he could barely keep up with the beating of his own heart. Landon's great strength rested in his ability to hand off the baton in a smooth exchange, as he did now with Mr. Cook.

In my mind, Charles was the most unreliable runner on the team, and not because of our personal history. He was blessed with strength, agility, endurance, and speed. But though he was light on his feet, he was weighed down by an arrogance that came to him through his heritage. Charles was the proud son of a northern family who had gotten rich on their investments in southern plantations. That pride made him likely to showboat on the field. And when he showboated, he made mistakes. On an all-important day like today, when the eyes on us sought grounds for criticism rather than praise, he would have done well to be a little more humble.

He did not.

I saw the expression on his face change as he neared his 200 meter mark. He put on a sudden burst of speed, lengthening his stride. His gait became jerky and uneven with the effort, and I knew he was overreaching. I held my breath.

When Charles hit the 200 meter mark, his feet slipped

and he toppled hip first to the ground. There was a collective gasp from the stands.

Charles scrambled to his feet and leapt after the pack, but the damage was done. Until his spill we'd been holding steadily at second—at one point he'd even edged into first—but his fall had put us in last place.

I took my place in the lane for the anchor leg and stood with my European competitors as, one by one they received batons from their teammates and sprinted away from me. Meanwhile, I stood there on that foreign field under the smug gazes of the spectators awaiting Charles. He eventually arrived, his left knee bloodied, and passed me the baton. I could see shame and humiliation beneath his sheen of sweat.

There would be no time for me to hang back today. No time to affect my opponents' pace. Even if I ran flat-out, it would still be a true come-from-behind victory—if it were a victory at all. Just to pull our team out of last place, I would have to run with every ounce of spirit I possessed. Anything less would be a failure.

I seized the baton and ran. In my head, Coach Robertson's words repeated like the tick of a stopwatch: Don't disappoint. *Don't disappoint.*

By the time I reached my 200 meter mark, I had already passed one competitor. At the 300 meter mark, one more. The crowd erupted in chaotic response. The lead runner, an Austrian, could have outrun me had he not looked over his shoulder in response to the crowd's frenzy. The moment he looked, he lost; that second of distraction cost him the race. I caught him in mid-stride and burned a hole right through to the finish line. The crowd roared like a herd of wild beast. We Americans were worthy of our reputation after all.

That is, with the exception of Charles Edward Cook. No one congratulated him for a race well run or consoled him for his fall. In the final analysis his fall and bloodied knee sweetened the win, making it seem near miraculous rather than merely extraordinary. He could own neither tragedy nor victory, for the miracle was mine, the victory ours.

Money can sometimes purchase grace, but all his wealth bought him in England was disappointment to go with the fancy souvenirs for friends and family. Yes, he was part of the team that had won the race, but his desire to show off and failure to pace himself had cost him a personal *victory*. Those of us who knew him understood that, though none of us dared speak of it—not even Coach Robertson, who called me a "hero" for the remainder of the trip. I could see Charles wither as I received words of praise from Coach and our teammates. He did not offer me his congratulations, nor did I expect him to. He simply lurked in the background.

I refused to get too caught up in the triumph of the day, though, for I knew that each new day brought an opportunity for triumph or tragedy, victory or loss. Like a character in a Shakespearean play, one could go from the peak of glory to the abyss of defeat in the blink of an eye.

17

Cheater

April 1905

The day began with the innocence of a newborn spring. The sun's warmth penetrated the chill swirl of the winds, but only sporadically. One moment it was so warm you wanted to pull off your jacket. The next, the wind would give you a chilly lick that made you pull your collar up about your ears.

We were in the middle of final exams and Coach Robertson had called a team meeting in the gymnasium before we began the new season. I entered the gym with a nod to Coach and sat down in the bleachers among my teammates, dropping my book bag—which was heavy with textbooks and term papers—onto the bench next to me. It was a relief to get it off my shoulder. I spotted Henry several rows up and nodded in his direction as well.

Coach Robertson moved toward us, nearly bumping into Charles, who was the last to enter and who appeared flustered. He mumbled apologies to the coach and hurried to take a place on the bench above me next to Landon Briar.

Coach raised one eyebrow in his direction and then

turned toward a new face among us—a young man I didn't notice until Coach called our attention to him. "Gentlemen, Nathaniel Cartmell will be rejoining our team," he said, gesturing at the "new man," who smiled and nodded at us. "I am most pleased to have this outstanding athlete back with us."

I gave Nate a firm nod, because I was most pleased, too. The importance of having another "friend" on the team could not be understated.

"Nathaniel will be running alternate third leg," Coach explained, turning hard eyes toward Charles.

It was then that I noticed how close Charles was sitting to me. He had moved several feet toward me along the bench in the time Coach had been talking, though he made no comment or fuss about the change in the relay team. He simply sat back against the bleachers and crossed his arms over his chest. In the entire two years of our co-existence on this team he had never sat so near unless he was trying to intimidate. As he was sitting above me, I assumed he was doing that now. Determined to show him I was not willing to be unnerved, I leaned forward and gave all my attention to the coach.

Coach Robertson then proceeded to give us a great talking-to, inspiring us all to return with quality running after our academic finals.

"Leave the finals in the classroom," Coach said sternly as he finished his pep talk. "The only thing that matters here is how fast your feet hit the ground. The only thing that should be on your mind is winning!" and with that he nodded and ended our meeting.

Charles rose with a smile, stretching as I stood up next to him. "Do well, John," he said.

My mouth nearly fell open in surprise. "You, too, Charles," I replied hastily.

He had surely not changed his mind about me in one afternoon, especially since he had never shown me anything but contempt. I could not fathom it, and I certainly did not trust Charles's new friendly smile.

Not at all.

Henry stood in the center of the gym, chatting with Nate, but his eyes kept darting between me and Charles, who was descending the stands next to me.

I adjusted my bag on my shoulder, showing no emotion. There was no way Charles would ever defeat me, not mentally, and certainly not on the field. I shook him from my thoughts and went to join Henry and Nathaniel.

★★★★

It was with great satisfaction that I had turned in my English Composition paper, which explored the exciting world of boxing generally, and the spectacular career of Jack Johnson especially. It had taken great effort and a tremendous amount of time to write the paper I wanted and to type it painstakingly in duplicate on a borrowed Underwood. When I thought my opening argument was sufficiently strong and was certain I'd done my very best, I dropped a pristine copy on Professor Ryan's desk.

Two weeks to the day, I entered class with anticipation,

anxious to see my grade after pouring my heart into that paper. I had carefully worded my opening statement, not wanting to appear biased. Though in my heart I knew Jack Johnson was the best—colored or white—I stuck to the facts and the results, simply stating the effect boxing was having on America and young sporting men. It was in my summation that I had taken the most liberty with my opinion and expanded on my opening statement that Johnson, whether admired or detested, would be the best candidate for the heavyweight championship.

I gave a nod to Henry, who sat several rows in front of me, and took my seat near the rear of the room as it filled with students and a buzz of nervous anticipation. Professor Ryan rose quietly from his chair and eyed the class. He looked from one student to another, and we looked back with great interest. His lips turned up in a small sneer as he turned his head in my direction.

Am I imagining things? I wondered. For surely I had done nothing but sit in my seat.

Professor Ryan turned his eyes away from me slowly, as if he wanted everyone to realize that he had been focusing on *me*. He came out from behind his desk and began walking down the row of students seated closest to the windows. I watched him, as did every other student, and followed his progress to the fourth chair in the row where he stopped directly in front of Charles Cook.

Charles looked up at him bemusedly. "Sir?"

"Lad," Professor Ryan said, his drawl thicker than I'd ever heard it, "you have been violated."

Charles's head snapped back and he stared up at the professor in apparent horror. "What do you mean, sir?"

Professor Ryan stepped back, raised his eyes, and slanted his body toward the other side of the classroom. With a slow, awkward gesture, he pointed his index finger directly at me. "John Taylor has taken your words and claimed them as his own."

I felt as if someone had poured ice water over my head. Never had I done such a thing. I would never take credit for another man's work. This was outrageous. Henry swiveled in his chair and stared at me, his face reflecting what I felt—a mixture of horror and shock.

Charles's lips twisted slightly before he said, "How could that be? What do you mean?" He sounded so sincerely outraged that his voice quivered, but his outrage was feigned; I suspected he was trying hard not to laugh.

I stared at him hard and cold. He turned in his seat and returned my gaze. There we sat like two Wild West fighters, guns cocked and ready to fire. I awaited the chance to deny these absurd charges.

It never came.

"You," Professor Ryan said, turning in my direction, "must leave my classroom at once. Dean Adams is waiting for you."

It took everything in me to maintain control. My blood was boiling so hot and strong I was certain that my complexion was somewhere between an outraged red and an embarrassed purple.

"Sir, I did not take any words from Charles Cook," I said.

A Novel by Craig T. Williams

"I would like to have some more details so that I have an idea of what you are implying."

"Are you questioning my capabilities?" Professor Ryan asked.

I could feel the intense gaze of the other students, but the only people I saw were my accusers—the outraged and the amused.

Hell, yes, I wanted to scream. *I'm questioning your capabilities, because you're insulting me by saying I would cheat from an ignoramus like Charles Edward Cook.*

Those were not the words that spilled from my lips. I had learned from one of the finest men in town to maintain my composure in the face of insult. If I had to summon the strength of John Taylor, Sr., I would. I would not be reduced to a stammering child over this injustice.

"Sir," I said, the words burning their way from my throat, "I am merely asking exactly what I am supposed to have done wrong and to be granted a chance to defend myself. I have a right to know what you think I have stolen from Charles and why you think I stole it."

"You are a cheater!" he screamed. "Now remove yourself from my classroom! I will not be questioned by a cheater!"

There would be no answers here today. I looked at the professor, and then gave one final glance toward Charles, who sat there staring at me with a Cheshire cat's grin. This had been intentional. I knew it as soon as I saw his face. Charles deserved applause; his performance had been that good. I contemplated clapping for him, for finally he had won, or so it appeared.

He could not beat me on the track, so it had come to this. He would defeat me by robbing me of my honor. I stared hard at him. There would be no backing down or away today. I wanted Charles to know that I was no fool, nor was I a victim.

I gathered up my bag and walked up the aisle, swallowing hard when I saw the kindness in Henry's eyes. He gave me a quick nod in support. I nodded in return, holding my head high as I left the hushed classroom.

I nearly ran to Dean Adams's office. My honor was at stake and I wanted—no *demanded*—answers. I took a deep breath before opening the door to the dean's outer office. His secretary looked up at me, and then returned her gaze to her papers as though the door had opened by itself and I was not standing there.

18

The Wall

April 1905

I suppose the accusations shouldn't have surprised me, given the poisonous hatred Charles had for me, but to dishonor a man without just cause or merit is one of the lowest of human acts. In this case, considering what it meant to our track and field team, it seemed especially senseless.

My most urgent task now was to clear my name of any wrongdoing, and leave it to the good Lord to reconcile my teammate's low deeds. I felt as if snakes writhed in my belly as I struggled to maintain my belief in God's grace and man's common sense, which suddenly did not seem so common anymore. It seemed vanishingly rare. How could a man who had always striven for integrity be accused of such unscrupulous deeds? If I were a champion on the field and a failure in the classroom, I might have understood the conclusion they leapt to. But I had a fine academic record—an exemplary one. Did they imagine that I had cheated my way to that and only now had gotten caught?

Now instead of walking in victory, I stood on Franklin Field, sweating out my frustration. It was an unusually warm spring, and promised a grand summer, but I didn't feel the approach of summer. My world was cold, and my prospects were in ruins.

I determined to escape the chill of this experience and so I ran. I ran like the black eagle flies, but the chill would not be outrun. It took up pursuit and forced me to run even faster, my feet striking the ground in a swelling rhythm. It was more than the chill I labored to outrun, I realized. It was hatred. A man's hatred of his fellow man, which is ultimately the purest form of hatred of *himself*.

I slowed to a walk and returned to where I'd dropped my duffel bag. I picked it up and started toward town. Out of the corner of my eye, I caught sight of Henry, who had come looking for me.

"John!" Waving, he jogged toward me across the field.

I hesitated and, for a heartbeat, deeply longed to be him. How much easier it would be to walk around with white skin. Even a man unable to speak English fresh off the boat got a fairer shake than any colored man.

"Henry."

He came to a stop before me. "What happened with the dean?"

I shook my head, then lowered my gaze from his bright, anxious face.

"What did you tell them?" he demanded.

"What *could* I tell them?"

"That they're wrong!"

"I told them that."

"Did they believe you?"

I raised one brow. "Do you think they believed me? Surely you can't be that naïve, Henry."

"It's not right, John," he declared. "You have to fight."

"Their minds are made up. They've already found me guilty. They want me to apologize to Charles Cook."

"*Apologize?* Surely you jest!"

"No, I do not."

"You've got to prove them wrong, John!" he pleaded. "You can't just lie down on this."

"I have nothing to prove. I did nothing wrong."

"Then what are you going to do?"

"I'm going to leave UPenn," I said. The words drove a shard of pain through my heart.

"You're dropping out?" he asked, aghast. "Oh, for God's sake, John …"

Dropping out. The words sounded harsh when said so flatly.

"And do what?" he prodded, angered by the injustice of it all. .

"I can't talk about it now, Henry." I turned and ran, leaving Henry talking to his own shadow.

"Prove them wrong, John!" I could hear him shouting as I faded into my own dark thoughts, now filled with drama, heartache, and lost dreams.

Prove them wrong, John. Prove them wrong.

★★★★

By the time I arrived home it was suppertime and Mama was busy preparing a "quiet feast." Music tumbled from the

Victrola and a jovial mood filled the house. But even with the salve of Scott Joplin's best, I had a feeling the sky was about to topple onto the roof of our Woodland Avenue home. Everything looked the same as it had when I'd left that morning, but in reality, everything was different—or perhaps only I was different.

The aroma from the kitchen would normally have had me singing heaven's praises, but tonight I wasn't hungry. In fact, I had barely enough strength to sit erect at the supper table. Across the table from me, Mama and Daddy seemed miles away. I picked over the food on my plate, unable to find the courage to share the events of the day and searching my mind for a way to say the words I knew I needed to say.

"Son," said Mama, peering at me, "you all right?"

Daddy turned his eyes in my direction and then set his fork down next to his plate. "Son," he said with obvious concern, "answer your mama. You okay?"

"Something happened at the university today," I said, barely able to get the words out.

"What happened, John?" Mama asked, eyes wide with trepidation.

I took a deep breath and began my descent into hell, fighting the urge to stutter. "Well, there was somewhat of a scandal at school today."

"What kind of scandal, John?" asked Mama.

"My English teacher called me a cheater."

"A cheater!" cried Daddy.

"Said I copied another student's paper … said I stole it and tried to make it my own."

"Dear sweet Jesus up in heaven," mumbled Mama. "Whatever would lead him to such a tall tale?"

"One of my teammates, Charles Cook, had the same opening statement in his essay as I had in mine."

"What?"

"The dean said we had identical opening statements and that I must have copied Charles's paper," I said. "But they got it wrong. He copied *my* page, I didn't copy his."

Mama lowered her head and Daddy got up from his seat and began pacing the floor, back and forth, deep in thought.

"Why?" Daddy asked. "What would possess this boy to copy your paper?"

"I'm a better athlete. He failed miserably in Europe … took a tumble right in the middle of the race…"

"You told us about that," said Mama. "*That's* the boy you mixed up with?"

"Yes, ma'am," I replied. "His jealousy got the best of him, and now he has set me up for a fall."

"Well, what's he saying?" Mama asked.

"Nothing. He's pretending to be shocked and outraged."

"Are you certain he's pretending?" Daddy asked.

"John!" Mama exclaimed, staring at Daddy. "You can't believe your son-"

Daddy raised his hand to forestall Mama's outrage and gave me a look that made me want to shiver in spite of the warmth of the evening. "You answer me straight, son. You take anything from this boy's paper?"

"John!" Mama repeated.

My ears burned with shame and dismay. "Daddy, I wrote

a paper about Jack Johnson. *Jack Johnson,* Daddy. A colored athlete. I praised him. I called him 'the best.' You think I stole that from a white student who's shown me nothing but scorn because of my brown skin?"

Daddy heaved a huge sigh and sat back down at the table. "No. No, son, 'course not. I'm just... This is ... this is hard."

"It's hard for me, too, Daddy," I murmured.

"So who's hearing your case?" he asked after a moment of hesitation. "For sure there's somebody who can straighten this mess out."

I shook my head. "I will find no justice there, Daddy. They've already settled on my guilt. The dean asked me to apologize for my actions. Guilty until proven innocent. There will be no hearing."

"What's that mean—there'll be no hearing?" asked Mama.

I took a deep breath and slowly pulled the Voluntary Withdrawal paper from my pocket. I laid it gently on the table. Mama snatched it up and Daddy leaned in to read it over her shoulder. They read the words silently. Tears began to trace the lines in Mama's cheeks. Daddy lowered his head in defeat, with an expression somewhere between distress and fury. I waited miserably for the words to come. When they did, they shocked me to the soles of my shoes.

"You go back to that school tomorrow and you tell those folks you're sorry," demanded Daddy. It was not up for negotiation. "You beg pardon of 'em."

Beg pardon? "I did nothing wrong!" I yelled, pushing my-

self from the table so violently the chair tipped backward
onto the floor.

Mama jumped at the sound of it, but Daddy moved to
meet me, towering over me and showing me that he still was
bigger.

"I ain't letting you throw away all your hard work!" he
thundered.

"Just apologize, son," pleaded Mama, looking up at me
through tears.

"For what?" I asked. "What would I apologize for?"

"Don't let this boy steal your dreams, John ... please." In
Mama's face, I saw torment. It saddened me greatly to see
her so torn up, but I could not back down from my truth.

"I—did—nothing—wrong!"

"You did nothing wrong?" roared Daddy. "Pride! *Pride!*"
He pounded the table with his fist, making Mama and me
both jump. "'Pride goeth before destruction, and a haughty
spirit before a fall.' That's the Bible! What're you gonna do
with your life if you leave that school? You go back and you
swallow that damned pride and you say 'sorry'!"

"What do you-" I began, but Daddy cut me off.

"You had to put yourself in the limelight. Had to be the
hero, the champion. You had to go and show that boy up.
Showboating on the track, rubbing his nose in his failure."

"I never said a word to him, Daddy!" I argued. "I never
once said a word to him after he fell. No one did. What did
I do to rub his nose in it?"

"You won."

"I did what I was *supposed* to do for our whole team. I

didn't have a choice when that no good for nothing show-off, up and tripped over his own feet!"

"You made him look stupid!" asserted Daddy.

"In the true spirit of what an athlete is—I did my job, Daddy."

Daddy said nothing.

The silence hurt my ears.

"I wouldn't be worth the salt of my own sweat if I had thrown that race, just to save some foolish boy's pride," I contended. "I'll apologize for *nothing!*"

"Make peace!" Mama begged. "Just make peace!"

"I'm not the one who broke the peace. *He* did. He lied. I will *not* surrender my honor or the honor of our family to a lie. I am an honest man."

"What d'you know about honor?" Daddy growled. "You think you're serving *our* honor?"

"Daddy, I chose this path to save this family disgrace. Fighting this or giving in to it I risk bringing shame to this family. This way-"

"This way you give up this family's dreams. Don't be no stubborn fool, John … Apologize. Have you forgotten whose world this is? This is the white man's world. You'll never win this kind of battle against *them*." Daddy retreated—his stance humbled in defeat. His tone was pleading. "You got the world at your feet, son. Like no colored I ever seen. Don't throw that away!"

"I can't do it!"

"You ain't here to start no uprising. You here for an education."

I knew what this was doing to them. I knew. It was tearing them up inside. But there was only so much sympathy I could feel. Beyond that I was numb. I had already been broken in two by my decision.

"Jesus!" cried Mama. "Help us, Jesus…" She started to sob in a way that I had never seen before. She put her head down on the table and wept, pressing her forehead against the hard wood.

Daddy tried to comfort her, but there was no comfort he could give or any convincing he could do to get me to return to UPenn and take on guilt that was not my own. To do that would have been true dishonor, and I would not live my life that way, regardless of what my father said or what Booker T. Washington said. I was no cheater, and that would be the admission I would make, the only words I would utter.

Not guilty.

19

A Grown Man

The next morning

Progress sometimes comes to a man slow and hard, and during the spring of 1905, I experienced the slow, hard progress of a life undergoing reconstruction. Away from formal education for the first time in my life, I was called upon to turn my attention to the secular world, where I was encouraged by Mama and Daddy to "make an honest wage."

In all honesty, I was certain that once the shock of my withdrawal from the university wore off, they would surrender their insistence on my going to work, but the next morning at breakfast, my parents only reinforced their stand on the matter.

"Since you're a grown man, I expect you'll be paying your way now," said Daddy, sitting at the head of the table, his expression serious. "It's time to get a job, John."

"A job?" I asked, swallowing a hard lump in my throat. "A job."

Mama, who was seated beside Daddy, offered up more of the same. "Home-cooked meals, laundry, and cleaning services run a pretty penny. Those things ain't free, son."

My heart sank.

"And then there's room and board," added Daddy.

My heart sank deeper.

"As well as the cost of fixin' your trousers," added Mama.

"Fixing my trousers?"

"Fixin' your trousers. Them trousers you wearing this morning wouldn't be holding up without that new, shiny button I put on 'em yesterday."

Despondent, I reached for a second helping of hotcakes, which Daddy quickly caught somewhere between the platter and my plate.

"And these hotcakes ain't free, neither," he said, placing the hotcakes on his own plate, "but they sure is tasty."

"You best move along, John," said Mama. "We don't want you to be late."

"Late for what?"

"Late for making your way," said Daddy with a tone of finality, followed by a long hard stare from both him and Mama.

"Late for getting a job," added Mama for clarity, just in case I hadn't gotten it already.

I got it.

I no longer felt welcome to linger here. Home was a place that didn't seem to belong to me anymore. I was sure that Mama and Daddy still loved me, but I wasn't willing to bet my last shiny penny that they *liked* me very much right about now. I excused myself without further delay.

Never before had I felt so heavy of body and soul as on the long walk back to my room. Getting a job didn't sound very exciting to me. In fact, it sounded like a lot of work. The only kind of job I'd ever had in my life was helping Daddy out here and there with his business. That was more like chores than a job. I sat on my bed feeling a little flustered and not sure where to go or what to do. It seemed like a man needed a starting point to end up somewhere, right?

But where do you go from here?

I settled into the soft feel of my pillow.

Yes.

This was a peaceful moment. I could feel a cool breeze dancing around the top of my head as I closed my eyes and leaned into the quiet of an unhurried day.

Yes.

I could feel myself begin to drift and float away on the chirping of birds and the lingering smell of hotcakes on the griddle.

Yes.

"No!" snapped Mama, nearly sending me straight up out of the bed and standing at attention. She and Daddy stood in the doorway, glaring at me. "You's a man now! A grown man ain't got time for leisurely napping!"

"No time at 'all!" declared Daddy from behind her.

"Especially when you gotta get a job," insisted Mama.

"But I don't have…" I began in protest, till Daddy raised his brow and gave me a hard look.

"You don't have no time to waste!" Mama said, finishing the sentence for me.

I surrendered on the spot, got up, and dressed.

Within minutes, I was heading toward the door. Mama

was cleaning off the breakfast dishes and Daddy was nowhere to be found.

"On my way," I said to Mama as I walked toward the front door.

I was hoping she would stop me or, at the very least, ask me where I was headed. But of course, she did no such thing. I don't think she even looked up one good time.

"On my way!" I said again, this time louder for emphasis. But again, she offered no response—not even a nod. I guess that in and of itself just about said it all.

Once outside, I saw Daddy urgently loading his horse and wagon with food to take to a party he was catering. I quickly offered a helping hand, thinking my kind gesture might buy me some time in figuring out where exactly I was supposed to be going.

"Thanks, son," said Daddy, "but I can manage."

"Oh," I said quietly, "okay."

"We all got to make our own way," he said, continuing to make circles around me, going from the porch to the buggy loading food. I just stood there in a fog and watched.

"Day ain't getting no brighter, John," he said sternly, looking up into the sky. "You best get a move on."

"Daddy, what do you think about me coming to work for you?"

"Nope."

"It's a *family* business, Daddy."

By now Daddy was done loading and climbed up into the carriage.

"It's *my* business," he said, giving me a good once-over

with his eyes. "And I've determined to settle the business on Hattie. I had meant William take it up after me, but both William and Clinton have gone off to make their own way in the world. You a man now, John. Time for you to do the same. Best get a move on."

"Yes, sir," I said, reading between the lines. "Best get a move on."

I swooped in to give my pal, Bean, a rub on the head before getting on my way, but even the horse turned away in the opposite direction as if to say, *Hhhhmmm … no time to offer a dropout.*

Daddy flipped the reins on Bean's rump and off he went. As he pulled away, Daddy waved and I waved back, but when I looked over my shoulder, I saw that it was Mama he was saying good-bye to and not me.

"I get it," I mumbled to myself.

I waved to Mama, who looked dead at me, closed the curtain, and walked away. I had never witnessed my parents so unlike themselves. Two stone hearts, closed against me. It hurt.

I turned and started on my way.

My first stop was a bustling restaurant near the UPenn campus. The eatery was filled with whites, but I didn't make too much of the situation. It looked decent enough, but once inside, I couldn't help but notice how intensely everyone was staring at me.

A big, burly-looking fellow wearing a white uniform made a slow approach.

"Deliveries in the back, boy," he said in a not-so-friendly manner.

"Afternoon sir," I said. "I'm inquiring about a job."

The restaurant fell silent.

"In this *here* restaurant?"

I nodded.

"Doing what?"

"Keeping books, sir. I'm studying finance at Wharton."

"There's no work for *you* here, boy," he said flatly.

I could feel the heavy stares of the cooks behind the counter and the waiters serving customers. Even from a distance, I could tell they were particularly interested in our conversation.

I nodded. "Thanks anyway." *No sense in making a scene.*

"Try 'cross the way," he suggested. "There's a hotel on the corner."

"Thank you," I said again, easing my way out of the restaurant.

The walk "across the way" felt like a million miles to my bruised ego. Perhaps the hotel would be more keen on the idea of hiring me.

The hotel was also decent enough, and appeared to be doing good business. However, the moment I swung the door open, time did that funny little thing again—stood still—and all eyes shifted in my direction. I tried to shake off my uneasiness and approached the main desk of this obviously all-white establishment.

"Afternoon, sir," I said to the tense-looking man standing behind the desk. He didn't speak, but his mustache did twitch a bit and twist to one side.

"I am inquiring about employment, sir. Might you be

needing a bookkeeper?"

His eyes blinked. His mustache shifted directions, but still no words came out of his mouth.

I looked at him.

He looked at me.

He said nothing.

"A bookkeeper?" I repeated a bit more loudly this time, reasoning that he might be a bit deaf.

"No jobs here, boy," he said in a deep, stern voice.

Even as he spoke, I noticed a small posting on his desk that read Help Wanted. The second I laid eyes on the sign, he tipped it over on its face and held it there like it might run off.

"We filled that position just this morning."

"I see," I said slowly, lowering my head in defeat.

"We'd love to offer you work, but like I said … there's none here. Maybe you can check in the Seventh Ward. I hear they got plenty … of *work*, that is."

"Thanks for your time," I said graciously, "and good luck on filling that position."

The man's eyes widened as I turned and walked out with as much dignity as I had entered with.

That scene was played again everywhere I went that day. I was fast approaching the realization that outside the doors of UPenn and off the track field, I was just another colored. And right about now, that didn't seem too impressive.

I had a whole gang of frightening thoughts and a new found appreciation for my dear friend, Pomp. Without education, what if the only job *I* could get was that of a janitor? Not that there was anything wrong with scrubbing toilets and floors, but the thought of doing that for the rest of my life was enough to stop my heart from beating. And for a moment, I actually thought maybe I should go back to UPenn and apologize.

By late afternoon, I needed to take a break. Clear my head ... or twist it back on straight.

I decided to go down to the Schulkyll River, where I would spend most of the afternoon sitting by the river's edge. I sat close enough to either jump in on purpose or fall in by mistake. I hoped to find peace in these tranquil surroundings, but I failed miserably. Peace was impossible, because it was nowhere within me. I couldn't help but think of Mary Agnes down by the river, and my heart weighed even heavier at the thought of what she might say about all of this ruckus. I think she would be very disappointed to know that I was no longer a student at the University. I could tell that she had a certain pride in my accomplishments. This could alter our relationship greatly. Then, there was Mr. Montier ... I shivered at the thought. If he knew what was going on, he'd bar their front door shut and never open it again.

Oh boy.

I needed to move my attention to easier thoughts. I was supposed to be somewhere *else* right now, but I just didn't know where to go. Truth be told, though I'd helped Daddy during the summer and done odd jobs, I had no idea of how to go about getting one. I wouldn't imagine that a good-paying job would just fall off one of these trees down here, so I knew I had to get going again.

The Olympian: An American Triumph

As I gazed across the western bank of the river, I caught a glimpse of the Seventh Ward. I could still hear the echo of the man behind the hotel desk. *They got plenty of work.* Maybe that's where I should begin this journey into manhood—where fearless colored men worked and lived. Though not far from our house, the Ward was a world away. I had heard all the tales and tragedies of this neighborhood. Even my father referred to it as "the slums."

"What's a slum?" William and I had asked the first time we heard him use the word. We were young boys to whom it sounded dark and a little scary.

"A slum is a place that in the dead of night, people up and disappear," said Daddy in a creepy-sounding voice, "and they ain't never seen or heard from again."

"Where do they go?" I gasped, mesmerized by Daddy's intensity.

Daddy'd shrugged his big shoulders. "Don't know. But it ain't no place for young boys to be hangin' about."

The Ward wasn't for young boys, but I was a *man* now. And men do what men have to do. And besides, hadn't W. E. B. DuBois written of the Ward? Hadn't he found in it something worthy of mention—worthy of study? In fact, hadn't Pomp also lived here?

I'd show Mama and Daddy just how much of a man I was. I'd go to the Ward and get me a good-paying job and start making my own way. Maybe being a man wasn't such a regrettable situation to find myself in, I mused. Maybe I could finally have a little personal freedom.

I got up from the riverbank, brushed the grass off my

trousers, stuffed my troubled heart into my breast pocket, and started making my way down the river road.

"Making my way," I repeated to myself.

The journey was somewhat intoxicating as I crossed the Chestnut Street Bridge, dizzied by the uncertainty of this forbidden voyage. I wasn't looking forward to the Ward itself, for I felt that the Ward and I had little in common with each other. However I was eager to establish my manhood and prove to my parents that I could get a decent job and make my own way. I must have walked for more than hour, heading to a place I thought I'd never go without permission.

Men don't need permission, I kept reminding myself.

I was familiar with the path, of course. After all, this was the route our family traveled to church every Sunday. But just one block from the Seventh Ward, I became intensely aware that once I'd taken a single step past our place of worship, the air changed.

Poverty has a smell.

The atmosphere grew heavier and breathing more difficult. I felt as though I had crossed over from my familiar world to *this* one. The sun was setting, and as it lowered toward the horizon, the neighborhood went through a slow transition. Corner stores closed and the respectable-looking folks moved inside for the night.

So much for getting a job today, I thought. *This looks like the kind of place that should be visited in the daylight hours.*

The Ward had a distinct *atmosphere.* I couldn't help but feel as though I had been swallowed up into the belly of a whale named "Hard Times."

I made my way as far as 7th and Lombard, telling myself to give up and go home with every step. But on that corner, I stopped, amazed, feeling as though I had fallen off the face of the earth and landed square in the heart of the imagined slum of my childhood terrors. I had never seen so many Negroes in such close quarters. Granted, the Ward was a small area of town, but the neighborhood looked or maybe just felt "bigger" because so much was happening in it. There was not a lot of actual activity, but lots of "mind chatter," for on every face I saw the same question: *How in the world do I get out of here?*

And here I was, trying to get in.

Everything was unkempt and dirty. The buildings were run down, and lines of row houses made of brick and wood were neglected beyond repair. The citizens carried their defeat on shuffling feet—young men and old alike. Eyes cast down toward the ground. Young women carried babies on their hips and burdens in their eyes. In one way or another, everybody seemed to be involved in some sort of struggle.

There was something about entering the Ward that felt permanent, as if there was no way out. Or rather, as if the way out was "invisible" to the folks who lived here. No one was barred from leaving, but they just didn't know that. So they stayed.

Again, maybe they couldn't leave. After all, where would they go, how would they get there and the biggest question of all—how would they sustain themselves once they had arrived? I suspected none of these people had ever stepped onto a college campus, and that they had the bare minimum education, if any at all. It was a new kind of slavery, I realized suddenly: free blacks corralled in a tiny area, enslaved by their own ignorance and lack of opportunity. That opportunity was lost to immigrants even though I'd bet these Negroes were willing to do the same jobs at a much lower wage.

I caught eyes with a stranger, a young man who looked to be around my age, but there the resemblance ended. Or did it? His eyes said he was filled with mischief, and his feet seemed to be moving purposefully, perhaps toward a heap of trouble. I was stirred with compassion. These people were just like me, but then again they weren't like me at all. I felt ... foreign.

I came upon a small diner and realized that Mama's hotcakes had long worn off and that I could feel the rumblings of my stomach. I went inside and was met by the unfriendly glares of locals sitting at the counter. These brown faces wore expressions of suspicion identical to the ones I'd seen on white faces earlier in the day. The realization stunned me.

I slowly eased my way to the counter and sat down.

The waitress, an older woman who wore a lot of years on her face, approached with an order tablet and a frown. "What you having?" she asked impatiently, as if I had already kept her waiting for two, maybe three, days.

"What's the special?" I asked.

She turned and pointed to a board citing Today's Specials as if I were a bit on the slow side.

"Fried chicken," I quickly responded and she walked away.

I felt about as uncomfortable here as I had on my first day at the university. Everybody in the room was colored, but we didn't feel the same, or at least I didn't feel the same. The natives could sense my uneasiness and were content to increase it with their distant glares and stares.

"You ain't from here, is you?" whispered an alluring voice into one of my ears, causing me to jump.

I turned to find a young woman laughing in my face. My eyes nearly popped out of my head when I saw her. She was glamorous but in a worldly kind of way. I had never seen a woman like this. She wore a lot of makeup, and had very long eyelashes that she didn't mind batting. She had shiny red lips and was wearing a dark green dress that fit so tightly that it seemed to scream *I am a woman!*

"I don't live too far from *here*," I said.

"But you ain't from here?"

"No," I said with a shy smile.

"You look real proper-like," she said with a southern drawl. "What you call yourself?"

"John."

"Name's Dorothy," she said, extending a hand. "But everybody calls me Dot. What business you got here in the Ward?"

"Just passing through," I replied.

"Hell … this ain't the kind of place you pass through," she said with a wink. "This the kind of place you get stuck in."

"I can see that," I murmured.

She laughed and brushed her fingertips along my shirt collar. "You ain't never been stuck a day in your life, I bet.

A Novel by Craig T. Williams

How long you plan on staying?"

"I … I don't know," I said, flustered. Dorothy—whom everybody called Dot—seemed to be breathing up all my air. Instinctively, I shied back—just so I could take a good breath. "And you're wrong about that."

"'Bout what?" she asked.

"About me being stuck," I said. "I've been stuck before."

She batted her lashes at me and flashed a white, pearly smile. *Wow!* She was some kind of pretty. But it was a different pretty from Mary Agnes. This was the kind of pretty that could get a weak fellow in trouble. This was not the kind of good looks that you bring home and show off to your mama. This was more along the lines of the kind you just admire from a distance.

"Why don't you c'mon down to Pa Bell's?"

"What's Pa Bell's?"

Dot laughed out loud. "Juke joint," she blurted.

"Juke joint?"

"You ain't never been to a juke joint, boy?"

"Can't say I have," I replied.

"Where you been all ya life, fella?"

"Fried chicken!" the waitress yelled, setting a hot plate in front of me and storming off.

"Listen up," said Dot, eyeing my chicken. "I'm going to the bathroom, and when I come back we going to the juke joint."

"Okay," I said, almost having to snatch the word out of the back of my throat. As I watched Dorothy walk away, my nerves took a turn for the worse. I had never been to a juke joint before, and I had a feeling it was the kind of place Mama and Daddy would hardly approve of. But I couldn't concern myself with that because I was a grown man now. And grown men didn't need permission. They needed jobs and the ability to earn an honest wage to pay for hotcakes and trouser repairs.

When Dot returned, I was ready to go. I had swallowed that hot chicken so fast that I had a stomachache on the way out the door. I probably left more chicken on the plate than I actually ate, but I was anxious to discover the Ward with my new friend, Dot.

The sky was pitch black as we walked to Pa Bell's, which was right in the middle of Spruce Street. Like I said before, all of the respectable folks were shut away in their houses, and I got the feeling most of the people I saw hanging on the street corners were up to no good.

"You all right?" Dot asked with a laugh.

"I'm fine," I replied quickly.

"You ain't used to being in a place like this, is you?"

"Of course I am," I lied.

She laughed again.

"You a schoolboy, ain't you?"

Those words seemed to hit me right where it hurt.

"Used to be."

"You look like a schoolboy," she said, sizing me up. "Haircut, nice clothes, decent-looking shoes, and no kind of scars on your face."

"What?"

"Yeah," said Dot. "You ain't nobody 'round here till you

been stabbed at least one good time."

"No, thank you," I said as politely as I could.

"You some kind of different," she said, shaking her head and chuckling at me.

It took us about fifteen minutes to get to the juke joint, which wasn't hard to find. All you had to do was listen for the sound of music and laughter. On the outside, the juke was little more than a crumbling shack, but the inside was full of life.

Couples were dancing in the middle of the floor, but it was nothing like I had seen before. Both the men and the women would have been labeled as "wild" or "raunchy" if they'd been behaving that way in public on my side of town. A small group of musicians with a variety of instruments, including a banjo and fiddle, were stationed in the corner, along with a big black man with a large belly and a grin to match. He approached Dorothy the second she stepped inside.

"Dottie!" said the man. "I see you got a new friend."

"This here's John," she said. "John, this be Pa Bell."

"Pleased to meet you," I said, extending a proper hand.

He just looked at me and laughed. "You ain't from 'round these parts, is you, schoolboy?"

"I don't live t-too far away," I stuttered.

"But you don't live *here*," he said, suddenly unfriendly.

It was then that I began to feel a little uneasy. In fact, a single glance around the room confirmed that I was the only outsider.

"He ain't got a single mark on him," Pa Bell said to Dot.

"He's decent … Don't you ride him, Pa." She tugged at my arm.

We made our way down a dark hallway at the back of the club. At the end of the hall, Dorothy entered a side door. "Wait right here," she instructed as she entered the room. Inside, men sat at a table playing cards and drinking hooch. Money sat atop the table, so I knew this was no friendly game of gin rummy.

As I waited in the open doorway, ready to crawl out of my skin, Dorothy went to the table and took one of the men by the hand. They disappeared through a door in the back.

My hair stood on end. I was utterly alone under the hostile regard of the gamblers, saved only by the fact, I supposed, that I'd showed up with Dot. I didn't know what to do or where to go and I was suddenly afraid, though I tried like the devil not to show it. I looked like a schoolboy who had never so much as broken a sweat a day in his life, whereas these people looked as though they had done so much living, they'd already died and come back twice.

I was at the point of leaving when Dorothy emerged from the rear room and came back out into the hallway with a smile and a few crisp bills, which she stuffed down the front of her dress.

"Where'd you go?" I asked.

She smiled, patting her ample bosom. "Girl's gotta make a living."

"Are you...? Do you...?" I tried to ask, but found that I was so shocked, I couldn't even get the words out.

"I got three kids, John," she said, looking me dead in the

eye, her mouth no longer smiling. "They gotta eat some-how."

And with that she took my hand and pulled me down the hall and out onto the dance floor. I was not really in a dancing mood, as I was trying to understand what had just happened and who Dorothy was, and why she had be-friended me.

"Don't you know how to do a rag, boy?" she asked.

Embarrassed, I shook my head.

She put her hands on her hips. "How about the turkey trot? I'll bet you ain't even done a cakewalk before," she added beneath her breath.

I shook my head again and she rolled her eyes, then set about trying to show me something called the Mississippi Rag.

"Com'on, boy! You gotta loosen up," she said, laughing at me. She glanced toward the bar and made a gesture at the barkeep. A moment later, a shady-looking man slipped across the room and handed Dot a drink, which she in turn gave to me.

I froze.

"Go on," insisted Dot. "Drink it!"

I couldn't seem to move.

Dot leaned in and whispered in my ear. "What are you so afraid of?"

I paused for a second, maybe two, before chugging the drink straight down.

"Sweet Jesus," I said holding my throat. It was so strong, it nearly burned a hole straight through to the floor. I gasped for breath while Dot just laughed at me.

"I like you better when you ain't being *you*," she said, rubbing her hand along my backside, caressing places on my body that I never knew women were allowed to touch.

"Can I have another?" I managed to blurt out, and immediately wanted to look back and ask, "Who just said that?" It surely couldn't have been John Taylor, Jr.

She led me to a tiny table just off the dance floor. Within minutes, another drink came.

Another.

And then another.

Each time it burned going down, but it got a little easier.

"Slow down, schoolboy," suggested Dot. "I got plans for you."

And with that she pulled me up and back out into the middle of the makeshift dance floor. By then, I was plenty loose and had even picked up a step or two from watching the others.

I felt *good*. So good that I didn't even notice the hours falling one on top of another, stacking up till it was two o'clock in the morning. By then the liquor was starting to wear off and I *knew* it was way past time to head home.

Dot and I left and I walked with her back to her place, a decrepit row house that smelled of urine and alcohol.

"Home sweet home," she said with a smile, staring at the trash on the front doorstep.

"Thank you," I said, not sure what I should say. "I had fun."

"Shit! You ain't never had real fun a day in your life," she said, laughing. "But I like you anyway, John."

She leaned into me and began to rub her hand along the inside of my thigh. I froze, too terrified to move. It felt good but at the same time...

"What's your hurry?" she asked, whispering into my ear. "Why don't you come inside?"

Come inside? Her words danced inside my head. "Right now?"

"Would it make you feel better to stand on my doorstep till sunrise, and *then* come inside?" she asked, kissing my neck gently.

Nervously, I pulled my pockets inside out and took out two pennies.

"But I'm down to my last two pennies," I said, offering what I thought was a good explanation for why I had to move on. After all, she did say that she was a "working lady" with three hungry mouths to feed. But Dorothy didn't see it like that, because no sooner had I pulled out my change than she smacked me right across the cheek.

"Ouch!" I said. "Why'd you do that?"

"'Cause you treatin' me like a damn whore!"

"Well ... I ... I..."

"You what?" she exclaimed. "Saw me go to the back room with that man?"

I didn't know what to say.

"I like you," she said. "This here ain't about business."

"I'm sorry ... but, I ... I have a real nice woman I'm courting."

She looked at me with a hard face. "Don't you get to

judgin' me. There ain't much else for us here and I gotta feed my babies." Her expression changed to disappointed. "Most schoolboys do got a "nice" girl they courtin, John."

"I didn't mean that you weren't nice, too," I hastened to add, but I knew I'd already damned myself.

"You best get on your way," she said, pulling back and drawing her arms up close to her body, "Sun'll be up soon." And with that she turned and went inside.

I stood there in front of Dot's run-down building feeling as lost as I had that morning when I'd left the house.

It was a long, long walk back home. By the time I arrived, the sun was up and Mama and Daddy were both in the window, looking tortured with worry. Mama's face was tear-streaked and Daddy's expression was outraged. When I opened the front door, Daddy snatched me by the shoulders, scaring the daylights out of me.

"Never again will you disrespect this house by staying out all night and worrying your Mama into an early grave!!" was all he said. "Never again."

I couldn't apologize.

My words were stuck.

Nothing came out.

I nodded and tried to catch my breath, and then I nodded again.

Daddy released me, and he and Mama almost fell over backward when they looked at my shirt and saw cherry red lipstick on the collar.

"Oh, sweet Jesus!" exclaimed Mama. "The devil has gotten hold of my son!"

"Dropping out of school and staying out all night," shouted Daddy. "What's gotten into you, son?"

"You have left the ways of the Lord! All's I can do is pray for your soul," said Mama as she disappeared into the kitchen without so much as a second look. Daddy followed close behind her.

Oh boy.

It didn't look like my morning was about to end up any better than my night.

20

Church Folk

May 1905
One week later

I knew I had to do something with my life. Being a grown man was getting harder by the minute. I had little choice left but to really begin my search for a job. It had quickly become clear that even in these progressive times, limited occupations were available to a Negro who had not completed his formal training. During my search, I was forced to look in all directions. The steady flow of immigrants were generally chosen first, especially if they could speak English. I might find work as a cook, janitor, butler, waiter, coachman, or valet, but those were not only a long distance from the hallways of Wharton, they were also sure pathways to poverty.

They were certain ways to get *stuck*.

All the decent-paying jobs I had imagined were out there—jobs as under-chefs or book-keepers—seemed to have vanished. I'd not even found a position as a hostler that was open to coloreds. Scarcity was everywhere, except among the wealthy, and my hunt for employment was fruitless. Perhaps, I told myself more than once, I was just being too particular. Still, with Mama and Daddy applying more pressure than ever, I had little time to contemplate options.

Daddy asked me why I couldn't simply go to my friends in the Boule. Surely one of those fine physicians, lawyers or business owners needed an accountant or bookkeeper? I could not seem to make him understand that, of all the people my new and lowly status might offend, I feared the reaction of my fraternity brothers almost as much as I feared Mary Agnes's. I could not, having fallen into such a quagmire of gray uncertainty, go to the members of that honorable body for aid.

In the midst of my trying to find myself, my brother William arrived from Illinois for what I could only think of as an "emergency" family gathering. He was scheduled to arrive one afternoon by train, and I offered to pick him up from the train station for several reasons. One, I was interested in hearing about something *other* than my awful situation, and two, I wanted to take a break from Mama and Daddy's distressing facial expressions. They looked like the Angels of Doom and Gloom these days, always in deep prayer and beseeching the Lord. They had barely uttered a word to me since I'd resigned from school, but I could tell they were both hoping that I would "come to my senses" and go running back to UPenn with apology in hand. And three, the ice between us had broken only when Mama mentioned that William was coming home for a visit. I was not above using my brother as a means of placing myself back in my mother's good graces.

I headed out to the railroad station hours before William's designated arrival, just to sit in silence with my thoughts. When he arrived, I swooped him up in a big hug.

"Look at you, brother," I said to William, smiling with pride. "Don't you look like a future druggist."

"Yes, yes," William laughed. "I'll have the cure for what ails you."

"What ails me ...Yes, *something* would be nice for that."

"How are you, brother?" he asked, pulling me to him for another embrace.

"I'm holding on."

"I heard all the news," he said carefully.

"Good news travels fast and bad news strikes like lightning. You know Mama don't hold back a thing."

William laughed out loud. "Whole neighborhood knows that," he said, then sobered. "So, where do you stand, brother?"

"On the outside of everything."

"What are you saying, John?" William asked, grabbing his bag and tossing it onto his shoulder.

I filled him in on the details of the past few weeks, words tumbling out of my mouth like water from a dam burst.

"And Daddy wants you to *apologize*?" William asked, his tone disbelieving. "Our daddy? The man who built his own business from the ground up?"

"He accused me of showboating—of trying to show up Charles Cook. What he means is I didn't keep my place. That I was looking too good. I guess I should've thrown a race or two, cheated *not* to win. I should have tried *not* to get good grades." Even I winced at the bitterness in my voice.

"I think you should fight the good fight," said William. "I think you should hold out for the truth."

★★★★

Mama and Daddy embraced William with a fierce joy.

Clinton had also made it home by the time we got there. I was relieved to see him, as he offered me solace through a big brother handshake and a strong pat on the back—while Mama and Daddy stood by stoically and watched. I could almost hear their thoughts out loud: *At least two of our sons are getting along.*

When we sat down to supper, Mama said, "It'll be right nice to have all my sons in church tomorrow. There's no better healing than calling on the name of the Lord."

"Is Hattie coming along?" asked Clinton.

"She's been under the weather this past week," said Mama. "Burning with fever last night."

"Is she all right?" William asked with concern.

"I went by this morning. Fever broke. She's doing better … leaning on the Lord for strength."

"I didn't even know she was sick," I mumbled.

Mama gave me a look that bordered on frosty. Subtlety was not Mama's strength. Ever since I'd come home with my withdrawal letter, she had called on Jesus so many times, I half expected him to return and sit with us at the supper table. The thought made me laugh.

"Sons," Daddy added, casting a glance in my direction,

"anytime a man needs to find his way in the world, he best find his way to the altar."

Can I get an "amen?" I thought wryly.

"Amen," said Mama.

"Amen," said Daddy.

"The Lord is my shepherd," said Mama, quoting Psalm Twenty-three.

"I shall not want," added Daddy.

"He maketh me to lie down in green pastures," continued Mama, and then turned to Clinton, who was expected to add the next line.

"He leadeth me beside the still waters."

"He restoreth my soul," chimed in William.

"He leadeth me in paths of righteousness for his name's sake," said Daddy.

"John?" asked Mama, her eyes closed.

A brief glance passed between William and Clinton before they turned their eyes to me, eloquent with sympathy. It was going to be a long, long night.

"John," repeated Mama.

I closed my eyes and cleared my throat before whispering, "Surely goodness and mercy will follow me all the days of my life, and I will dwell in the house of the Lord forever."

When I opened my eyes, Mama, Daddy, William, and Clinton were staring at me. I had purposely skipped the middle of the passage and gone straight to the last line.

"What happened to the rest of the psalm, John?" asked Mama.

"The way I see it," I said, "the last line sums it up quite nicely."

"Oh, dear God up in heaven!" said Mama, exasperated.

Clinton, William, and Daddy just bowed their heads out of respect for Mama, and I sat there feeling like a heathen because of my incomplete participation.

Dear God up in heaven, indeed.

★★★★

Come Sunday, the Taylor family made its way to the African Episcopal Church of St. Thomas in fine fashion. Hattie was still under the weather and did not join us, but of course we all held her in our prayers. Mama wore the beautiful pearl earrings Daddy had saved up to give her for their anniversary. She had her hair piled high on her head so that everyone would see the gift shining from her ears. Despite being displeased and distressed by the son who followed in her footsteps, Mama walked with a grace that pretended all was well. Daddy had his arm linked through Mama's and he strolled, apparently without a care in the world, showing off his beautiful wife.

To arise out of the dust and shake themselves, and throw off that servile fear, that the habit of oppression and bondage trained them up in.

As I did every Sunday, I paused in the narthex to read Absalom's words—to allow them to settle into my body and soul. They never failed to stir me, but *this* Sunday they stirred me to the depths of my soul and filled me with a sudden certainty that I, too, would arise out of the dust. Born of a people burdened by bondage and weighed down by oppression, I would rise. I would shake off confusion and hopelessness. I would shake off the fear that was trying to envelop me and the uncertainty that threatened to cloak me. I would shake it all off, and walk the path of Absalom Jones and make my way faithfully to the light of peace, grace, and clarity.

Daddy placed his hand gently on my shoulder. "You will find your way, son. Sometimes the tide of life turns in a way we can't explain and the best we can do is hold on to who we are in order to navigate the waters. I raised you honest, so I know you ain't no cheater.."

"I just want to be respected as a man, Daddy," I whispered. "As a *man*."

Mama somehow gathered us all to her bosom, and there we stood, the dignified Taylor family, having a private moment in the very public entry of our church.

"The Lord is with you, John. Know that," Mama whispered in my ear.

I could only nod in agreement. All would be well, one way or the other.

21

Misery

The previous day's familial embrace did not mark the end of disagreement, by any means. Thinking perhaps it had, I asked Daddy again to let me work with him and Hattie at the catering business, despite the fact that I had no cooking skills and found no joy in feeding other folks what I'd rather be eating myself. Again, Daddy refused me in no uncertain terms.

"I won't have you in the business, John, and that's that."

I was floored. "Are you still punishing me?" I asked. "Well, this is irony—I won't do things your way one time so you won't *let* me do it your way now?"

He ignored me, continuing to read the newspaper.

"So what am I to do?"

The paper, which concealed his face from me, rattled. "You *know* what you're to do, John Baxter. You best to go about *doing* it."

"Why? Why can't I work in the family business?"

He looked at me over the top of the paper. "Because you

199

don't love it and you don't deserve it." He rattled the paper and disappeared behind it once more.

"I don't love it? And d'you suppose I'll love waiting tables or cleaning floors?

"Daddy, even the prodigal son was welcomed home after he sinned."

The paper rattled again. "You *are* home."

"No, I'm not. Not really. Not if you insist on pushing me away, on keeping me out, on punishing me for something that was no fault of mine."

The paper came down, revealing a dark and stony face with eyes like cold chips of brown glass. "You brought this on yourself, John. You made this bed, now you have to lie in it."

"I did no such thing. This was done *to* me. I did nothing wrong."

He set the paper aside. "You showboated, son. You showed up that white boy—made him look a fool. And you *enjoyed* it. More than that, you tried to show them all up by writing that fool paper. Going off about how a black man is the best candidate for heavyweight champion. You might as well have waved your arms and yelled, 'Look at me! I'm a Negro and I'm just as smart as you are.'"

"But I *am* just as smart. And as fast. And as strong. What's wrong with that?"

"You didn't have to draw so much attention to it, John. You didn't have to make it so big and so loud. Just like that damned Johnson," he muttered, flicking an article on the boxer with the tips of his fingers.

A Novel by Craig T. Williams

"Oh, I see," I said, anger stoked so hot it made my cheeks burn. "I'm supposed to bob and dance like Jim Crow and say, 'Yessuh, massa,' and keep my place like a good black boy. Is that it?"

The paper fell flat to his lap and he glared at me. "Don't you speak to me–"

"Don't speak to you that way? What way, Daddy? Don't speak to you like a man? If I can't speak to you—another colored man—that way, then to whom can I speak like a man? Not *them*—no, I'm to bow and scrape to *them*. You want me to bow and scrape to you, too? Then how am I supposed to be a man, Daddy? If I have to act like a *boy* to everybody?"

"I didn't say–"

"You *did* say it, Daddy. You said don't show them up. Don't let them see how smart you are, or how fast, or how capable. You sound *just like them*."

He said nothing to that, but only stared at me with rage in his eyes. Slowly, like the melting of winter snow, his expression changed. The anger leached away to leave only a grim despair. Finally he cleared his throat and said, "This is the way it is, son. It may not be right or good, but it *is*. Be smart. Be strong. Be fast. But don't point at yourself and call yourself those things, because the moment you do, you will get slapped down. There is only one way for us to rise in this world, John, and that's to do it slow and quiet. So that one day, the white world will turn around and see us there and believe we have simply always deserved to share those heights with them."

I shook my head. "I can't wait that long, Daddy," I told him. "Should I wait until I'm old and gray or until I'm dead and gone?"

He looked at me for a moment with a shadow in his eyes that I couldn't name, and then the paper hid him from me once more.

I received my first official job interview that very afternoon at the Seventh Ward Central Hotel on 1300 Lombard Street. The job posting was simple. It read, "Opportunities for work." but there were no specifics as to what kind of work. I guess that's what the interview was for.

By daylight, the Seventh Ward showed another side of itself. It was a community in which wealthy white folks and poor Negroes lived almost side by side. In fact, they could almost lean out of their windows and shake hands. On one side of the street a man might have a butler, and on the other side a man might *be* a butler. This irony of coexistence flourished within a distance of a few hundred feet. If I worked here, I would get a good look at both sides, without having to strain my eyes.

On the day of my interview, I dressed in fine church clothes and made my way to see Mr. Thaddeus Brown, who was in charge of hiring for the Seventh Ward Central Hotel. I was ushered in for my appointment to find Mr. Brown seated behind a rather bland desk. Upon my entry he did not speak, nor did he look in the least pleased to see me. I handed him my letter of introduction and he waved me to a seat opposite him. I sat and waited for his inspection of my accomplishments. He reviewed my resume with a critical eye and unmerciful sluggishness.

"Brown Prep," he said, reading it over with his spectacles pulled low on his nose so he could peer at me over the rims.

"Yes, sir."

"Star athlete of the track and field team."

"Yes, sir."

He shot a sharp glance my way, and it was then that I figured it was best to sit in absolute silence.

"University of Pennsylvania…" He read the rest slowly and carefully before setting the paper down and removing his spectacles. "It seems as though you have kept good company, son."

"Yes, sir," I said, sounding like an echo. I searched my vocabulary for words beyond *yes, sir.*

"We do a good business down here in the Ward," he said proudly, "and we like to think we keep good company, too, by way of the standards we uphold for our workers."

"Yes–" I started, then caught myself.

"I can see where you've been," he said, "and that reads swell on paper, but I need to know what you can do … in a practical sense."

"I can do anything," I said confidently.

"I'll level with you, son. I don't need a bookkeeper. I do that work myself. Can you clear a set of dishes from a table?"

Dishes?

Even among my own kind, the jobs I trained for were unavailable to me. I considered turning on my heel and walking out, but something stopped me. Maybe it was Daddy's despair, or my own. Whatever the reason, I said, "Yes.

God knows I've done enough dish clearing in my day."

"And wipe a table down so clean that you'd be willing to eat off its bare wood with no cloth to cover it?" There was so much passion in the question, I thought he would have me scrub his supper table right there on the spot.

"Certainly."

"Then John Baxter Taylor, this is the place for you. Welcome aboard." He extended his hand.

As we shook, I felt as if my personal world had been squeezed down to the size of a dinner plate.

"You start with the dishes and the table," he said with such a burst of enthusiasm that I imagined a drum roll might accompany him, "and in no time, I will make you one of my finest waiters."

"Great," I said with the kind of smile you offer when you finally feel the weight of the world lift from your shoulders.

Well, I told myself on the way back home, at least it was a start. A weekly salary somewhere around a dollar and a half didn't seem like such an honest wage, but it was at least an opportunity to "pay my way" in this world. It would be a narrow way for a time, but it was a way to show Mama that all hope was not lost and to show Daddy that I was my own man no matter what he thought.

This job would also provide me with a good perspective on things. What would I do in the practical world? Running track would take me only so far; then I would have to pick up some type of business sensibility along the way. Maybe working at the Seventh Ward Hotel was a good opportunity for me to see what I *didn't* want to do.

Beneath all of this thought, I couldn't help but hope that somehow this whole mess would clear up at the university and I'd be able to return with no apology necessary—not on my part, at any rate.

Wishful thinking, that's all it was. And somewhere, deep in my heart, I knew that.

★★★★

June 1905

Several weeks had passed since I had seen Mary Agnes, but it was not for lack of effort on my part. I had made my way to the "prettiest row house in Greenville" at least three times in the past month, but each time I arrived, Mr. Montier met me at the door with a pile of excuses. I knew that news of my disgraceful exit from UPenn had reached the Montiers, possibly through Cousin Algernon.

The excuses were thin ones.

She's not feeling well.

She went to the market with her mother.

She's resting.

I had even traveled to the Porter's, where Mary Agnes worked during the week, but still I could not find her. In fact, the door went unanswered there, though I thought I saw a curtain move in one of the gleaming windows.

I already knew that I was more than fond of Mary Agnes. In fact, I would say that I had been crazy in love for some time—possibly from the first moment I laid eyes on her. So it was on a hot Sunday morning that I put on my best suit and traveled to the Montier's with a fierce determination to see Mary Agnes in person. I stood on the Montier's now-familiar porch and knocked three times, which was a great surprise since Mr. Montier usually started for his front door right about the time I stepped off the front steps on Woodland Avenue. I got the feeling that my visits caused quite a stir in the Montier household, but I didn't want to acknowledge the cause for the disturbance.

Mr. Montier at last came to the door, and it creaked opened at a slow pace. In the meantime, I had ample opportunity to rehearse my lines. Once he opened that door, his face stern and uncompromising, I instantly forgot why I was there.

"Mr. Taylor," he said, in the most formal of greetings.

"Mr. Montier." I nodded politely and removed my hat, as was customary. I had not brought him another box of chocolates, for even I had noticed the widening of his girth. Maybe, I thought wryly, the best gift would be to refer him to a good tailor. "I was hoping to have a word with Mary Agnes," I said humbly.

Mr. Montier looked at me a good long while before responding. "She is unable to have a word with you today, young man."

"Perhaps tomorrow?"

"She will not be speaking with you tomorrow either," he said.

"Perhaps at week's end."

"I don't see her speaking with you at week's end."

"Pardon me for asking," I said, clearing my throat, "but is she stricken with laryngitis?"

Mr. Montier's eyes widened and he seemed a bit inflamed by the remark. "Son," he said, "Mary Agnes is no longer available for courtship."

My heart clenched in my chest. "Why?"

"She's on her way to Cheyney University in the fall."

"Cheyney," I replied, "is not unbearably far away from Philadelphia."

"Dr. Jackson told us about your situation at school," he said, with eyes that cut into my bone, making me feel awkward and embarrassed. "My daughter was distressed about it. More so that you never came round to explain about it yourself."

"I'm here now. And I've come before. "

"A bit late, wasn't it, son?"

"This has nothing to do with her going off to school, then, does it, sir?"

"Mrs. Montier and I think it best to…" He could not even finish the feeble sentence.

I drew myself up straighter, taller. "Sir, let me assure you, I did nothing wrong."

"It's not that you did anything wrong. You're a good, decent fellow. What bothers me most is that you didn't do anything to make it *right*."

The words stung. Was I about to hear one more person tell me I ought to apologize for being the victim of a lie? But no, Wilton Montier took a completely different tack.

"Sometimes, you have to do more than just maintain your innocence in this life. Sometimes you have to fight for what's right. Sometimes you have to fight for the truth."

I raised my head. "I *did* fight, sir. That's why I'm out of school."

"I heard you resigned from school."

"Well, I ... yes. I–"

"That you didn't defend your position."

I felt my temper rising. "I didn't feel I should have to defend my position. The accusations were false!"

"And you did nothing to prove them so ... or so Dr. Jackson tells me. It never went before the school board of regents."

"It would have humiliated my parents to have it be so public."

He gave a snort that I realized was laughter.

"I hear you got a job busing tables at the Seventh Ward Hotel," he said.

"Yes, sir," I responded, taken aback by the abrupt change of subject.

"What do you make—about a dollar a week?"

"A dollar fifty," I said, trying to raise my value, which seemed to be dropping like the temperature in December.

"We're looking for a *brighter* future for our Mary Agnes. She is going to be a woman of letters, Mr. Taylor. Now, you're good people and all, but Mary Agnes is from a family of *free* Negroes. It is not in her nature to hide her light under a bushel as you are content to do."

"I'm not content," I protested. "It's just ... it's a decent enough job for now."

"Hell of a trade, son," he said.

"It's not my trade." I mumbled. "I'm just…"

"I'm talking about trading Penn for the Seventh Ward Hotel. Trading business school for busing dishes."

"It's temporary."

He laughed out loud and shook his head. "Do you know the definition of misery?"

Aside from this miserable conversation on his porch, I had not a single definition in my head.

"Misery is a man's inability to reconcile himself to the torment of a *permanent* destiny born out of a temporary decision." He gave me a keen look. "Ask yourself what you were dodging when you made that decision. Then ask yourself how successful you were."

The silence that fell between us was weightier than it had ever been. I was almost relieved when he said, "Take good care, son," backed away from his threshold, and slowly shut the door.

22

Fighter

August 18, 1905

I ran to work each day, so as not to lose the "athlete" completely. I had already been shriveled in size in more ways than I cared to recall. And on this particular day while running, I was lost in my own head, not paying much mind to the horse-drawn buggies, carts, and wagons on the road. I did not even pay particular attention to the few automobiles rumbling by, though I was still fascinated by their ability to transport a man with the speed and grace of a horse and buggy—albeit with more noise.

My experience gave me a new appreciation for all of Daddy's hard work. He surely must love what he did—there could be no other reasons to do what he did than love or survival. These past three months had clearly shown me that this was not the way to be extraordinary, and I wondered how I had gotten off the road and into the ditch.

"Hey there, now!" a man shouted.

I looked up to see a man dashing across the road, weaving between the various vehicles. I smiled, wondering if he would make it without losing his hat ... or his dignity. Some of these cars went nearly ten miles an hour and could land a man swiftly on his buttocks if he was hit. With horses on the road as well, getting from place to place was becoming tricky. A man had to stay alert at all times nowadays.

A car moving immediately to my right along the curb stopped short to let the pedestrian cross. I glanced into the car and was forced to blink. Were my eyes deceiving me? I would swear the man behind the wheel of that vehicle was the "Big Smoke" himself.

Is it possible? I wondered. *Could that really be Jack Johnson?*

Well, who else could it be? There were not too many ebony-colored men driving brand new cars, smoking fancy cigars, and wearing finely tailored suits to boot. My heart jumped in my chest, my throat swelled up, and I stood there not remembering how to put one foot in front of the other. Folks flowed around me as I gawked at a true American hero sitting so close, I might reach out and touch The Champ.

You could have knocked me over with a feather when he pulled his vehicle over and parked right in front of the Seventh Ward Central Hotel. I put my hands up to my eyes in disbelief, then glanced about to see if other folks were as moved by the presence of this man as I was. No one took much notice, as if it was a common occurrence for a black man, accompanied by an entourage of white men, to pull *his* car over and enter an establishment for a meal.

I was more than ten minutes early for my shift, hoping for a chance to be in the presence of a man who knew no fear.

The Olympian: *An American Triumph*

When I entered the dining room, I found the champion sitting at a table as if he were the king of Philadelphia holding court. The lunch crowd looked on with fascination while Jack Johnson sat among his entourage joking, telling stories, and eating up the attention. I recognized Sig Hart, one of the whites in Johnson's crew, who glanced from the energetic crowd to Jack with an amused grin. He appeared to be a bit taken aback by how much Jack was loved by the residents of the Ward.

Not every face was smiling and shining in Jack Johnson's direction, though. There were some colored folks who appeared to be puzzled by this loud and boisterous man. One thing was certain, when the Negro Champion was around, you felt *and* heard his presence. The energy in the room shifted as if making way for a man who could alter the course of Negro America if he so chose, simply by refusing to bow down and back away. No, Jack Johnson breathed in all of his air without apology and left his impression in the space he occupied.

Some folks looked at him in admiration and some with envy, as if they wished to be this type of man. As if all their lives had been just fine until the second they saw Jack with his big, happy smile and fancy new car. Suddenly life wasn't "just fine" anymore. Suddenly it wasn't enough to make a few dollars a week. Not when right in front of you stood a man who looked like you but made thousands in one night. He made a man wonder about his possibilities and was proof that more was possible.

He made me wonder.

A Novel by Craig T. Williams

I was mesmerized by Jack Johnson. I strained to hear the words tumbling from his mouth as he laughed about James Jeffries's recent retirement.

"I told him to come on now and take this last fight, make world history!" Jack said, with a glance that took in the whole room, his gold teeth gleaming. "But he won't fight a Negro. Took the title and went back to his farm. I think someone is *bock-bock-bock-bock*." He laughed, got up, and strutted around like a chicken.

I shook my head and laughed. James Jeffries, the white heavyweight champion, had retired undefeated and said that there were no more "logical challengers" left for him to fight. Yellow! I was a bit amused by his choice of words, particularly since just two years before, the *Los Angeles Times* had written the very opposite. I found this conversation ironic—not that it was happening but more so that I was listening to it. For this had been the very theme of my term paper.

Johnson was the logical opponent for Champion Jeffries, the paper said, adding: "The color line gag does not go now. Johnson has met all comers in his class and has defeated each and every one. Now he stands ready to box for the world's championship ... When they meet, the world will see a battle before which the gladiatorial combats of ancient Rome pale into childish insignificance. And meet they someday will. It is up to Jeffries to say when."

I admired Jack Johnson greatly for taking Jeffries's inability to say "when" in stride. He seemed focused on the title, not just on the man holding the belt.

Sam Fitzpatrick, the other white man in Johnson's court,

appeared sincerely appreciative of Jack's humor. When he met Jack's eyes, I felt a genuine connection that reminded me of my friendship with Nate. Some relationships transcended race and color and were forged by a mutual appreciation and respect. I sensed this was one of them.

This man will help Jack Johnson go even farther with his boxing, I thought.

Funny how much easier it is to look into the life of another man and see his path. When it came to figuring out your own path, it wasn't nearly so clear. In fact, I was sometimes convinced that the biggest obstacle to my progress was me.

"Excuse me, son—do you work here or are you one of the customers?" a voice said from behind me. I turned into the straight face of my employer.

"Well, sir, I was a bit early and…" He interrupted my flow of words with one look at his pocket watch.

"I do believe you're right on time now," he said, tossing me a dishrag. He pointed in the direction of Jack Johnson and friends. "You can start with wiping that table off so we can keep these folks happy. No point in entertaining the champ if you can't keep the lager and food coming. Know what I mean?" He clapped his hand to my shoulder and then walked away.

It seemed as though the noise stopped, everyone froze, and the only people in the building were Jack Johnson and me. My footsteps were slow and deliberate as I crossed the dining room to his table. I knew I was supposed to wipe the table and allow Jack Johnson to entertain his folks in peace, but a part of me wanted to shoo all those people out of the way, sit in front of Jack, and beg him to tell it all: his way of handling life, the secret of his strength, how he dealt with defeat. Just a few words could help me make it through the day.

I swallowed hard and veered toward the table to clean it for him—for the champ.

"John Taylor!" Mr. Brown shouted from the front entryway. "I have to head upstairs for a moment."

I nodded.

The champ watched our little exchange and our eyes met. He smiled brightly at me. "John Taylor?" he asked with a southern drawl, drawing all attention toward me. "Are you *the* John Baxter Taylor, Jr.?"

"Yes, sir," I said, finished wiping table and straightened, shocked that he would recognize my name. "How … how did you know?" I wanted to pinch myself. I was having the beginnings of a conversation with Mr. Jack Johnson.

Johnson's face lit up. "Well, I'll be," he said, turning and looking at everyone around him. "We will be served by a great young man here. John, you're going to be my waiter today!"

Reginald, the head waiter, paused in the act of seating a trio of customers and shot me a fiery look. Obviously, he was not pleased. I hadn't meant to take his job—thought I did want it. But you don't say "no" to Jack Johnson regardless. I ignored Reggie and gave Jack my whole attention.

"What can I get for you, sir?" I asked, hands trembling so bad I couldn't have written down the order even if I'd had a pad to write it on.

"We'll have the special," said Jack, taking it upon himself to order for everybody at the table. "And beer all around."

I was relieved because it made my job a lot easier; and when they all nodded in agreement, I quickly scrambled for the kitchen.

Moments later, I returned, bringing glasses of cold beer for Jack and all of his guests. "So, what's the best quarter-miler in the country doing getting my supper?" Jack Johnson asked.

I managed to smile. "I'm having some difficulty at school."

He frowned at me. "For every point I'm given, I'll have earned two—you know how it is."

"Yes, sir. I know it."

"You still in school?"

"I, uh, I…" I could not say the words.

He snapped his head back and looked at me hard, raising one eyebrow at me. "You haven't quit school, John Taylor."

"Yes, you know how it is in this white man's world." I quietly responded trying to echo his sentiment.

"White man's world?" questioned Jack. "Listen, us Negroes have fought and died in every war this country has ever had."

"Yes, sir," I acknowledged.

"We are as American as anyone else—if not more so—for the blood, sweat and tears we have given this country. Don't you let any man or anything get in the way of you chasing your dream."

"Yessir," I briskly responded.

"See your dream through or die trying!" Jack asserted. "So, why did you quit school?"

"I was wrongly accused of cheating," I said, adding pointedly, "but I am no cheater."

He nodded, then listened as I continued to explain my situation.

"So," I concluded. "I withdrew before they could accuse me of something inflammatory like that, mark my record, and embarrass my family."

"You withdrew?"

I raised my head and pushed my shoulders back. "I was set up, sir, and I refused to apologize for something I didn't do."

"So let me see if I got this," he said. "You got knocked out before you even threw a punch?"

"No, sir–"

"You up and quit before the fight started?" His face wore a look of complete disbelief.

"No!" I protested, then found that words had deserted me. Wasn't this exactly what Mary Agnes's daddy had said?

Words had not deserted Jack Johnson. "You're a quitter."

In that moment, I felt condemned by the group-at-large. Not only did Jack think I was a quitter, but the sentiment was echoed through the eyes of all the onlookers at the table.

"I … uh … no…" I fumbled with my words, trying to find some that made sense. I must have looked ridiculous, shaking my head and wringing my dishrag, because Jack started mocking my movement. He was right to do so. I had been so intent on saving face, on not living a lie, that I had missed the fact that I was not living the *truth*. Truth was more than refusing to mouth a falsehood, and by that standard, I had not been true. Not to myself, not to my family, not to my race. I had lied by omission. Jack Johnson was right.

Mr. Montier was right.

With a great laugh, Jack said, "Son, you *never* stop the fight unless you've given it everything you've got! You dance around that ring and wear your opponent out. You don't go withdrawing from anything, ever! The worst way to lose a fight is *No Contest*." He sat back, pointing a strong, black finger at me. "I've seen you in the same papers I been in, winning championships, running in Europe. Everybody has a place and *this* ain't *yours*." He emphasized the statement with a sweeping gesture at the room around us.

There were no more words to be said. I simply nodded in embarrassed gratitude.

When the champ left, I followed him with my eyes until I couldn't see him anymore. The very "air" in the room itself had changed—simply because Jack Johnson had breathed it. A man of true wealth and grace, I was most humbled by his words and equally grateful for the $10 tip he left me on the table.

★★★★

A Novel by Craig T. Williams

Wear your opponent out.

I walked home that evening in contemplation of Jack Johnson's words. I understood that when it came to running. It was my strategy, my signature. How had I failed to apply it to my life?

Well, that was about to change. I had decided to fight. I would request a committee review and defend my honor. That would be my way of saying, "I won't let you knock me out."

I was a born fighter, I told myself, just like Jack Johnson. I saw that now. It was as if he had sparked my memory, as if his simple words had turned me inside out and helped me see that in order to be crowned the champion, you had to fight for the title.

As I reached our front walk, I looked up to see the smoke rising into the twilight from the chimneys of the buildings near Franklin Field. I smiled with a knowing "I'll be back."

"Well, it's good to see a smile on your face," a friendly voice said.

I turned to look up into the warm eyes of Henry Smith, who stood on my front porch, grinning at me.

"Henry?" No student had ever been to my home during my years at UPenn, though I lived within walking distance of the campus.

"How are you?" I smiled, taking a seat in Mama's favorite rocker. "What are you doing here? Didn't you go home for the summer?"

"Did. But the track team got a new coach and the new

coach ordered us to report early for practice. So, I'm here getting settled back in."

"New coach, huh?" I repeated. "I've heard rumors."

His grin widened. "They're all true. It's Mike Murphy, John. Just like the rumors said. The man who trained the first American heavyweight boxing champion, John L. Sullivan. That's who's going to be coaching us this year." He paused, then added, "Coaching you."

"Me? What do you mean?"

"Well," Henry said, sitting down next to me in Daddy's chair, "the truth has come to light."

"What truth? What are you saying, Henry?"

"The team checked in at the gym yesterday. Coach wasn't there, I guess—at least he didn't introduce himself, but we all showed up for roll call. Charles Cook was there and when one of his buddies wondered why you *weren't*, he bragged about nicking the opening of your paper. He laughed at the way he sat right next to you and copied the first page while Coach Robertson talked." Henry shook his head and frowned. "Said he wanted to teach the 'uppity nigger' a lesson."

I sat back heavily in the chair, setting it rocking. "He bragged about it? Out loud?"

"Out loud. The man thinks he's invincible, John. He thinks nobody can do anything about it now. I want to prove him wrong. I want us to go to Dean Adams and tell him what Charles Cook said."

My mind raced. I could go back now and force the truth into the light. I would be vindicated. Dear God, this was the perfect ending to my day *if...*

I looked over at Henry. "Will your word be enough? They all know we're friends, you and I. And I'm sure none of Charles's friends would repeat what he said."

Henry's brow furrowed. "I hadn't thought of that. But ... there were a few other people there. In fact, there was an older gentleman—he may have been a professor—I know he overheard Charles. He was looking right at him. I suppose we might track him down if we had to. But I'm hoping that my word will be enough."

"Henry?" My voice came out in an awed whisper. "You would do that for me?"

"A great man, whom I am honored to call a friend, once said, 'Loyalty is an admirable trait,'" Henry replied, leaning toward me.

I remembered the conversation in which I had uttered those words. This was a true mark of a friend—one who stands with you when you are up and helps to pick you up when you fall. I had no words to express how touched I was by this gesture of friendship.

"What ... what can we...?" I began, at a loss for words for the second time that day.

"We get Charles into the dean's office and you have your day," Henry said emphatically.

That *we* meant the world to me. Henry Smith had a permanent place in my heart. I jumped out of my chair, filled with more hope than I had felt in months. I nearly lifted Henry Smith right out of his shoes and spun him around my front porch.

"Thank you!" was all I could say to the Lord and to Henry.

I was making such a ruckus that Mama and Daddy both peeked through the windows and stared at me with grave concern. I saw them trade glances in an exchange that suggested their son had just lost what was left of his fragile mind.

I calmed myself. "Did you say anything to my parents?" I asked.

Henry shook his head. "I just said I came by for a visit."

"Good. I don't want them to know until ... until this is over. Until the truth is out and I've won back my place at UPenn." I would say nothing of this to them until victory was in hand and I could proudly show them that their son was neither cheater nor quitter.

Meanwhile, Henry and I came up with a plan.

★★★★

August 20, 1905
Dean Adams's Office

I walked quietly, but without hesitation, into Dean Adams's outer office and was amused to see his secretary, Miss Francis, standing with her ear pressed gently against the dean's door. I stifled the urge to laugh and merely cleared my throat to gain her attention.

She straightened so fast she nearly toppled over. She reminded me so much of a vaudeville slapstick character that

A Novel by Craig T. Williams

I had to swallow my laughter a second time. She huffed and walked away from the dean's door to seat herself behind her desk. Where she recovered her poise.

"How can I help you?"

Just then a loud, familiar voice issued from behind the closed door of the dean's office. "Why would I do that? Have you completely lost your mind?"

I smiled with satisfaction. The plan was in progress.

"I need to see the dean," I said.

"As you can hear, the dean is busy."

"Yes, ma'am, but I believe his business pertains to me. Henry Smith is in there and is expecting me to join him."

The secretary eyed me skeptically, but rose to usher me into the room. She knocked, opened the door and said, "Excuse me, gentlemen. This young man says he's expected."

The men in the room—Dean Adams, Professor Ryan, Charles, and Henry—immediately turned their attention to the open doorway in which I stood, hope and anticipation elevating my heartbeat. Henry, seated in the swivel chair before the dean's desk, looked relaxed enough, but Professor Ryan seemed confused, and the dean and Charles Cook wore expressions of extreme annoyance.

The secretary murmured an apology and withdrew, but only a step or two. I suspected her curiosity had gotten the better of her.

"What is going on here?" Dean Adams questioned.

Henry swiveled in his chair toward the older man. "I believe John Taylor has just requested an urgent conference with you."

"What?" Charles's annoyance flared to anger. "You," he said, pointing at Henry, "brought me here to hear false accusations and now this…"

It was now or never. "I would like to thank you all for being here," I said, stepping farther into the room. I knew what Henry had said, of course. He had turned the tables on Charles, accusing him of being the cheat. I saw the stunned look on Charles's face as he realized my sudden appearance was no coincidence.

I turned to the secretary. "Could you bring my file, please, Miss Francis?" I asked. "It contains my term paper and, I'm certain, a copy of Charles's paper as well."

She hesitated for a moment, peering past my shoulder at the dean. When he merely shrugged, she looked deeply into my eyes. After a moment, she afforded the dean another glance, sighed, and returned to her own office. In her absence, no one moved or spoke. I closed my eyes and prayed for Miss Francis's speedy return, and when she announced her presence in the doorway by clearing her throat, I nearly jumped for joy. She brushed past me and went to the dean's desk, handing him a brown folder and a sheet of paper that he merely glanced at and set aside.

"Thank you," I said as she turned back toward me. I do believe she smiled as she left the room.

"Mr. Taylor. Mr. Smith. This is not the appropriate method of bringing something to my attention," the dean said curtly. "This business is closed. I have no inclination to revisit it."

Henry turned slightly toward the doorway where I was

still standing and we locked gazes for a moment. When he blinked and looked past me, I became aware that someone was standing in the doorway behind me.

"Ah, but I do," said a man's voice I did not recognize.

I stood to one side as a middle-aged gentleman entered the room. He was of average height, wiry, and wore a fine gray suit and a bowler hat. His most prominent feature was a most luxurious brown mustache. Peppered with gray, it set off a pair of pale, keen eyes. He gave me a quick smile, then sailed past me into the room, where he deposited himself in an empty chair between Henry and Charles, not even waiting for the dean's invitation to do so.

Henry turned about in his chair and pointed at the gentleman, mouthing, "That's the man!"

Dean Adams leaned back from his desk, his eyes warily on the newcomer. "Coach Murphy ... to what do I owe the pleasure?"

Henry gasped aloud.

"I had been wondering," said the coach, removing his hat and settling it in his lap, "why I was not to have this fine athlete on my track and field team." He gestured back over his shoulder at me, then turned and said, "Come here, won't you, John?"

I obliged, stunned and mute, to take a place between his chair and Henry's.

"As I said," continued the coach, "I had been wondering about this when a rumor came to my attention that he had withdrawn under a charge of cheating. I found this hard to believe. When Mr. Cook, here, excused himself from a meeting with me to attend this conclave, I figured it was in my best interests to be here too. So, here I am—I've come to find out, first hand, why an athlete I had greatly hoped to work with is not on my rolls."

"Coach Murphy," protested the dean, "this is most irregular."

"I agree, sir. It is indeed. Which is why I am asking John Taylor to explain to me why he is not on my track and field team." He turned his gaze to me and nodded.

"Just a minute!" objected Charles. "He has no right to speak!"

"He has every right to speak, young man," Coach countered. "And I have every right to hear him. I will hear you, as well, because I believe you may confirm an astonishing statement you made yesterday."

Charles turned to the dean. "Sir, please," he said. "I protest."

"As do I," said Coach Murphy. "Speak, John."

"Sir, thank you. Thank you. The truth of the matter," I said baldly, "is that Charles Cook copied from my term paper, then told our professor-" I nodded toward Professor Ryan, who was seated at the dean's small conference table. "-that I had copied from him."

Charles protested. "Why would I copy from some colored boy who thinks Jack Johnson could beat James Jeffries?" He turned on Henry. "How dare you call me here so you could stand up for him?"

"You *said* you copied from him," Henry said coyly, glancing at the coach. "I heard you."

A Novel by Craig T. Williams

"What? Do you listen in on conversations now? Has it come to that, Henry?"

The dean cleared his throat, Professor Ryan went pale, and Charles reddened as he realized what he had just admitted.

"It's my word against his," Charles said, turning to the dean. "Who will you believe?"

"It's my word, too," said Coach Murphy. "You see, I also overheard Charles Cook claim to have copied the opening paragraphs of John Taylor's paper during a team meeting."

"I-I-I was joking," stammered Charles.

"Indeed?" Coach Murphy raised an eyebrow. "Dean, did you read both papers in their entirety?"

"Well, no ... I did not."

"Dean Adams," I said, jumping into the sudden stillness, "if you will read both papers, you will see that it makes more sense for that opening statement to be mine. Charles just said as much."

The dean glanced around the room with annoyance in his eyes and then opened the folder in front of him. As he pulled out the two papers and scanned the words with his eyes, I continued my plea.

"On page one, the introductory paragraphs suggest that the sport of boxing may do well to open the ring to a new breed of champion, and concludes that the new breed of champion might be represented by men like Jack Johnson. The conclusion of *my* paper follows logically from that: it suggests that if Jack Johnson were allowed to compete at the same level as the current champion, he might well win. I ask you—given what Charles Cook just said to me about Jack Johnson, does it seem likely that he would have come to that conclusion? Does, in fact, the conclusion of his paper support his opening statement?"

Professor Ryan looked away from us all and peered out the window as if he might escape through it. Dean Adams flipped to the last page of each paper and scanned it. Then he looked up directly into my eyes.

"This is absurd." Charles rose from his chair, shot me a furious glance, and started toward the office door.

"Do not leave this room, Charles Cook."

Charles stopped in his tracks. He did not acknowledge the dean. He did not turn his body. He simply tilted his head and looked back at me. I felt his anger and hatred pummeling me, but it failed to knock me down.

Dean Adams rose from his chair. "Honor. Trust. Integrity," he erupted, banging a fist on his desk with the pronouncement of each word. "Tell me, Mr. Cook. Tell me of your belief that Jack Johnson would be America's heavyweight boxing champion were he to fight the current champion."

At last Charles turned to face the dean. "I—believe—no—such—thing."

"Yes, well, after that rather suggestive opening, your paper seems to go in another direction altogether. In fact"—he turned his gaze to Professor Ryan—"his conclusion seems to bear little relationship to the opening statement. I am puzzled as to why this was not a subject of discussion between you and your student, professor."

A Novel by Craig T. Williams

Professor Ryan didn't respond—in fact, he seemed to find something outside the window of greater interest instead.

Coach Murphy, meanwhile, sat back in his chair, taking it all in like a silent judge.

Just as I wondered if I should say something, Dean Adams turned in my direction. "It appears that the Office of Academic Studies needs to make a correction in your transcripts and reinstate you to this school." He hesitated, then added, "That is, if you choose to return to this university. In view of your treatment, I would understand if you did not."

"Well, I wouldn't understand it," said Coach Murphy with a smile. "Who else should he run for if not UPenn?"

I wanted to jump up and shout, praise the Lord's name, and fall on my knees in prayers of gratitude—all at once. I merely cleared my throat and nodded. "I do wish to return, sir."

"It will be done," he said, resuming his seat. "You may go. I need to have a word with Professor Ryan."

Henry and I rose so quickly you would have thought we were being timed. Grinning like madmen, we turned toward the door. Charles made an effort to follow, but a loud clearing of the dean's throat stilled him. We stopped as well.

"I intend to start proceedings to have you expelled, Charles Cook." The dean's words were quiet and precise.

"What?" said Charles in disbelief.

"Money does not buy honor," Dean Adams told him. "Integrity is essential in both the student *and* the teacher." He settled a look of cold fury on Professor Ryan, but Ryan did not turn from the window.

"A man may have his imperfections," the dean continued, "a university may have its flaws, but my office does not tolerate or condone the misuse of authority." He looked up at me solemnly. "John?"

He had never before called me by my first name; he had always called me Taylor.

"Sir?"

"You will need my signature on this form," he said. He took a pen out of his case and added his signature and stamp to the paper Miss Francis had brought in with my file. He hesitated, wrote something further next to his signature, then picked up the paper and held it out to me.

Dazed, I gently took the page from him. It was my request for reinstatement. My resurrection. My return to the land of the living.

"Thank you, Dean," I said happily, and then turned and walked out of the office, drawing Henry after me. As we left, I saw Coach Murphy rise and return his hat to his head.

Once outside we stood side by side as we read the committee review form. Dean Adams had written, "This student resigned under duress due to false accusations of impropriety." He had underlined the world *false*. Just like that, I was once again part of the University of Pennsylvania—a man with a clear record.

The secretary looked up slightly as Henry and I exited the dean's office. I smiled in her direction, and this time she clearly smiled in return. Out in the hallway, I grabbed Henry and hugged him as if he were my brother. When I held him at arm's length, I saw he had tears in his eyes.

"You deserved your chance, John," he said, his voice rough with emotion. "You deserved justice."

"Thanks, Henry. Thanks! And thank *you*, sir," I added as Coach Murphy came out into the hall.

He doffed his hat and gave me a cock-eyed smile. "I'll see you at the next team meeting. You let him know when and where, Mr. Smith."

"Yes, sir. I will, sir," Henry assured him and together we watched him whistle his way tunelessly down the hall.

23

If I Could Do
One Thing

August 20, 1905

It was all I could do not to fly home to share the good news with Mama and Daddy. The Taylor family would be proud to know that the "miracle child" had made a comeback one more time. But my family would know soon enough. There was one other person whose good opinion of me was of utmost importance—Mary Agnes—and in her case, time was of the essence. For all I knew, she might already be back at school.

I left the university campus with a promise to Henry that I would not miss the next team meeting and went to the prettiest row house in Greenville ... by way of the Schuylkill River, where I hoped to gain the appropriate words and some fortitude. I will not lie and insist I was not quaking in my shoes at the prospect of seeing Mary Agnes's formidable daddy again. But I had to try to let Mary Agnes know—to let her family know—that I had been vindicated.

I climbed the steps to her door, praying that she would not yet have returned to Cheyney and that she would be the one to answer the door when I knocked. I prayed so hard, I was almost murmuring the words aloud as I raised my hand and knocked once, twice, three times, but the door went unanswered, and not even Mr. Montier appeared to disapprove of me.

My heart fell. Perhaps they were not home. How ironic it would be if the Montiers were taking their daughter to the train station to-

But wait—someone was coming.

I stilled my lips, praying silently now to see Mary Agnes framed in the doorway. For a moment, I thought my wish had been granted, but when the sunlight crossed the threshold, I realized it was her mother who looked up at me from the foyer.

"Why ... why John! Such a surprise!" Her words were not unkind and her expression was—well, it seemed gentle, if a little sad. She glanced behind her down the hallway, stepped over the threshold and pulled the door to a bit. "John, you know Mary Agnes can't see you."

My heart leapt at the words because they meant she was here!

"I need most urgently to speak with her, ma'am," I said. "You see, something's happened. I'm to return to school. My name has been cleared."

She gazed up at me, wide-eyed. "Why John, that's marvelous news!"

"So you see," I continued. "I have to tell Mary Agnes. I need her to know. It's ... important," I added.

She smiled at me. "Well, of course it is. Come in."

I stepped into the hallway, eager and wary at once. "Is Mr. Montier home?"

My expression or tone must have telegraphed my concern, for she laughed softly. "Yes, but he's napping in the parlor. Why don't you come back to the kitchen with me? I'll fix you a cup of tea. Mary Agnes is snapping beans for supper," she added, then put a finger to her lips and moved silently away through the large dining room toward the back of the house.

As I followed her, hat in hand, I peered quickly into the parlor. Mr. Montier, looking no less formidable in his sleep, was snoring in his comfortable chair, reading glasses slid down his nose, a newspaper half-crushed in his lap.

I wished he might wake to a headline that read: *UPenn Athlete Stands Up to Accuser: John Baxter Taylor, Jr. Exonerated.* If I were a braver man, I might wake him and tell him myself, but I figured to let Mary Agnes do that.

She was at the sink when I entered the big sunny kitchen in her mother's wake.

"Mama," she said, hearing the tread of our feet, "what do you want me to do with the rinse water? Shall I pour it on the- Oh!" She had turned and seen me. "John!" was all she said.

"Mary Agnes," I said and became tongue-tied.

Then, "Mama?" She looked to her mother for some explanation.

"John has some news," Constance Montier said and turned to the stove. "I'll just make some tea."

"What news, John? Nothing's wrong with your family...?"

I grinned at her. "Nothing's wrong, Mary Agnes. Everything's right. Right as rain. I'm going back to school. To UPenn. I've been reinstated."

She came from the sink to the kitchen table, pulled out a chair and sat, her eyes never leaving my face. "But, how?"

"I met with the dean today," I said. "I and witnesses who knew what Charles Cook had done. I spoke to the dean myself. This time he listened to me. This time I proved myself innocent. He apologized, Mary Agnes. He apologized and he signed me back in to school."

She smiled and the sun got significantly brighter. "That's wonderful news, John. So, you'll be picking up where you left off, then?"

"Well..." Now I came to the other path my mind had trodden during my sojourn by the Schuylkill. I had known for some time that finance did not inspire either my mind or my heart. And I had determined that I should pursue another calling. "I'll be at UPenn, but not at Wharton. You see, this whole thing has made me think about what I really want in life. What I really want to do."

"And what is that?" she asked gently. "What is it you really want to do?"

"I want to be a veterinarian, Mary Agnes." I rushed on before she could comment. "You know how it's always been with me and animals. How I get such satisfaction from caring for them. And I thought, if there were one thing in the world I'd like to do besides run, it'd be that—helping animals, large and small..." I tried to read the expression on her face, but she had turned her pretty head to exchange glances with her mama.

"Well," she said, turning back to me, "I suppose I'll now have to call you, 'Doc,' won't I? Doc Taylor." She smiled.

"Doc Taylor," repeated her mama, turning an almost identical smile on me. "That does have a nice ring."

"Well, it has a better ring than 'bus boy,'" said a new voice.

I turned to see Mr. Montier standing in the kitchen doorway. "Sir!"

"Glad you finally came to your senses, son. Found that backbone of yours. Knew it had to be in there somewhere." He held his hand out to me and I shook it. "Now, sit down at the table and drink the tea my wife has just set out for you. Talk with us a spell."

I did, still feeling, I must admit, a bit shaky in his presence.

"Tell me," he asked as he lowered himself into a chair across from me, "what caused you to take up the fight?"

"I am surrounded by wise men, sir," I told him. "Wise men and loyal friends. That's what made me take it up. So, thank you."

"Thank *me*?" he repeated with some surprise. "For what?"

"For reminding me that sometimes a man gets as much or as little as he expects. So it's best to expect big."

The corner of his mouth curled slightly upward. "Drink your tea, son," he told me.

24

Calling

September 1905

A funny thing happens when a dream is snatched away when you least expect it—when the choice is thrust upon you: fight for it or let it go. You find out about yourself then. You find out what's important to you. Something guides you to what feels right. It was this same inner guide—this same voice that had talked me through all my races—that had tugged at me this summer, pushing me to be more accountable to myself and my journey. It was this same voice that guided my steps toward my destiny at the University of Pennsylvania's School of Veterinary Medicine on 39th Street—just up the street from my home.

My parents had been overjoyed—especially Mama. I'd hoped for a bit of an apology from Daddy for advising me to beg forgiveness for something I hadn't done, but it didn't surprise me when the furthest he was willing to go was to say, gruffly, "Well, I'm pleased they were in a listening frame of mind, John. Surprising the dean that way might've backfired, though. Did you think of that?"

A Novel by Craig T. Williams

I hadn't thought of that. "I wasn't on my own, Daddy. I had one good friend and the coach, himself, to back me up. To believe in me."

I wished to call those last four words back as soon as they left my mouth, but he only looked at me gravely and said, "It wasn't *you* I didn't believe in, John. You gotta know that."

I suppose I did know that, but it didn't make it any easier. For him, either. So I let him change the subject. "Mike Murphy, huh? You gonna be coached by Mike Murphy? That's fine."

So we talked about Coach Murphy and the changes he'd made to college track and field programs in his time at Yale.

★★★★

Fall found me installed in new classrooms, learning a new subject that was not really that new to me. I had been the "horse doctor" since I was a small boy and why it came to me so late that I should be that as a man, I did not understand. There were certain facts I knew about my life, and one of them was that finance bored me to pieces. My heart did not belong in New York City. I was not born to focus on the ups and downs of the stock market. Apart from running, my joy was in caring for an animal and seeing the mute gratitude that lingered in its eyes for such small kindnesses as feeding, grooming, or tending an injury. There was a kinship between animals and me, an understanding of the fine line between being caged and running free. The animals in the Philadelphia Zoo reminded me of myself. At some stage of life they'd been free to roar, stomp, and run with all their might, only to find bars and wire limiting them to a finite amount of space. I couldn't change that. My mission in life was to doctor them to health, to help them enjoy what freedom they were allotted, however wide or narrow it might be.

I realized that I'd learned something from my Daddy, and from Jack Johnson, and from working in a restaurant in the Seventh Ward—and that was that a man should do what he loved if he could. Daddy did what he loved. Jack Johnson did what he loved. Every time I stepped on the track, I was doing what I loved. And when that part of my life was over, I wanted to continue to do what I loved. I wanted to do more than just survive. I owed it to myself, to my family ... to Mary Agnes, whom I'd seen off to her fall semester at Cheyney with hope that our relationship would be reborn without the shadow of shame between us.

When I said that animal doctoring was familiar to me, I don't mean to suggest for a moment that I knew everything, or even most things. I knew folk cures. Good cures, mind you, but folk cures nonetheless. Now, in the classrooms of UPenn veterinary school, I was learning more. I was learning why those cures worked—what substances worked in the body to take down a fever, kill an infection, clear breathing or heal a wound.

Then there was the vocabulary—now that was part of animal doctoring that was not familiar to me. I'd grown up with the common names for animals and their various troubles. Now I must learn the proper words. A horse wasn't just a horse, he was an equine. Sleeping sickness was more properly called *equine encephalomyelitis* but was deadly by either name. I got to see animals in a whole new light—as marvelous flesh and blood machines that physically had so much in common with human beings that it was no surprise to learn that in frontier towns the village doc took both human and animal patients.

I loved it. I loved learning it all. And as I contemplated my future, I saw that it was going to be a very good future after all.

In and around my contemplation and discovery of my calling, I wondered if Charles Cook was having moments of contemplation and discovery about his life since being expelled from school. His family had been outraged, of course, and had offered to donate a substantial amount for a proposed statue of Benjamin Franklin, but Penn declined the offer and instead clung to the integrity of the honor code. After all, a university, like a man, was only as good as its word. Coach Murphy quoted that to me. He claimed the dean, himself, had said it and I suppose he might've, but I learned of my new coach that he never let the truth stand in the way of a good story.

★★★★

The Olympian: An American Triumph

December 1905

When I'd left UPenn and suspended my relations with the Montiers, I'd also suspended my relations with the Boule. I had received letters from them that I had not even opened. And while I had re-established myself among the student body and the Montier family and the athletic team, I had not done so with my fraternity brothers simply because I didn't know what to say. I had no idea what had been said about me in my absence. I had been shamed and afraid that I might bring dishonor to that honorable group of men.

It was Christmas week before I saw one of the members again and that member was, of course, Mary Agnes's relation, Dr. Algernon Jackson. I had gone to supper at the Montier home the two days before Christmas, taking one of Mama's pies and a baking dish full of candied yams from Hattie's kitchen and was surprised when I saw Dr. Jackson seated in the Montier's parlor. I don't know why I should have been. He was a member of their extended family, after all. I hesitated inside the parlor door, feeling suddenly at a loss.

I felt Mary Agnes take the containers of food from my grasp and carry them away to the kitchen. I longed to follow. Instead, I stood with empty hands as Dr. Jackson rose from the chair next to Mr. Montier's. I removed my hat and clutched the brim tightly enough to bend it.

"Dr. Jackson," I mumbled.

He took a step toward me, thrust out his hand and smiled. "John, it is a pleasure to see you again. Wilton was just telling me your good news. Congratulations on your rein-statement. Dare I hope we'll see you at the next meeting of the Boule?"

"Well, sir," I said, licking my suddenly dry lips, "I wasn't certain I'd be welcome."

"Not welcome?" He seemed puzzled. "Did you read none of the letters we sent expressing our support?"

"Ah, no, sir. I was rather afraid to open them. I figured I was to be expelled from the fraternity as I was from school."

Dr. Jackson glanced at Winton Montier, then returned his gaze to me, looking very grave. "John, the members of the Boule stand together. Personally, I did not believe for a moment that you had cheated on a paper."

I looked up sharply, startled. "How did you know-?"

Again the glance at Mary Agnes's daddy. "Winton knew. He explained the situation to me."

"But he..." I turned my own gaze to Mr. Montier. "You wouldn't let me in the house, sir!"

Mr. Montier snorted. "Not because I thought you cheated, son. Because I knew you hadn't but wouldn't defend yourself. You knew that."

I nodded. "So I'm still a member of the fraternity?"

"Indeed," said Dr. Jackson. "We will be pleased to have you among us again, John. Very pleased."

"And I'd be pleased if you all would come to the table," said Connie Montier, appearing in the foyer.

We obeyed immediately. I spent the evening basking in the warmth of their acceptance.

The Olympian: An American Triumph

★★★★

February 1906

"John Baxter Taylor," Coach Murphy said, rising to offer me his hand. "Pleased to see you. How did you feel during practice today?"

"I felt fine, sir," I replied, marveling at how different the full five syllables of my name sounded coming from his mouth instead of my mother's. "Why did you wish to see me?"

Coach Murphy pointed to the chair opposite his desk, and I sat down, feeling at ease in his presence. He sat back and clasped his hands behind his head.

"I have a question for you, John."

"Yes, sir?"

"Have you been following the Olympics?"

My mind flashed back to my discussion of the last Olympics with Coach Robertson. "Yes," I said warily.

"I served as a trainer at the 1900 Olympics in Paris, and I expect to take a few of my Penn boys to the next Olympics in '08."

I could have leapt out of my seat with excitement.

Coach Murphy tilted his head slightly. "My favorite novelist, Honoré de Balzac, said, 'Nothing is a greater impediment to being on good terms with others than being ill at ease with yourself.' Do you have enough confidence in yourself that you can look beyond what others think of you and focus merely on the needs of your soul and your team?"

I felt like I was suddenly in front of the Reverend Cartier from St. Thomas. Our insightful rector asked similarly pointed questions.

"Yes, *sir*," I answered.

"Well then, lad, you keep showing up for practice with that attitude, and we'll see if you can head out to the Olympics in '08. Is that a goal you would like to meet?"

"Yes, sir. Thank you, sir."

He rose again and stretched out his hand to me. "Fine then, I wanted to be sure. Your previous coach didn't have many kind things to say of the Olympics, Of course, he had not many kind things to say of you, either, after losing you for his team at the end of last season. It was, I think, a great blow to him and to the school's track and field program. I imagine you will not let it happen again."

"No, sir." I rose, shook his hand and went home with my mind a-buzz. "Oh-eight," I mumbled over and over to myself. "Oh-eight will be here before I know it."

★★★★

April 1906

My life had begun anew in earnest—on the field and off—and I found myself sucking up knowledge like a sponge. In the classroom, I learned the art of healing; on the field, I learned to run better, faster smarter. Coach Murphy was a fountain of knowledge and taught me many things I didn't know—about running and about myself. I didn't, for example, know how much pride I had in my running "style" until Coach Murphy challenged it.

"You like to come from behind," he observed one day at a meet. "You've given that thought, have you?"

"Yes, sir," I responded, proudly, for I had. "But it's more than just coming from behind, sir. I leap out and set the pace, get everyone off to a fast start. Then, I pick the best runner in the field—the one most likely to contend—and push him through the beginning of the race. I find if I do that, he often won't have anything left for the stretch."

Coach nodded. "I see. You've thought about it a great deal then."

"Yes, sir."

"Hat's off to you, John. That's intelligent running. A lot of runners just flat out run, trusting instinct to carry the day. But what happens if you choose the wrong runner?"

"What?"

"What if you're so busy pushing the fellow you think is the 'best' that you miss a dark horse in the field—a fast dark horse?"

I hadn't honestly thought about that. "I suppose I've never done that, sir. I've never guessed wrong."

His eyes glinted. "Never, John? Never? I can't believe that. You do lose the occasional race, don't you?"

"Of course, sir. Everybody loses now and again."

"Tell me, who is it that most often beats you in these times? It the runner you're watching or the one you're not watching?"

Well, I had to think about that. And as much as it pained

me, I had to allow that most often when I was beaten, it was by a dark horse, as coach put it. A sleeper. Someone I hadn't expected to win. Now I only admitted this to myself, you understand, because it galled me to have to admit it to my coach.

"When I lose," I said, "it's got nothing to do with the other runners. It has to do with me just not being there—mentally, I mean."

"Or physically?"

"Maybe."

"John," he told me in all seriousness, "there are going to be times when your come-from-behind style isn't going to work. There are going to be times when the only thing standing between you and first place is how fast you got off the mark. There are going to be times when the field is so deep or the stakes so high or the track such that you will have to run your heart out from the first shot. As I recall, you had a moment like that at the international meet back in '04."

I remembered that even as he said the words "run your heart out."

"I guess so, sir."

"So, in these coming months at practice, I want you to learn a different style. I want you to learn how to come out fast and keep going—rely more on stamina and less on acceleration. And less," he added, "on the other runners' state of mind and body. I want you to learn how to win the race in the first five seconds."

"Win-?" I shook my head, grinning. "Now you're joking with me. That's not possible."

He gave me a shrewd look. "I'm telling you it is. Are you going to argue with me about it?"

In the sparkle of his eye, I saw the reminder of how foolish that argument would be on my part. *I've forgotten more about running than you'll ever know, that look said.*

I made a sort of compromise in my head. If Michael Murphy said I needed to work on my starts, then I would do just that, but I was certain as could be about my running style. I'd practice whatever he'd like, I told myself, but I'd keep my signature running style for meets.

25

A Fine Gentleman ...

1907 Season
Intercollegiate Association of Amateur Athletes of America
(IC4A) Championship, Harvard University, Cambridge,
Massachusetts

It was the best of times, it was the worst of times, it was the
age of wisdom, it was the age of foolishness, it was the epoch
of belief, it was the epoch of incredulity, it was the season of
Light, it was the season of Darkness, it was the spring of hope,
it was the winter of despair, we had everything before us, we
had nothing before us, we were all going direct to Heaven, we
were all going direct the other way ... —Charles Dickens

★★★★

I continued to play Dickens's words over and over in my
head that day, and not because I had recently finished reading *A Tale of Two Cities* in English literature class, but because
upon this day at the IC4A Championship meet in Massachusetts, I caught hold of the great irony of life that Dick-

ens referenced in the opening of his novel. This was the book that my Mary Agnes was reading when we first met. I thought of her as I read every line of it.

I was a Negro—a colored man—and therefore was deemed by some to be inferior. And yet, I was enrolled in a white institution of higher learning, I was a member of a prestigious fraternity—Sigma Pi Phi, and I had just been invited to join, of all things, the Irish-American Athletic Club (the Winged Fist), notwithstanding I had not one drop of Irish blood in my veins.

There I had renewed acquaintances with several of my classmates from Brown Prep, including Mel Sheppard who, I suspected, had been instrumental in the invitation. He'd shaken my hand at my induction, winked at me and said, "Welcome aboard, Doc."

Doc. I did like the sound of that.

Tensions were high at the Harvard meet; I felt it the moment we stepped onto Harvard soil. Those who came to compete today came to win. Second place in any event would be a disgrace, and though no one uttered those words out loud, it was etched on the face of every athlete in attendance. That was especially true of Nate Cartmell, who had returned to school proud of the two silver medals he'd won in the "sideshow" in St. Louis. Despite the fact that Coach Murphy's attitude toward the '04 Olympics was less caustic than Coach Robertson's, there was a certain amount of defensiveness in Nate. He was a man with something to prove and he'd every intention of returning to the Olympics in '08 to do it.

A Novel by Craig T. Williams

As we UPenn athletes made our way across the field, we traded glances with the boys from Princeton and the boys from Harvard. It was an ugly exchange even without verbal confrontation. Beneath the heavy tension we all knew just how much was riding on our performances today.

Coach Murphy sensed our tension and offered support in the strength of his giant presence. "All eyes ahead," he said, leading the team across the field. "Be of a single mind— nothing on the sidelines is real."

Coach Murphy was one of the smartest men I knew, and his style of motivating was nothing less than genius. He had done something that Coach Robertson in all of his years at Penn had not been able to do—gain the respect of protégés and opponents alike.

Once we made it to our area of the field, the coach called us to form a huddle. "This is what we've been work-ing for, boys," he said, "and every single one of you is about to stand in the glory of the moment." He looked right at me and winked.

I tried to remember those words when it came time to draw a position on the field. That, and what Coach had by now drilled into my head about getting off the mark quickly. I had a bad draw on the outside. Though that meant I would be obliged to run yards farther than my opponent, I would not allow it to discourage me.

I stand in the glory of the moment; nothing else is real. With that thought in mind, I took my position on the track along with my rivals, all thirsty for blood and glory. I could feel them looking at me, assessing me. I ignored them. *Nothing else is real.*

Marks. I positioned myself on the track.

Set. I dug in my front foot just as Coach had taught me, shifting my weight forward just so.

Drive.

The starter fired his pistol and I leapt into motion, paying no attention to what lay on either side of me, nor the distance I would have to run in order to make up for the bad draw. I adjusted my strategy a bit, placing myself between and just behind two big runners from Harvard. I kept my eyes focused on a win, and my feet in motion.

As I approached the 200-yard mark, one of the Harvard boys dropped back a step and jostled me. He nearly threw me off balance. At the 300-yard mark he jostled me again with more vigor, this time with an elbow to the rib cage. Pain shot down my side, but I didn't let it distract me. This was my moment of glory and I wouldn't be denied it. I pressed forward, feeling nothing but the interlocking rhythms of heart and lungs and feet. Faster. And yet faster. The other runners slipped behind me one after another.

I caught my fastest opponent in the last 100 yards and passed him. I won by three yards and set a new record: 48.8 seconds. It was mine to break. I'd set the old record in '04. I also proved something to myself—it was not merely sound strategy that won races. Desire won races, too.

This was only the beginning of what I would refer to as the "frenzy of the championship." The 1907 IC4A Championship was one of the greatest meets of all time. Records were set in seven of the thirteen events. My teammate Guy

A Novel by Craig T. Williams

Haskins won both the mile and the half mile at the IC4A, becoming only the second runner in history, aside from Princeton's John Cregan back in 1898, to accomplish such a feat. Another teammate, Tom Moffitt, set a meet record in the high jump. I, too, had experienced my personal best that day.

Our entire team left the meet with triumph etched in our hearts. As we headed home to Philadelphia, I reframed the opening of Charles Dickens's novel:

It was the best of times. It was the age of wisdom and the age of truth. It was the epoch of belief, it was the epoch of miracles. It was the season of light and the spring of hope. We had everything before us … and we were all going directly to heaven … every single one of us …Yes … every single one of us was going…

★★★★

September 7, 1907
Amateur Athletic Union Championships –
Norfolk, Virginia

The AAU National Championships in Norfolk, Virginia, fell on a crisp fall day. The championship was held in conjunction with the Jamestown Exposition, the tri-centenary of the founding of the Jamestown Colony. There were many in attendance, and the mood was competitive. I had come to participate in "my event"—the event for which I was best known, the quarter mile.

As we took our positions on the field, I sampled the tension and excitement buzzing in the air around me. Taking Coach Murphy's philosophy to heart, I rarely made eye contact with the opponent, because to acknowledge their presence beside me would be to make them "real." I had a decent draw from earlier that day and, as a result, had a good starting position. As I mentally prepared for this race, I recalled other words Coach Murphy had spoken: "There is nothing out there on that field but you and your personal best."

If that was the case, then I was in a position of privilege from the beginning. My personal best was the national record, and that simple thought gave birth to a smile.

Marks.

Set.

Drive.

And with that my opponents leapt out onto the cinder path to do battle with each other Not I. I battled only myself and my previously set record.

Well, J. T., I said to myself, *I'm gonna beat you today.*

Let the others tire themselves jockeying for the front of the pack. I was content to follow … for a time. My pacing was especially good that day. I gave my opponents their lead and lingered a while in their dust, just nipping at their heels. Then, as we neared the 330-yard mark, I made my push.

We were pelting down the homestretch when an opponent from a local university crossed my path deliberately. I saw him glance back at me before he altered course. He all but fell across me, giving me an elbow to the groin as he staggered forward again. The pain nearly toppled me, but the collective gasp from the crowd pulled me up and kept me moving.

I heard cries of "Foul! That's a foul!" from our bench, but no foul was called.

Should I retaliate? A well-placed knee or elbow, perhaps? I considered it for a heartbeat before Coach Murphy stopped me—or rather his words did. "The opponent isn't real," he'd told us many times as we nursed bleeding knees and lacerated palms, "and neither is your injury."

Nothing was real but winning the race, and winning the race was my desire.

It was one of the sweetest victories I had ever tasted. As I passed the man who had grossly fouled me, I found the wind at my back pushing me harder than I had ever been pushed before. My legs flew by will and my spirit soared by grace. As I crossed the finish line in first place, the crowd came to their feet with the most thunderous applause I had ever heard. And it was mine.

It was a day of reckoning, a day in which I knew beyond all knowing that justice always rises into the light, just as it had done with Charles Edward Cook and his preposterous claims of me being a cheater.

Justice always rises.

Always.

And as I stood in the victor's circle, scores of white

Southern gentlemen lined the field for an opportunity simply to shake my brown hand and call me "a fine gentleman" to my face.

★★★★

February 1908

If sports are egalitarian in nature, so, too is the need for healing. An animal does not care what color the hands are that give it medicine or soothe its pain, and I found that I was not alone in realizing this. Even before I received my degree in veterinary medicine, I had been asked to doctor animals. In school, I found this was part of our learning process. Farmers would cart their sick sheep or pigs or horses into town or we would be carted out to visit them and to see, first hand, the sorts of places where we'd be practicing our speciality.

I recall one trip we made out to a local dairy farm where we were asked to diagnose a sick cow and attend the births of a trio of calves. Each of us in the group— there were eight of us—were asked to examine the ailing cow and take notes. I was the third student to examine the patient.

"Mr. Taylor," my professor said and I moved toward the poor creature.

I cannot forget the war in her owner's eyes as he realized that a Negro was about to lay hands on his property. He started forward, causing me to look up into his eyes. I saw unease, uncertainty, acceptance and embarrassment flash through them in quick succession.

I hesitated.

My professor—Dr. Mulcahey—noticed this. "John, here, is one of my most dedicated students," he told the farmer, the accent of his motherland lilting on his tongue. It seemed a bit more pronounced than usual, which I suspected had something to do with the fact that the farmer's name was O'Riley. "He tells me he's been nursing sick animals since he was a lad."

"Do tell," said Farmer O'Riley, who suddenly relaxed.

I moved to examine the cow. She seemed low—droopy. Her belly was slightly distended and her udder was full to leaking. One of the teats seemed inflamed. I took note of this, then stepped back and watched as my classmates took turns checking her. When we had done, Dr. Mulcahey asked for our observations. All of us caught the inflamed teat—most that she was running a slight fever. Not all noticed the distended belly—cows aren't the most elegant of creatures and all look to have swallowed a balloon of some size.

Dr. Mulcahey then asked for our opinions as to what was wrong with the old girl. Mastitis, fever, or digestive problems were the most popular suggestions.

"Mastitis, yes," said our professor. "But caused by what?"

I waited until everyone had spoken, nodding when I heard something I agreed with. Then, Professor Mulcahey asked if there were any other observations, possible causes, unnoticed symptoms.

I raised my hand. "May I ask Mr. O'Riley a question?"

"By all means."

"Well, sir," I said, "has she been eating normally?"

"Now that you mention it, no."

Those in favor of digestive problems smiled.

"In what way are her eating habits different?" I asked.

"She's been eating me out of house and home. Pushing other cows out of the way to get at the hay."

"That doesn't sound like a stomach ailment," said one of my classmates. "Unless she's got worms. Is her manure normal?"

The farmer nodded.

"She's pregnant," I announced. "And her udder's swollen with milk. But because she's got a clogged teat, there's inflammation and a slight fever." I looked to the professor. "Am I correct, sir?"

Mulcahey and the farmer exchanged glances. "That is correct. Can you tell me how she might have come by a clogged teat?"

"Well, that could be caused by a number of things," I said, "but in this case, I think it's because she got kicked by another cow. There's a cut across the base of the teat."

"And how," Mulcahey asked, "would you recommend treating this ailment, Taylor?"

"Clean the wound and sterilize it. Milk her to relieve pressure in the udder and apply heat." I glanced at the farmer. "And you might want to fix that hole in your fence."

"What hole?" he asked.

"The one the bull got in through."

My classmates and professor laughed and, after a moment of surprise, the farmer laughed too. He had no reaction to me helping to birth one of the three calves due that day, and when we left he shook my hand and called me "Doc."

26

An Open Call
on Hearts

March 1908
Schuylkill River

In my search for solitude, serenity and strength of purpose, I was compelled to go down to the river's edge today. With graduation just around the corner and Olympic pretrials coming up in June, there were plenty of things to tend to, but there was one thing that eclipsed them all—a goal I had set myself, a quest of the heart I must make. As I released myself to the simplicity of a river walk, I smiled at the whimsical thought of living life as a tree, a leaf, or even something simpler than that—a blade of grass.

There were other people at the river, but I paid them no mind and they paid me none. Gentle breezes serenaded me with songs that promised a warm summer as I searched quietly for my perfect spot. The spot where I often met Mary Agnes.

It was here, down at the Schuylkill River, that my life changed once more. I caught just a glimmer of sunlight on raven hair and knew it was Mary Agnes Montier. She was home just now on a break from school. I paused to admire the way the sun shone softly on her skin, the tilt of her head, and the set of her shoulders. Yes, that was how I studied her—like a careful hunter or an artist.

My knees threatened to buckle as I made my way slowly over to her, for I had a question to ask this day. I stood behind her as she sat on our bench by the river and gently cleared my throat. I could tell by the sudden stiffness of her posture that she knew me, though I'd spoken no words.

"How have you been, John Baxter Taylor?" she asked, without turning around to face me or offering a smile.

"I have been well," I said in reply, settling into the false formality that had become a game between us.

"I've heard good things about you."

"And I of you. How are your studies at Cheyney?"

"Rewarding."

"And how are you finding your break from school?"

"My father's not well," she said without great emotion, "so it seems I shall be busy helping my mother."

"I'm sorry to hear that—about your daddy, I mean."

"Hmm," she said, eyes never leaving the river's spangled surface. "Well, it was his own doing that landed him flat on his back unable to move. Specifically, it was his stubborn insistence that he would rebuild a house that had already been built quite well the first time around."

Now she turned and offered a smile. That smile was like dewdrops on a parched leaf.

"So it's nothing too serious?" I asked, relieved on two counts. I took a seat beside her on the little wooden bench.

"No. His back is out for a bit … but it will be back." She caught her own pun and burst into laughter.

I laughed, too. It was funny to think that anything could level Mr. Montier.

We sat in companionable silence for close to an hour before any more words were said. It felt quite as if we had not been separated by school at all and had not seen each other since Christmas.

Then Mary Agnes said, "There's something I haven't told you about that summer before I left for school."

"And what's that?" I asked.

"I came to see you at the hotel where you were working."

I frowned and turned to look at her. "I never saw you."

With a reflective look in her eye, she recalled it in vivid detail. "There was a lot of commotion in the restaurant that day, and you were hovering over this table, waiting on this man hand and foot … and catering to him like nobody's business…"

"What?" I asked in disbelief. "Couldn't have been me. I wasn't a waiter."

"You think I don't know your face, John? I came in and waited for you to look up at me, and I stood there for a long time, but you never did. So, I left because I thought if you didn't have the good sense to look up one time … then you deserved not to see me."

"Mary Agnes," I said in shock, "how would I have known to look up?"

"I know. Silly, isn't it? Those are the kinds of tricks the

heart plays when it's hurt. I got it into my head that because I was calling on you with my heart you'd hear me," she said, tears forming in her eyes. "My daddy had forbidden me to see you, and I wanted to know if love was stronger than his rules. So, against Daddy's wishes, I went to the Ward to call you with my heart … and you didn't hear me speak to you."

I did not know what to say, for no one had ever said such a thing to me. It seemed unfair.

"Of course," she continued with a lighter voice, "when I returned home that evening, I learned that Jack Johnson was at the hotel that day, and that it was him you were listening to."

Oh. That day she could have walked up to me and planted a sweet kiss upon my lips and I would not have felt a thing.

"Then I laughed," she said, "because Jack Johnson has a really big mouth, so no wonder you couldn't hear me. And … because I knew I'd been silly."

We both laughed then. Laughed until we ran out of laughter.

"I never wanted to stop seeing you, you know," she said, "but Daddy…"

"It's done," I said, grabbing hold of her hand. "It was the best of times and it was the worst of times."

She smiled. "It was the age of wisdom and of foolishness."

"It was my season of light and my season of darkness."

"It was my spring of hope and my winter of despair."

"We had everything before us," I said, looking deeply into her eyes.

"And we also had nothing before us."

"We were going direct to heaven."

"And we were also going to Cheyney University in the fall."

I laughed.

She didn't. Her eyes, as she looked up at me told me that this was the time. The time to say out loud what I had been feeling for quite a while.

"I am in love with you, Mary Agnes. And I would like to call upon your daddy and ask for your hand in marriage."

A lifetime was spent between my asking and her answering.

"Are you sure, John?"

"I am sure," I said, "that I do not wish to miss the call of your heart a second time."

27

Olympian

June 6, 1908
Olympic Pre-trials

New York Times
Three trial meetings will be held by the American Com-
mittee for the London Olympic Games. The cities selected for
the tryouts are Philadelphia, Chicago, and San Francisco. The
selection of Philadelphia in preference to New York is because
of the fact that the University of Pennsylvania tendered the
use of Franklin Field, whereas there was no available athletic
track in New York.

★★★★

The events leading up to the Olympic pre-trials of 1908
hinted at destiny. With the previous year on record as my
best track and field season ever, I entered 1908 seeking a permanent place in history. With such aspirations, I found it difficult to heed the warning of my general physician, who had
advised me to be "extremely careful." It seemed I had de-

veloped a hernia. I first noticed it after the IC4A Championships the year previous, but was determined that it wouldn't deter me. I told myself that Doc Foxworthy was a worry-wart.

"Doctor," I said during one of our many conversations on the subject, "I'm about as healthy as they come."

"I didn't say you weren't *healthy*, John," he said, eyeing my records with care, "except for the fact that you have a hernia."

"But I feel fine," I protested.

"You might feel fine ... for now."

"I led the Penn relay team to victory this past year."

"Good for you, son."

"I won the quarter mile at the IC4A Championship for the third year in a row, so I think that makes me a little special. I'm only the third person in their whole thirty-three-year history to do such a thing."

"Well, you are some kind of special, John," he said with a hearty laugh, "but I still have some concerns about your running with a hernia."

"Have you ever run a race?"

"Can't say that I have." He continued his fact-finding and figure checking.

"When I'm running, I feel as if I'm having a conversation with God."

He finally stopped what he was doing and turned to face me. "Then I guess that is some kind of special. I know I feel that way when I deliver a baby. I've always believed there are other ways to pray besides words."

"Well, there you have it," I agreed. "And I doubt God wants either of us to stop talking to Him."

That handled Doc Foxworthy pretty effectively, Coach was another matter. The day the official announcement was made of his coaching the Olympic track team after months and months of rumor, he had gathered us all together in the gymnasium to give us the news. Though we had known it, or at least known of it, for some time, still we leapt to our feet to applaud.

The act of rising so swiftly irritated the hernia and it gave me a sharp, insistent tug. I doubled over before I could catch myself and sat back down. I was able to stand again, more slowly, in a moment and joined in the ovation, but Coach had noticed the behavior and called me into his office after the team meeting.

"Let's talk about the Olympic Games," he said.

"Okay."

"Are you going to be able to compete?"

"Why wouldn't I?"

"I saw that wince of pain when you stood up just now, John. What's wrong?"

"Just a stitch."

He shook his head, making clucking sound with his tongue. "John, John. You have a hernia."

"How do you–?"

"Do you think I could take my athletes to London without reviewing their medical records? I spoke to Doc Foxworthy personally. He has some concern for you."

"He needn't have. I'm fine. I barely notice it."

"That's not what I saw just now," said Coach.

"It doesn't bother me at all when I run," I fibbed. It was a small fib, because the truth was that nothing bothered me when I was running.

"You're not Hercules," Coach warned me.

I grinned at him. "Father of the ancient Olympics."

"John."

"Seriously, Coach. I know I'm not superhuman. But it's really not much of anything. Doc Foxworthy is an old mother hen."

"Indeed? What does that make me?"

"My coach."

"That's right. So, if I tell you to take it easy during practice today, I expect you to obey me. Are we clear on that?"

"Oh, yes, sir." Another small fib, perhaps.

He pointed a finger at my nose. "I know you, John Taylor. You're a stubborn man. Don't be too stubborn for your own good. If I tell you to stand down..."

"Yes, sir."

Coach paused to study me. "You didn't compete in the last Olympics because Coach Robertson was so dead set against it."

I was glad of the change of subject. "More like he was dead set *for* me competing in Europe that spring. He ... he called the Olympics a sideshow. Said we wouldn't be really representing America."

"He had a point there. But that won't be true this time, will it?"

I grinned. "No, sir! This time we'll wear U.S. uniforms.

This time we'll be the main event."

"Maybe you can tell me how many Negro athletes represented the United States of America in those Olympics."

"Sir?"

"I think the question was pretty clear."

"None," I said cautiously. I wasn't sure where he was going with this.

"None," he agreed. "Not one wore the uniform of the United States or represented this country. It was every man for himself. Until now. Until *this* Olympics … *if* you go, John. And if you go, you will make history simply by being there in U.S. colors." He fixed me with a sober gaze. "Did you realize that, John? Had you thought of it?"

I had. If I went, I would make history.

"I understand that you're highly motivated to compete in this Olympics," he said soberly. "Don't let it make you blind to trouble."

"You're not saying I shouldn't compete," I objected.

"No. I'm simply saying you should compete wisely."

If you go, you will make history. Those words were in my mind now as I prepared to take the track for the Olympic pre-trials. The anticipation had built up in the East and the promise of an intense battle had made the headlines in the previous month's *New York Times*:

MANY STAR PERFORMERS WILL
COMPETE AT FRANKLIN FIELD FOR OLYMPIC
TEAM. MEN IN GOOD CONDITION.

The Olympian: An American Triumph

The article boasted of a rivalry amongst New York's premier athletic organizations, all vying for the honor of being selected to represent the United States in London. It said, in no uncertain terms, that "athletes capable of carrying off victories at this meet will be sent abroad." So it was with great anticipation, with the history of the Games crammed into our heads and riding the high of our personal bests from the year before, that the UPenn athletes arrived on the soil of Franklin Field, June 6, 1908, to compete with the best of the best.

As I prepared for the quarter mile run I reminded myself that this was no different than any of my other meets, though the athletes who came for these Olympic pre-trials were certainly at the height of distinction compared with our typical opponents. They seemed to exceed the *New York Times* description, *Men in Good Condition.* The general atmosphere met my expectations, equal parts anticipation and desperation. Everyone was hungry for the honor of representing the United States in London. Far from engendering camaraderie, this patriotic passion made them downright unpleasant this afternoon. That did not discourage me, for I was certainly no stranger to friendly *and* unfriendly competition.

I took my position on Franklin Field knowing I had an advantage. This was my home turf; I would not be running on foreign soil today, as most of my opponents were. I glanced into the stands and saw my family, and seated among them, Mary Agnes of the soothing smile, who had come to lend her support and good cheer. A smile warmed my lips at the sight of Hattie, sitting in the stands beside her, holding her Bible with both hands and smiling in my direction, my mother and even Daddy, looking proud, but nervous on my behalf. Well, good. Let them be nervous for me. I had nothing in my heart but quiet confidence. I offered a confident nod to them. They were all I noticed of the outside world before going deep within to ignore it ... and the occasional pinch from my hernia.

I closed my eyes and awaited the call of *Marks*. I had no recollection of anything after that, just running shoes against hard ground. Each of us leapt to his own call of destiny.

Within 110 yards I could tell it would not be an easy sweep. My competitors brought a superior will fueled by blood, sweat, and dreams. I pressed on with focused determination, cutting through the wind. Today it seemed to fight back, howling in protest. It kept up its protest throughout the race, pushing and pulling my body.

Somewhere around 320 yards I became aware of a sound outside of my head. The spectators had risen to their feet to shout and applaud. They were not applauding me—I was not in the lead. In fact, I was at a substantial disadvantage—more so when I was forced to run wide on the turn.

Run, John. Run.

I could hear the words as if they were carried on the wind from the lips of family and friends.

Run faster.

Run.

Faster.

I could feel my heart pounding in my chest, urging the rest of my body to rise to the occasion.

The Olympian: *An American Triumph*

Win, John.

Win.

It was earlier in the race than I normally made my move but something told me it was now or never. That something insisted that it be now.

I focused on the lead runner and began to close the distance between us. My competitor was unwilling to surrender, though. As I drew up to him, he surged ahead—once, twice. I finally pulled abreast of him and glanced fleetingly at his face. I saw fierce determination in his eyes. I could hear his breath coming hard and fast and the trailing flutter of air that was released from his lungs as he lunged, thrusting his body forward in an attempt to capture the win. But he did not have nearly enough. Just twenty yards from the finish line, I passed him as though the wind and I had at last formed an alliance. I could say it was by will, by sweat, by prayer, and by power that I crossed the finish line first, but it was by the grace of the wind that I crossed it by so much.

I began shouting as the thrill of victory penetrated my body. It felt like mere seconds before my winning time was placed on the scoreboard as 49.8 seconds.

John won it!

John won it!

John!

I could hear my name amid the shouting and applause as I looked into the stands where Mama, Daddy, Hattie, and Mary Agnes were all cheering and crying at the same time. Oh, yes, many others stood and cheered as well, but of them I have only a vague memory.

A Novel by Craig T. Williams

My win qualified me for the Olympic Games in London. I would run with athletes I knew only through the newspaper clippings I had saved—Amateur Athletic Champion Horace Ramey, John Atlee from Princeton, John Carpenter from Cornell. Two colored men had earned medals at the St. Louis games in 1904. Joe Stadler won a silver medal in the standing high jump and George Poage won two bronze medals for the 200 meter and 400 meter hurdles. But I would be the first Negro to represent the United States of America in Olympic competition and held the distinction of being on the first team to wear the American uniform.

When it was announced that I would represent America in the Olympics, I saw the culmination of all my hard work and perseverance. I had never given up. I had never looked back. I had never given in. I had done what I did best.

I ran.

And for that I had become an Olympian. I would go and I would make history.

28

Graduation

June 17, 1908
One Hundred and Fifty-Second Commencement
University of Pennsylvania, Philadelphia

Yesterday had been Class Day—an infamous rite of passage for the senior class, a time for us to laugh, present awards, perform skits, and transfer the cap and gown to the junior class president. Our class presented Edgar Fahs Smith, the vice provost, with a silver loving cup in appreciation for his services. He was so surprised, he turned a blushing red, because it was the first award ever seriously presented to a faculty member on Class Day. Class Days in the past had spoofed and mocked the faculty, so it was a change of tradition for us to show our gratitude.

The best part of Class Day had to be walking with my head high, wearing my cap and gown, and strutting down the street with my fellow graduates as thousands of families and friends watched our procession. I had found Mama and Daddy's smiling faces as my class marched into the Triangle of the Upper Quad for the planting of the ivy.

A Novel by Craig T. Williams

Every graduating class planted ivy as a symbol of planting roots and growing great and strong through the years. The applause had been long and loud when the dirt was dug and the class of 1908 planted its vine in the soil. Then we'd burst into the loudest version of "Hail Pennsylvania" ever sung in the history of UPenn. We swayed from side to side, nearly shouting the last stanza:

"Hail Pennsylvania, guide of our youth. Lead thou thy children on to light and truth. Thee when death summons us, others shall praise Hail Pennsylvania through endless days!"

On to light and truth. Every muscle in my body could relate to those words. I was ready to graduate and begin my life operating one of the finest veterinary practices for wild and domestic animals in Pennsylvania. As I stood before the mirror this morning of my graduation brushing my hair, I looked into the eyes of a man certain of his purpose in life. I had fought my way through some trying times and now here I stood in my graduation gown, smiling with pride at the gray border of my stole, signifying my degree in veterinary medicine.

My chosen calling was a fine blend of the practical and the spiritually satisfying. It was also a balance and a blending of two streams of life philosophy that I had once been certain could never be reconciled. The prospect of me becoming Dr. John Baxter Taylor, Jr., DMV was pleasing to both my father and Mary Agnes's. I was certain that it would have pleased the man who had introduced me to the thoughts of DuBois. Pomp had, after all, been a man of great soul and great pragmatism.

Mama entered the bathroom behind me and smiled. She turned me to her, happiness radiating from her face like rays of sunshine. I felt her love embrace me. She didn't say a word, just took the black tassel of my cap in her hands and placed it gently on the right side of my head. Then she stood back and clasped her hands.

I was a grown man, but even a grown man is humbled when standing in the presence of the woman who loved him before he fully knew how to love himself. Words refused to form in my mouth. I simply smiled at her like a child being praised for his latest drawing.

Mama turned me back to the mirror and stood beside me with a big grin. We caught eyes in the glass and just laughed.

Daddy popped into the doorway behind us with a broad smile. "You ready, Doc Taylor?"

My smile could not stretch wide enough. I left, for the moment, the fact that Daddy and I had never talked about my confrontation with the dean and Charles Cook, had never discussed my reinstatement, what it meant to our relationship, or how it reflected on our disparate philosophies. He was clearly proud of me now, and I was more than content with that.

"Yes, I am, Daddy. Yes, I am."

William was in the middle of his internship and unable to leave his post as a druggist. Clinton was also unable to attend but sent a letter of congratulations. Hattie and her husband, James, joined Mama and Daddy in the stands to view my graduation.

I took my seat in the oval center of Franklin Field and enjoyed the music and speeches. Then the words were read that melted me from the inside out: *"Degree of Doctor of Veterinary Medicine conferred upon John Baxter Taylor, Jr."*

I stood and moved my tassel to the left.

My classmates responded with thunderous applause, and I am sure my cheering section was clapping the loudest. The applause pulsed through my body, and I was filled with so much joy, I felt as if I had won a thousand races in a single day.

★★★★

Later that evening we had a special supper, indeed, at the Taylor house. Mary Agnes came to meet my parents for the very first time, and I was about as nervous as a young man could be. I had wanted to invite Hattie and James but thought it might be a little overwhelming for Mary Agnes, so I kept it simple, with just the folks.

We gathered around the Taylor table in joy, wearing our Sunday best. I was seated beside Mary Agnes, and Mama and Daddy were seated across from us, eyeing every movement and noting every expression. Mary Agnes looked especially lovely that evening, and I could tell that both of my parents thought she had an exceptional kind of beauty.

"Mary Agnes," said Mama, "John tells us you're a student at Cheyney."

"Yes," I said quickly, "she's a great student."

Mary glanced at me, then turned politely to Mama. "Yes, ma'am," she said with a touch of pepper in her voice.

"You like the school?" asked Daddy.

"She *loves* the school!" I bubbled, before Mary could respond.

She looked at me again with a gentle eye, and then turned her attention back to my parents. "It's quite nice," she said. "I'm studying English literature. I'd like to be a teacher one day."

"Oh," said Mama, impressed, "that's a very noble career choice."

"Well, she's a very noble lady!" I interjected, nearly tripping over my tongue.

"Tell us about your parents," said Mama.

Before Mary Agnes responded, she turned to me and gave me a look that said, "Not a word, John Baxter Taylor. Not a single word."

All I could do was grin and blush.

"My daddy's a master craftsman woodcarver," she said. "He creates the most beautiful pieces you've ever laid eyes on."

"Oh, and they are…" I began, but was silenced by a single stern look from Mary Agnes.

"He creates custom pieces for Philadelphia's wealthy," she concluded.

"And your mother?" Daddy asked.

"She takes care of Daddy. He's a handful."

"Yes, he is!" I said with a roll of my eyes, and with that all three of them turned and looked at me. I could feel myself shrinking down into the seat.

"Anybody care for dessert?" I asked.

They all laughed. I got a wink from both Mama and Daddy after Mary Agnes returned her attention to her plate, and knew that everything was going to be just fine.

29

Magic

There was much to do before leaving for London, and each day the preparation list appeared to sprout a new set of obligations. I would have to be wise with my time if I was to check off all my tasks before leaving. One thing took priority, and it required its own advance preparations.

First, there was a private conversation with my parents behind the closed doors of the Taylor house, and a request for their blessing. There Daddy extended a congratulatory hand on my becoming a man and Mama's eyes swelled with pride, and the bittersweet emotion of releasing her boy into adulthood.

Second, I spent the next several days in and out of jewelers' stores with Hattie, who dragged me around like she was choosing a ring for herself. She and I were having great difficulty agreeing on one that we *both* liked and that I could afford.

Third, I paid an unexpected visit to Mr. Montier, who seemed as grumpy as ever. I entered with gifts, and left with his blessing. Granted, it was a long time coming, as I did a lot of "fast talking" and he offered a handful of slow responses. Ultimately, I left with three nods, two grunts, one handshake and one blessing.

Fourth, I withdrew the funds I had received while working at the hotel to purchase the "one perfect ring" that Hattie and I had agreed upon without argument. I figured that if I could find something that she and I both liked, Mary Agnes would absolutely love it.

And last, I took a sunset walk hand-in-hand with Mary Agnes down by the Schuylkill River.

"I can't believe you're leaving tomorrow," she said as we walked along the river's edge.

"Me neither," I said.

"You excited?"

"More than you know."

"You nervous?"

"A little," I admitted after a pause.

"Don't be, John," she reassured me. "Just don't lose your socks and you'll be fine."

Huh?

She started to laugh. "Remember the day I met you? You had lost a sock."

"Oh, yes," I said, still slightly embarrassed at the thought of her having to return something so personal as that upon our first meeting. It seemed a lifetime ago: me, Mary Agnes, and the sock.

"You are possessed with it. I hope you know that, " she said.

"Possessed with what? A sock?"

"Magic."

"Magic?" I repeated.

"Of course, John."

"What do you mean by magic, Mary Agnes?"

She paused a bit in contemplation. "Well, I don't know because it's hard to put something so abstract into words."

"What are you saying, woman?" I cried melodramatically. "You have no Mary Agnes poem on magic to share with me? And you dare to call yourself a poet?"

She laughed. "Okay, okay. Magic is the silver lining in the clouds at the end of a rain."

"And?"

"And … it's the stuff that makes a wound scab over."

"And?" I repeated, wanting more.

"It's what keeps us going long after we should have crumpled up and expired," she said, looking at me.

Her words literally brought me to my knees at her feet.

She looked at me and laughed. "Get up off the ground, John Baxter Taylor, before you tear up your knees—and then how will you run your race?" She gave me a gentle push, trying to topple me over into the dirt.

I could not laugh because my heart was on the line. Before another word could be spoken, I took hold of her hand, pulled out that delicate garnet ring, and held it up to the backdrop of the dimming sky.

"Mary Agnes Montier," I said, "will you marry me?"

I had never seen her so still. She stood as if made of stone, eyes fixed on the ring. I knew it was more humble than showy, more simple than fancy, but it was the most honest gift I had ever given to anyone in all my life.

"Will you marry me?" I asked again, just in case she hadn't heard.

"YES!" she cried, almost ripping me out of my suit coat as she pulled me up into her embrace.

As we held each other down by the river where it had all begun, I murmured, "Our life together will be so grand."

"*Yes,*" she whispered.

"We'll plan our wedding when I get back from London."

"Yes."

"Anywhere you want," I said.

"Yes."

"As big as you want," I promised. "And as magical as you can dream it to be."

Yes, said her smile.

Now, this truly was magic.

★★★★

June 29, 1908
Aboard the Steamship Philadelphia

My second trip to Europe on a steamship was even more thrilling than the first voyage. We were a large group—one hundred and twenty-two strong—and the excitement was infectious. The Olympic team had booked passage aboard the *SS Philadelphia*, a splendid ship, sleek and black with a knife-sharp prow. My first impression of her was that she was in motion even as she floated quietly at her New York Harbor dock. Like me, she was built for speed. And also like me, she had won her share of races. She was a holder of the Blue Ribband, which is sort of like an Olympic medal for ships, given only to the fastest liners to cross the Atlantic. Made me feel right at home ... and as if God were sending me a message. She was fast, she was a winner, and she was named for my hometown.

Life aboard Philadelphia was pleasant. The weather was fair, which meant we could spend a great deal of time above-decks on the promenade. In fact, they had installed a cork track there for us so we could run—and run we did, around the ship's gleaming white superstructure with the sea to the opposite side, sparkling in the sun. Other athletes practiced there, as well, the shot-putters had a range set up on the fore-deck and javelin throwers made a game of tying lines to their spears so they could hurl them at the sharks who came to pick through the ship's wake for garbage.

These were heady days and I admit I didn't get nearly as much sleep as I ought. My hernia whined a bit as well but I was determined not to let it bother me. Our days were given to practicing, playing shipboard games and reading. We had no cares about being fed or housed. Nate had asked Coach to let us bunk together. He was comfortable with me. We had known each other a long time and we were both different—me the only colored member of the team and he with his half-hand. We were pretty well inseparable, taking all our meals together. Those meals were indeed memorable. They fed us curried lamb, spaghetti, roast beef and mutton, coconut custard tarts so tasty that I'd half a mind to beg the recipe for Daddy.

After a hearty meal, our conversation was almost always turned toward the shores of England and the games. We talked about what we would do, how we would run, and how many medals we would win.

"Aren't we being a bit arrogant to count our medals before we've won them?" I asked Nate as we strolled the deck after a fine lunch of curried lamb and roasted potatoes.

Nate looked at me sideways and said: "Do you doubt how good we are as a team? And as individuals?"

"No. I just ... I just don't want to jinx us, is all."

Nate laughed. "Oh, there'll be no jinx on us. We'll bring home medals. I know it." With that Nate slapped my shoulder and excused himself to "hit the head." I stood there by the rail and saw myself breaking the ribbon in the 400 meter final over the Atlantic.

"What do you say, Taylor?" came a quiet voice that pulled me back to the deck of the *Philadelphia*. There, seated on a teak steamer, was Bill Hamilton, reading the *Police Gazette*. Bill was a sprinter. He ran the 100 and the 200. He was mighty fast and generally kept pretty much to himself. I guess this was his chance to take the measure of me.

"Hi, Bill."

"So, you're not so sure of our chances, eh?"

"No, sir. I just like to let my feet do the talking, if you know what I mean." I smiled amiably.

He studied me for a few ticks and then went back to the *Gazette*. Just when I thought we were through he broke the silence.

"Says here that coon champion, Johnson, is stalking the real Champ half way around the world demanding a crack at the belt. He's in England right now, to face Ben Taylor, but he wants a shot at Tommy Burns. He sure as hell don't let his feet do his talking. He's got a loud mouth on him."

His fists speak louder, I thought. Aloud, I said, "Is that so?"

Bill began reading the article aloud, but I could only see his lips moving because suddenly all I could hear was the ring of heavy feet on the metal stairs coming up from the lower deck and heavier laughter booming out through a doorway. He just kept on reading as the "Irish Whales," Ralph Rose, John Flanagan and Martin Sheridan—a ton of men, taken altogether—squeezed through the little opening out onto the deck between us. Their laughter stopped at the sight of me just in time to hear Bill finish reading the article.

"'...and Edward VII has chimed in to call on Tommy Burns to give up the title if he won't give Jack Johnson a shot at it.' Imagine that, the Prince of bleeding Wales." he said in his best cockney accent. Then he asked the question: "So Taylor, do you think the big Ethiopian has a chance against good ol' Tommy Burns?"

"What?" snorted Ralph as he glanced at his two companions.

Now understand that Ralph Rose was a shot-putter—a giant of a man six-feet-six-inches tall and weighing more than three hundred pounds. John Flanagan was another

A Novel by Craig T. Williams

mountain-sized fellow, a tough New York City beat cop, and the World record hammer thrower. Martin Sheridan threw the discus. He was also a NYC beat cop, stood six-feet-three-inches tall and had to weigh much more than 200 pounds himself. He was also our team captain, which meant everyone else naturally deferred to him, including me. All three of these cracks were members of the Winged Fist, and none seemed too keen on me being one of them.

There I stood, 175 pounds soaking wet, wishing I were Harry Houdini.

"I asked," reiterated a suddenly impatient Bill Hamilton, "if Taylor here thought the Dinge could beat Burns. He hasn't answered me."

I licked my lips. How could I put this in such a way it would not get me thrown overboard? I smiled, trying to show a good spirit about it all. "Well...I... ah. He *is* the Big Smoke, right? I mean Jack Johnson is one heck of a pugilist and..." I paused as a shadow had come over all of their faces. John Flanagan's right fist balled up and cracked its knuckles in his left palm.

"Why I oughta..." he said.

Just as I figured I was going swimming, Nate and Mel came strolling around the corner, all smiles.

"What's all the hubbub, gents?" said Nate.

"This bony nigger here was just saying that that big Sambo boxer, Johnson, or whatever his name is, is gonna be the next heavyweight Champ of the world!" said Flanagan.

"And we mean to make him eat those words." added Ralph.

Nate laughed and made a "crazy" gesture—his finger going round and round by his left ear. "Humor them," he stage-whispered to me.

"Humor them?" repeated Ralph. "I'll put a whoppin' on the both of you! Nothing worse than an uppity nigger."

Mel turned on him sharply, eyes glinting dangerously. "Except maybe an uppity Irishman. Listen, Doc's got the goods, and you know it. So don't you go callin' him names, you hear me?"

Ralph reddened down into the collar of his shirt and clenched both fists. "Why're you defending this colored boy, Mel? I've heard you go on, yourself, about niggers that don't know their place."

"John is different. He's one of us. He's a runner and a UPenn man and on top of all of that he's a Winged Fister."

Flanagan snorted. "He's about as Irish as this boat."

Nate paused to point to a small plaque on a nearby stanchion. "Can't you read? This boat was refitted in Belfast."

I bit my lip, trying not to laugh aloud at the expression on Flanagan's face.

"Yeah," said Mel, a slow grin pulling his mouth to one side. "Guess he's *Black* Irish."

Nate snorted, then burst into laughter, and I did the same. The other fellows, however, didn't think it quite so funny.

"Come on now, fellas," said Mel, seeing their dark looks. "It ain't worth getting riled over. Taylor here is part of the US team. Besides, he's a healer, not a fighter. Right, Doc?"

"That's right," I agreed..

Martin Sheridan shrugged his big shoulders. "Okay, enough of this guff. We're all here for the stars and stripes. Let's grab some chow before they stop serving." He swung about and led the Whales and Mel to the dining salon. As they walked off staring, a sheepish grin lingered on Bill Hamilton's face. In a moment, he rose too, tucked away his newspaper and hurried after the others.

"What the hell?" said Nate. I just wiped my brow and tried to imagine that finish line over the Atlantic.

30

Olympic Games

July 1908
Games of the IV Olympiad
White City in Shepherd's Bush, London

I was no stranger to Britain, but when I arrived in West London, I did my best not to gawk at the elaborate white buildings and the throngs of people. Blood rushed through me at a frantic pace as I imagined the crowds that would come out to see the contest of the greatest athletes in the world.

Unfortunately the bulk of the eight million people milling about were not there as spectators of the Olympics; their interest was in the Franco-British Exhibition. We were competing for attention with Britain's largest fair, which looked like a winter wonderland because of all the white faces. There were people in the crowd who turned their attention to me with such intensity that I felt like one of the "features of the fair," as I was the only Negro wearing an American uniform.

An ordinary man would find it difficult to be comfortable under such inspection, but in the land I'd come from, I was accustomed to being stared at like a sideshow oddity, examined like a lab specimen, or ignored as though I were invisible. I had crossed the line between the high visibility afforded by my athletic talent and the invisibility conferred on me by the color of my skin. But on this great day, there was no stare that could halt my steps or cause me to lower my eyes. I was here to see this beautiful city and the Great Stadium that loomed ahead.

It was my earnest desire to stop time and carry this moment back to the United States with me, to share it with friends, family, and the children Mary Agnes and I would one day have. Perhaps this moment of great privilege was a taste of what a man might aspire to without the impediments imposed by a society blinded by the color of his skin. I thought of the great Jack Johnson, himself here in England preparing to fight Ben Taylor. I imagined him looking about himself, taking in the sights, and wondering if his pursuit of the new heavyweight champion, Tommy Burns, would result in a final fight for the world championship. What would he say if he could see me now? I'd come a long way since our one conversation. A very long way.

As I moved through the swelling crowds, weariness tugged at me like a sudden weight. Looking ahead to the competition, it was clear I was going to have to draw deeply on my internal resources. We were up at seven o'clock each morning to train and had a curfew of ten o'clock at night. The early mornings were particularly tough for me, as I was not at my best; I had found sleep aboard the *Philadelphia* difficult and so, was fighting travel fatigue and some discomfort from the hernia. I had, perhaps, exaggerated when I promised my doctor I was in "top shape for running." I met the weariness by reminding myself of the significance of my place on this team—an athlete selected to represent my country.

Through Coach Murphy's mandatory requests that we know Olympic history, I had learned that the games were to be held in Rome initially, but were rescheduled when Mount Vesuvius erupted two years ago, devastating the city of Naples and causing Italy's Olympic funds to be used for general reconstruction. The role of host city fell to London, and the Great Stadium had been built especially for the games. Within a year "the Great White City" had gone from a 140-acre farm tract to a spectacular area filled with twenty pavilions, hundreds of buildings, rides, waterways, pagodas, and the most advanced stadium in the world.

The Great Stadium was nothing short of extraordinary, designed for running and cycling tracks, an open-air swimming pool, and space for football, hockey, rugby, and lacrosse. It gave the appearance of a field in which giants would play while the world watched, seated comfortably in the stands.

We were all in awe of the place, and as we toured it, learning where the different events would be held, Nate noticed the flags.

"Wow!" he said pointing, and we all stopped to take in the beauty of the display. They fluttered from standards around the stadium in a rainbow of hues and patterns. The blues of Argentina, Australia, and New Zealand, Finland,

A Novel by Craig T. Williams

France, Greece, Great Britain, the Netherlands, Norway, Russia, and South Africa, gleaming brightly against the reds of Belgium, Bohemia, Canada, Denmark, Germany, Hungary, Italy, Switzerland, and Turkey...

"Wait, a minute..." said Mel, frowning.

We glanced at each other, puzzled, and then counted the flags again ... and again, as though with only twenty-two to account for, we might have missed one. Twenty-two countries were participating in the games, but only twenty flags flew above the field. Two were missing: the Swedish flag and

...

"Where's *our* flag?" asked Nate.

Ralph Rose scowled at the display. "Yeah. Where is the American flag?"

"I don't know," I said, scanning the Great Stadium.

"Surely it must be..." murmured Nate.

"... here somewhere," I finished.

But it was *not* here. The United States flag was not on display.

"It *must* be here," commanded Mel, as if he could make it appear from sheer desire.

"Did they forget us?" I asked.

"How could anybody forget America?" asked Nate.

A wave of shock and outrage washed over us. Was it truly possible to overlook a country as great as ours? Could we possibly have been overlooked by accident, or was someone making a statement about the United States that we, in our arrogance, could not even imagine?

This set the tone for these Olympic Games. We now

prepared to compete without the honor of having our flag displayed like the other countries in attendance. The oversight was a bitter pill to swallow, but in our mouths it became a tonic that would make us work harder, smarter, and stronger. We promised ourselves that if that flag was still not flying on opening day, our resiliency and victory would reveal to all how great an oversight it truly was.

★★★★

July 13, 1908
Opening Ceremony of the IV Olympiad

The downpour of rain, which had threatened to delay the opening ceremonies, gave way to a calm gray sky. The stadium filled with spectators, with newspaper reporters placed prominently and many well-known writers gracing the stands, eager to capture the event. The royal box was populated by the Crown Prince and Princess of Sweden, the Crown Prince and Princess of Greece, and the Duke and Duchess of Connaught and Argyll.

Not so calm as the weather were the hearts of the athletes gathering to pass before those notable folks. Swedish athletes also felt slighted by the absence of their flag and there was some grumbling from that quarter about a protest. None of the participating teams was happy with the fact that all the judges—every last one—were British. The measurements, however, were European—everything was measured in meters. That meant that instead of running 400 yards in a foot race, we would run 400 *meters*, which was 437.4 yards. We had further discovered that all were obliged by Olympic rules to wear knee-length running shorts. We were used to wearing shorts that came only to mid-thigh. Coach Murphy simply said that there were seamstresses in London, by God, so at least that could be remedied.

But there had been no remedy for the flag. When Nate and I entered the stadium for the opening ceremonies, it was still not flying atop the stadium wall. We stood in a chaotic assemblage of athletes watching and waiting our turn to parade out onto the field. We were among the fortunate ones. We got to witness the opening ceremonies with our own eyes and would not have to rely on a secondhand description of the exciting events. Coach Murphy had held back many of the athletes in Brighton, where we were staying, with offered assurances that they would join the Games "when they were called upon for more serious work." I was grateful to him that Nate and I were among the privileged few to attend the opening of the games.

Precisely at 8:00 AM King Edward VII of Britain, along with the Queen, arrived with a train of forty guests. A bugle announced his regal entrance and an anthem was played in his honor. The crowd rose and cheered so passionately that I had to believe King Edward was quite the popular monarch. I stood in awe. It must be something to be so important that trumpets sounded and official anthems were played wherever you went. I surely couldn't imagine it.

The opening ceremonies had the air of the sacred about them and I quickly found myself caught up in the excitement of it all. Whenever Nate and I exchanged glances, I could see that he was as affected by the solemn splendor as I was.

Once the king settled into the royal box and the strains of British anthems had faded into the silvery sky, the competitor gates opened and athletes from all over the world began to march out onto the field to parade before him, two thousand and thirty-five strong. We were proud to be wearing the colors of our countries and aligned behind our respective flag bearers. As I looked into those shining faces, I realized that differences of language were as nothing here. They were no impediment to understanding—patriotic pride shone from every face. We were all on the same ground, sharing the same goals.

I sighed and looked up at Old Glory waving gently on her standard. Our flag bearer, shot-putter Ralph Rose, caught my glance and grinned, giving the standard a shake. The flag rippled in the breeze.

"Where are the Swedes?" asked Nate.

I pulled myself out of my reverie and peered about the group gathered outside the stadium. There was no Swedish flag and no Swedish team. "The Swedes protested after all," I murmured. "What do you make of this madness, Nate?"

He shook his head, baffled. "I don't know. But I don't think they were forgotten at all, John. Nor were we. I think it was intentional."

"Surely they haven't withdrawn from the games," I said. I noticed the Finnish team, just then entering the arena. They marched behind their flag bearer, but he carried no standard. Instead he held his arms tightly to his sides, his expression grim and proud. I called Nate's attention to this.

"What's going on with the Finns?" I asked.

"Coach said they were expected to march behind the *Russian* flag," Nate said, "and they refused. So they're walking without a flag. And when the Irish were ordered to compete for Great Britain, many of them withdrew right on the spot."

"You've got to be kidding," I whispered. I couldn't imagine forgoing the Olympic Games for political reasons.

"That's what Coach says: know your history," he concluded with a wry grin, parroting Coach Murphy. He shook his head. "Staged chaos."

"Indeed it is." So many tempers and nostrils flaring at once, I thought, feeling my own nose twitch with suppressed resentment. There certainly was enough insult to go around. I could not believe that the Olympic Games were getting started on such a bad foot. I had no idea then that it was going to get worse.

Suddenly it was our turn to join the parade. Ralph held our flag high as we formed ranks and entered the stadium. Our entire team took one swift look at the large flags in a row along the stadium walls, nearly in unison, to draw attention to the fact that our flag had still not been raised there.

Then I was overcome by the moment, by the vista of that huge, sweeping oval with its bright green central sward of grass and its grandly rising rows of seats, every one filled with spectators—most of them Brits. I felt the crunch of the track's cinders beneath the soles of my shoes and longed to run headlong past the orderly stream of athletes and taste the place—to feel the breezes of England in my face as I ran my heart out for America.

I did not do that. I contained myself and settled for absorbing everything about this moment—us marching in US uniforms, following Old Glory around the stadium.

When we arrived at the royal box, Ralph hesitated. It was customary, we'd been told, for each flag bearer to dip the head of his flagstaff as a sign of respect of the royals. Ralph looked directly at King Edward as we marched past the royal box, then faced forward and led us on around the track. He did not dip, bow, nod, wave … *nothing*.

We followed suit, holding our heads up high, amused by the fact that we had just said, in a public, but nonthreatening manner, *"To hell with your customs—where's our flag?"*

Our countrymen in the stands (and I imagine any Swedes, Irish, and Finns present) burst into laughter while the English stiffened in their seats. Surely they thought we were a wild bunch indeed, Yankees to the core—disrespectful and obnoxious. Perhaps we were, but it was tit for tat. If they were going to slight us, we could certainly return the favor.

I could barely keep the smile off my face. "What do you make of that, Nate?" I mumbled.

He grinned unrepentantly. "Very bold."

As we left the stadium later, we were mobbed by reporters asking about the absence of a ritual nod. Martin Sheridan, our team captain, gripped the flagstaff and told them, "This flag dips to no earthly king."

A Novel by Craig T. Williams

Well, as you might imagine, this caused a great fuss. It was a bit intimidating—all that negative attention, all those hostile questions—but we supported Martin. The English had shown no respect to us or our flag. Why should we show respect for their king?

"Ever get the feeling the water you're in is far deeper than it looks on the surface?" I asked Nate.

"Yeah," he replied with a slow, steady nod, his eyes on the ring of clamoring reporters. "And this is starting to look like an ocean."

If the British officials now looked at us as though we had an unpleasant odor, the British press surely had its own unflattering opinion of us. The Yanks were whiners, they said. Whiners and ruffians who showed disrespect for the British crown and who thought they were God's gift to the world of athletics. The British team, the newspapers said, would put us in our place.

I knew then that these summer Olympics would be more than an enjoyable challenge—they would be a battle of wills.

★★★★

July 14, 1908
Men's 1500 meter Final

It was Mel Sheppard who took up the challenge in the Men's 1500 meter race. He ran his first heat on opening day (wearing shorts tailored to our specifications) and won a place in the final, setting an Olympic record while he was at it. Nate and I would not have missed the final for the world and so found ourselves trackside watching from behind Coach Murphy when they called *Marks! Set! Drive!*

We suspected the British runner, Joe Deakin, would not contend as he might be saving himself for the relay. He didn't. It was his teammate, Ivo Fairbairn-Crawford who came out of the blocks first and set the pace.

Oh, but he didn't set it fast enough for our Mel. Crawford was white hot, surely, but he spent himself in the first 500 meters and couldn't shake Mel Sheppard, who breezed past him and settled into his stride. That was when Vince Loney, another British runner, took over the lead, but Crawford had forced everyone to run that first 500 meters hotter than they'd probably meant to and Mel was dogging him step for step.

Dear Lord, what must it have been like to hear those footsteps right behind you, knowing that you had to hold on for another 1000 meters, knowing that, in that last stretch, you might not have anything left to give!

They were in a loose pack with 300 meters to go. It was anyone's race, if only they had the speed left in them to make that last push. The Brit, Harry Wilson, thought he had it. He made his move on the final turn, pumping for all he was worth. He led out of the turn and into the straight, his teammate, Norman Hallows, on his heels. The British in the crowd went wild—roaring victory … until Mel Sheppard made his move.

Coming off the turn, he sailed—he soared. Flying for

the finish line and that blessed tape. He moved past Wilson and Hallows as if they were walking, and broke the tape with at least two meters between him and Wilson.

Nate and I had been jumping up and down, yelling ourselves hoarse through that entire final 300 meters. As the tape broke we threw our arms around each other and danced around, pounding each other on the back.

"Mel's golden!" I shouted, and Nate picked up the cry: "Gold! Gold! Gold!"

Coach Murphy, standing several feet closer to the track, turned and gave us a raised eyebrow. "Gentlemen," he said sternly, though his mouth threatened to smile, and his eyes gleamed with pride, "I would advise you not to spend your best energy in celebrating Mel's victory when you have your own to think about."

We subsided with silly grins and bobbing heads and mumbles of "Yes, Coach." But we danced our way out of the stadium.

★★★★

July 17, 1908
Tug of War

I had never personally thought of tug of war as an "athletic" event, yet there it was on the program. We had put our strongest men in the event. That meant the Irish Whales and some of their equally massive peers were entered. Other than the British teams—all policemen, I gathered—there were only us and the Swedes in the contest and we were confident of a win, or at least Ralph Rose was.

"We've got it all over them for size," he said, casting a critical eye on the team of British "bobbies." "And what's that they've got on their feet?"

What they had on their feet were their service boots—or rather retired service boots, for these were worn and scratched and disreputable, and looked outlandish with the sports gear the Brits were wearing. We hid our smiles, Nate and I, and nodded astutely at each other.

"We'll soon teach those lads a lesson," said Bobbie Cloughen, who'd come to join us in the stands.

"What's the news, Bobbie?" Nate asked. "Are you on the team?"

Bobbie grinned. "I am. Coach put me in as a late entry."

Bobbie was quite the story. He hadn't made the team during the trials, but out of sheer determination, he'd made his way to England on a tramp steamer and petitioned the team manager, Mr. Sullivan, to let him join in. I don't know what was said or how he did it, but he did it. I had to admire that about Bobbie.

"What events will you run, Bob?" Nate asked.

"I'm to go in the 100 and 200 meters." He just got the words out before succumbing to a fit of coughing.

"You all right, Bobbie?" I asked. "You look pale."

He waved dismissively. "Ah, the sea air don't agree with me is all. That and I didn't sleep so well on the way over. Everything smells of garlic in steerage." He laughed, then coughed again.

I had to admire that, too. Bobbie Cloughen was a man after my own heart—not one to let a little ailment knock him down. I told my hernia to profit from his example.

"Look, look!" Nate pointed. "There go the Whales!"

There they went, indeed. Sheridan, Flanagan and Rose, supplemented by six other worthies: Burroughs, Dearborn, McGrath, Talbot, Coe, and Horr.

"Ah, now what do they need those other guys for?" asked Bobbie. "Those Englishmen don't stand a chance against our boy-Os. They look like kids out there."

I had to allow that our men had superior size and while I'd read that these policemen used this skill of theirs on the job for rescues and that it was not all about strength, I was skeptical. Sounded like bluster to me.

The two teams lined up, took up their ropes and got set. The thick rope was elevated and a judge moved out to make sure that the tape marking its center was over the center mark on the ground. That tape was the thing to watch, for when it moved twelve feet to one side or the other and crossed into a team's territory, the game was won.

Nate, Bobbie and I settled ourselves back for a hard-fought battle.

"Who'll wager that our men pull them straight over?" asked Bobbie.

"Now, I hear it's not all about size and strength," I cautioned.

"In a pig's eye."

Nate nudged Bobbie in the ribs. "They're starting."

The judge stood off to one side, checked the center tape over its mark, checked the two teams then shouted, "Heave!"

I could scarcely believe what happened next. The Brits pulled as one—and so swiftly, so vigorously—that the Americans literally fell onto their faces. There was a moment of stunned silence, then the crowd around us went wild with jubilation.

"They yanked the Yanks right off their feet!" cried someone close by.

I blinked, then looked over at Nate and Bobbie as blood rushed to my face. They were both redder than radishes and I knew that if I were as pale-skinned as they I'd look equally embarrassed.

Out on the field, as the Liverpool bobbies were awarded the first heat win, the Irish Whales marched from the field of battle, humbled. The three of us scrambled to meet up with them in the locker area beneath the stands.

"What happened, Martin?" asked Nate of our team captain.

Martin looked like a vengeful god, a towering Thor or Odin. He was so beside himself, he couldn't speak and it was John Flanagan who answered, pounding a beefy fist into his palm.

"They cheated is what," he snarled. "Cheated plain and simple."

"Aye," agreed Ralph Rose, who'd been third on the rope behind Martin. "They must've done. Pulled early."

Some of the others nodded and murmured in agreement, but Martin was shaking his head.

"No. No, I saw 'em. They didn't pull until after the judge gave the go. It wasn't that they went early."

"Well, what then?" asked Bobbie. "How'd they beat the Flying Fist?"

Ralph looked around at the others, his face grim. "Those boots."

"What?"

"Those silly boots they were wearing. They're not regulation. For all we know they might have hobnails or spikes."

More nodding.

"I say we protest," said Flanagan. "We protest those boots. Make the judges check 'em."

Every one of us looked at Martin to see what he would say. He was silent and still for a long moment, then he nodded, grim fury in his eyes. "We protest the boots."

★★★★

July 21, 1908
Men's 400 meter Race, Preliminary Heats

The US tug of war team had protested the Brits boots that very day, but we heard nothing official for the better part of a week. The newspapers had gotten hold of it, of course, and spoke of how we Yanks would no doubt attribute every loss to cheating, such whiners were we. We were being laughed at, and we knew it. It wasn't pleasant.

As I stood on the sidelines for the preliminary heats of

the 400 meter run with some of the other American runners, watching Paul Pilgrim get set, Nate appeared at my side. The fact that he had news was written plainly on his face.

"What is it?" I asked, one eye on Nate and one eye on the track where Paul loosened up.

"They ruled on the tug of war team's protest. The boots were legal. No spikes. No hobnails. No advantage. That's what the judges said."

"What did the British team say?"

"That they'd be happy to do the contest again in their stocking feet if that's what the Yanks wanted."

"And?" I took my attention off the field.

Nate shrugged. "Our team dropped the protest."

I leaned closer to him. "D'you think the boots were a cheat, Nate?"

"Nah. I think our guys were just caught by surprise."

We got caught by surprise then, too, as the starter's gun went off and the first round of heats commenced.

Paul didn't win his heat, which was disappointing since there was only one other runner. He lost by yards. There was no one in the second heat and only one runner in the third due to folks pulling out, but we had a field of three in my heat. I admit, though, that I felt as if I was the only one who had come to race. It was my first official run on English soil and I was keyed up and eager.

I flew.

I soared.

I felt strong … and I won by a dozen yards, making my

move late in the race as was my habit. And the hernia? It seemed to have given up plaguing me. At least I didn't feel it while I was running.

In the second round of heats, we Americans were a mixed bag. J. C. Carpenter won his heat, the British runner, Wyndham Halswelle, won the second heat. Halswelle was an impressive athlete. I had heard he liked to come from behind as I did. But in this race, he flew to the lead and kept it, pulling away from there to win by at least a dozen yards with a time of forty-eight and two-fifths seconds. This then, was a man to watch. I'd no doubt I would face him in the medal round and knew that if he ran that way in the finals, I would be hard-pressed to wear him down.

This didn't worry me. I had learned under Coach Murphy that I could adapt. If Wyndham Halswelle forced me to do that here, I would.

I went into my own heat, running against another American, Horace Ramey, a Brit named Ryle and a Frenchman—Georges Malfait. At the starter's shot, it was Malfait who took the lead. I leapt after him and pushed, Horace pumping hard at my heels. As I ran, I thought about Halswelle. About how he'd run his semifinal heat. The temptation was great in me to push forward now, just to see if I could take the lead early and hold it. But I didn't. I didn't make my move until just about 300 meters. Then I lengthened my stride and struck out for the finish line, drawing Horace with me. In the last fifty meters, I could hear another runner pressing us—I suspected it was Ryle—but he had no chance. I was almost laughing as I crossed the finish line with over five meters to spare. In two days, I would run against the best of the British runners. I would go for gold against Wyndham Halswelle and I would win. I could taste the win.

★★★★

July 23, 1908
Men's 400 meter Race Final

The field for the Men's 400 meter race was composed of myself, J. C. Carpenter and William Robbins of America, and Wyndham Halswelle of Great Britain.

"I'd say we have a good chance at a medal," quipped J. C. as we huddled with Coach Murphy on the sidelines before the race.

The rest of us snickered, but Coach shushed us up. "You see those men along the track?"

We turned and looked. There was, indeed, an official posted every fifty yards.

"What's that about, Coach?" asked William.

"They're umpires. They're there to make sure we don't cheat."

"We?" I asked. "You mean … the American team?"

He nodded soberly. "You know how it's been since the games began. The flags, the protests…"

"The fact that we've already shown we can win big," interrupted J. C.

Coach silenced him with a look. "The fact that there are three of you to their one. Three of our best, to one of theirs."

He smiled. "Run your hardest."

That went without asking.

"And above all, run fair," he added, tilting his chin toward the umpires.

We understood what the coach was saying very well. The Brits didn't trust us, which meant we had to be more than cautious. It was not friendly air in which to run, but I had been trained to focus on my race, not on my opponent.

In a drizzle of rain, with time stilled in the heavy, moist air, I moved into position and took my mark—fourth from the verge. It was a bad spot. It gave away valuable yards that I knew from the beginning would be tough to regain, but I would not whine about it. J. C. had a good spot—number one, right on the verge. Halswelle was in the second position and Robbins in the third. I thought again of the race Halswelle had run two days ago. Would he try to take the lead and hold it or would he let one of us set the pace?

And as I hovered between stillness and flight, I felt a surge of confidence. It didn't matter, I told myself. Regardless of my place on the track, no matter how well Halswelle ran, I could still win this race. I *would* win it.

Marks.

Set.

Drive.

The starter's pistol fired, and with a wind born of rage, fire, and fury, we flew from the blocks. William Robbins, who'd had the fastest qualifying time, edged out in front. By halfway through the race, he had opened up a twelve meter lead. The crowd was in a frenzy, shouting, screaming, roaring.

Their movement was a multicolored blur at the edges of my sight.

I didn't care about Robbins. I was thinking about Halswelle, watching him, gauging what he would do. I had the uncanny sensation that he was doing the same thing with me. I had met his eyes as I moved past him to take my position on the track. We each knew the other as THE rival—the one to watch, the one to beat. And so we both hung back.

At 200 meters, he made a move that left me in last place, pushing past me and past J.C. I took my attention from Halswelle and focused all my attention on the back of J.C.'s jersey. Out of the tail of my eye, I could see Robbins begin to fade. He'd pushed too hard from the beginning. In a few strides, J.C. and Halswelle were past him, and then J.C. edged out in front of Halswelle and began closing in on the final turn.

Then Halswelle made a mistake. Instead of taking an inside path, he swung wide on the last turn in an attempt to pass J.C.

It was time. *My* time. I made my move, plotting an inside route.

Suddenly, along the sidelines, one of the British officials flung his arms over his head and pulled off his hat. "Foul!" he cried, wildly waving his head gear. "No race! Foul! No contest! *Stop the race!*"

Out of nowhere one of the umpires blindsided me, tackling me from the sidelines, and shouting in my ear, "Foul! Foul! No race!" As I fell I saw a second official stepped for-

A Novel by Craig T. Williams

ward and cut the finish tape, nullifying the race. He too began to shout, waving off the runners with emphatic gestures. *"No contest! No contest!"*

From the ground I watched the tape float to the track in utter disbelief. I didn't know what to do, and in a cruel moment, the decision was taken from me. One of the umpires blindsided me, tackling me from the sidelines, and shouting in my ear, "Foul! Foul! No race!"

John Carpenter ran on, unfazed, with officials trying to catch up with him and hold him. It would have been funny under any other circumstances—a bunch of middle-aged gentlemen trying to capture one of the fastest men in the world. It was like watching a bunch of milk cows trying to run down a thoroughbred. J.C. crossed the fallen tape with a time of 47.8 seconds. Robbins, too, crossed the finish line unimpeded, barely eluding the grasp of the officials who tried to pull him from the track.

I was the only one they had stopped. The only one who never made it to the finish line. I was shocked and hot with anger. Words of rage leapt to my tongue, but I swallowed them down, bitter as they were. I wanted no charge that I was "unsportsmanlike." I had never been pulled from a track while running in my entire career. I don't know anyone that had. Why had it happened now?

I shrugged off the sweating umpire and made my way to where the United States team officials and athletes had gotten into a head-to-head confrontation with the British officials, who continued to cry "foul." What sort of foul did they imagine had been committed?

I found out soon enough. Amid the loud protests and finger-pointing, the charge emerged that J.C. had cut Halswelle off by crossing into his "lane" on the final turn.

"Carpenter all but pushed him off the track!" said one of the men. "He ran wide on the turn and forced Halswelle to the outside."

"Why did you wait until we were thirty yards down the stretch to call it, then?" demanded J.C.

"More to the point," said Robbins, "why didn't your man simply run to the inside? J.C. always goes wide on the turns. He did it during his heats and you didn't call it foul then."

"What do you say to that, Mr. Badger?" one of the other judges asked the umpire.

"I say they were pocketing him. They'd done it on the first turn as well, only it was this other man, Robbins, who went wide."

"Pocketing him!" cried Robbins. "We were running our race, just like Coach told us—hard but fair. We knew you were watching us, waiting to catch us out. Why would we foul anyone?"

"It's ridiculous," said J.C. in a quiet voice that somehow cut through the chaos. "How can you imagine that we might pocket as good a man as Halswelle? We simply raced him off his feet."

The Brits responded with a thunderous protest and the crowd joined in. They began to pour onto the field to take up the argument. In mere moments, I was drowning in people, being pushed and shoved, spun about. The noise was unbearable. It was as if all the world's winds and thunders and roaring waterfalls had come to this place—as if every train rumbled through my head. Men ripped hats from each other's heads and stomped them into the ground. Fists flew. The officials were overcome.

I fixed my eyes on the grandstand and, hands over my ears, began to make my way toward the spot where a gate opened up into the facilities beneath the rows of seats. Other athletes had reached the safe haven before me and watched the crowd in shocked amazement, awaiting some form of direction from coaches or officials. In all my years of running I had never seen such a chaotic mess. It was a vast sea of boiling humanity. Finally English bobbies appeared on the field in an effort to restore order. I saw their dark blue hats as they moved through the crowd, blowing shrill whistles, prodding and poking with their truncheons. It took nearly an hour of hysteria before they gained control of the rowdy mob and sent it from the stadium.

Later, officials on both sides thrashed it out—the British leveling a foul against John Carpenter for interfering with the "natural outcome" of the race, our team officials protesting such a conclusion. In our eyes it was the umpires who had interfered with the race. The British maintained that the rules set strict guidelines on when a man was allowed to leave his lane, and that we had violated them. We counter-protested that this was not a rule in US athletics and that we had never been informed of it.

Our protests fell on deaf ears—the rules were the rules. Photographs taken by the event's chroniclers were called for, and statements taken from every one of the umpires. Of course, J. C. had run wide on the turn. He always did. And though we protested that Halswelle had ample room to pass him on either side if he'd had the stamina and speed to do so, the foul was upheld, It was ruled unintentional by the judges, but even so the British coaches labeled it "unsportsmanlike" and declared that such behavior was "not to be condoned." The Olympic committee was wise, they said, to have posted those umpires along the track. The Yanks were every bit as underhanded as the newspapers had said—no more than a bunch of hooligans dressed up in athletic garb.

John Carpenter was beside himself. "This is an absurd allegation!" he protested to the bevy of reporters on hand. "It was called to save the British the embarrassment of a loss. Halswelle made a mistake in judgment and it cost him the win. That's all." He wrapped himself in his stylish raincoat— for the sky had opened up again as if to express its opinion of the situation—and swept dramatically from the field.

The British still in the stands stood and booed him. They were making a habit of booing American athletes and had halted at least one competition, upsetting the contestants with their jeers to the extent that the event had to be postponed.

I watched, dejected, as J. C. left the field holding his head high. Having been accused of cheating myself, I understood his outrage. We were not cheaters. We were damn good runners. The best! We had no need to resort to underhanded tactics. What seemed underhanded to me was this on-again-off-again applying of the rules. If it was a foul to cut across the lanes, why had we not been informed of it? More to the point: why hadn't they called us (or anyone else) on it when it happened during the heats leading up to the final? Or when William Robbins had gone wide on the very first turn?

By the end of the day, the chairman of the London Olympic Games had announced that the 400 meter race was officially nullified and would be rerun two days later. John Carpenter would not be allowed to participate. That left it to William Robbins and me to carry the flag for America.

Nate, Mel and I tried to exorcise the demon Fury by cheering for Bobbie Cloughen in his semifinal for the 200 meter race. I have to admit, the sport worked its spell on me, at least. Bobbie had won his preliminary heat with a time of 23.4 seconds. He posted a time of 22.6 seconds to take the semifinal. He was ecstatic and accepted our congratulations sincerely, his eyes aglow.

"Goin' for the gold, John," he told me. "I'm goin' for the gold."

It was in a mixed atmosphere of celebration and disappointment that we returned to Brighton for the evening and settled into the parlor of our hotel. After everyone had congratulated Bobbie, we fell into an uneasy silence. William Robbins broke it.

"Well, I suppose we're lucky the Brits didn't consider Bobbie's win cheating."

J.C. snorted. "Maybe they'll wait for the finals tomorrow."

"It's a damned injustice!" William slammed his fist onto the arm of his chair, his face dark with fury.

"It's absurd," agreed J.C.

"It's the rules," I said. "Theirs are different than ours and I don't think that's fair. Seems to me, there ought to be Olympic rules that everyone has to follow no matter what country the games are held in."

"Or at least," said Mel. "If they felt the damn rules stood a chance of causing a nullified race, they ought to have made damn sure everyone knew what they were. No one told us you couldn't cut to the outside. In fact, runners have been doing it right and left until now."

"They want to win," I said simply. "As much as we do, I guess."

"Then let's let them win," said Mel. He turned his steely gaze to J.C.

I saw the spark of comprehension in John's eyes just as I felt it creep into my own mind.

"I couldn't ask it," J.C. said. "I *wouldn't* ask it."

William leaned forward in his chair. "Then I'll ask it: Why should we run in a travesty of race? I say we boycott it. We don't run." He looked at me. "What do you say, John?"

What did I say? This was my chance at an individual medal. Yes, I was to run in the relay later in the games, but this—this was my sole chance at an individual Olympic medal. And I knew that if the race went forward the next day, Halswelle didn't stand a chance against us. He would medal—we all would—but he would not take gold. I knew it in my heart.

I turned my eyes to John Carpenter. He had done nothing unsportsmanlike. He had not deserved to be suspended from the race. They had applied their "rules" unfairly and with bias. I knew that in my heart too.

My place is with my team, with my countrymen.

"I say we boycott," I said. "I say we stand together and Halswelle runs alone."

"Are you sure, men?"

We looked up as one to see Coach Murphy watching us from the doorway, his eyes steady and more solemn than I had ever seen them.

We took stock of ourselves, trading glances, then I said, "We're sure, Coach."

"Then I shall not protest the decision of the USOC."

"What decision?" asked J. C.

"Our Olympic Committee has issued a formal statement to the Brits that our team will not participate in the 'do-over' two days from now. I'd have protested it, or at least gotten your opinion of it. But it seems you have come to the same decision on your own. We will not run where the rules are applied haphazardly or with prejudice."

Final, then. It was final. There would be no individual gold medal for John Baxter Taylor, Jr. in this Olympics.

I realized something in that moment. While the idea of not running was painful, more painful still was knowing that we were viewed as whiners and cheaters when we were neither. And there was no way to prove ourselves.

Except, perhaps, to continue to win. Fair. Clean. Uncontested.

"So do we just not show up?" asked J.C. "Won't they take that as cowardice? I won't have you all taken as cowards on my account."

"I say we suit up and go," I said. "I say we go to the venue and stand in silent protest so they see it's not cowardice, but justice driving us."

"Here, here!" said Nate from the corner where he'd been watching us all. That was followed by a round of affirmations.

Coach cleared his throat and said, "Gentlemen, I am as proud of you at this moment as I would have been if one of you had won that race. I approve your plan. The day of the race, dress down, go to the track and stand in silent protest … together."

Later, as we went to our rooms for the night, Coach drew me aside, his gaze steady and piercing. "You all right with this, John? I know how much this means to you, especially."

He did not add "because you're the only Negro athlete here," but he didn't have to say it.

"I've been at the wrong end of injustice before, Coach. What sort of man would I be if I didn't stand up for someone else in that same position—a fellow American, a teammate? J. C. didn't cheat. He didn't foul Halleswelle."

Coach smiled at me. "All for one and one for all, eh?" He patted me on the shoulder. "Good man. Now hit the hay."

I did "hit the hay," but sleep made itself a stranger that night.

★★★★

A Novel by Craig T. Williams

Saturday, July 25, 1908
400 meter Run-Off Event

Two days later, I woke with a pit in my gut. Two nights of broken sleep had done little to soothe the fever of anguish within, and as we made our way back to the stadium for the rerunning of the 400 meter race, we moved in silence. Sometimes doing what you know is right is hard. Sometimes there are no easy choices, or painless choices, or good choices—there is only the *right* choice. I wish I could say that once that decision was made, peace would come. But that's not always so. And there was plenty going on to wreck our peace in any event. Word of the outcome of the original race had hit the papers, pubs, and gossip mills hard, and there was plenty of opinion in the air about the matter of the Brits and the Americans.

"Where do you stand, men?" asked Coach Murphy as we gathered at trackside.

"On our own two feet," I said in reply, and the others said "Aye" and that was the end of it.

When we were called to take our mark for the race, William Robbins and I stood just off the official field, with our arms down at our sides in protest. In that moment, I knew with all my being that it was the right thing to do—the right and *only* thing—regardless of the fact that the race would be called and go on without us.

Then peace came.

Marks.

Set.

Drive.

The starter fired his pistol and the Brit, Wyndham Halswelle, began the 400 meter race alone and looking unhappy but resolute. The British newspapers said that evening that he ran with "personal dignity." Perhaps he did. I certainly held no grudge against him. He had merely run. He had never claimed he was fouled nor said anything about us pocketing him.

In the end he would win the Olympic gold with a time of 50.2 seconds. J.C. had posted a time of 47.8 two days before.

★★★★

Later in the Day
1600 Meter Sprint Medley Relay

We had secured for ourselves one last chance of redemption in the eyes of the world. We had a position in the last race—the 1600 meter medley relay—before the queen's distribution of the gold medals. By the time I took my position on the field, tension and emotion had reached a boil. This, notwithstanding the general sense of exhaustion from the heightened drama surrounding the men's 400 meter race. All of the theatrics had caused such a ruckus that I was beginning to feel scattered and out-of-focus, and a little weaker of body and spirit than before. Still, we were buoyed by other victories as we took our marks for the relay. Bobbie Cloughen had taken the silver in the 200 meter final the day before and Nate the bronze. And Mel had not only won the 1500 meter, he had set a new world record doing it.

We were staggered to run the sprint medley in the following order: Billy Hamilton from the University of Louisville, who would run the first 200 meter leg, followed by Nate, who was the IC4A sprint champion in the 100 yard and 220 yard dashes that year. And though J. C. Carpenter had led the Americans at the finish of the disputed 400 meter race, I was assigned third leg on the sprint medley instead, with strong direction from Coach Murphy.

"Run flat out," he ordered, "none of this coming from behind nonsense. You won't have time for it."

I opened my mouth to protest, then simply nodded and said: "Yes, sir."

The 800 meter leg of the relay belonged to Mel Sheppard, who was the undisputed world record-holder in the 800 meters.

"Let's make it a clean sweep," said Nate as the four of us made our way to the field, "and take back what belongs to us."

"Take it back," I agreed wholeheartedly.

"You bet," said Billy Hamilton.

"No foul." Nate looked through my eyes and into my soul.

I returned his gaze. "No foul."

Mel held out his hand, palm down. "Go for the gold."

The Olympian: An American Triumph

"Go for the gold," the rest of us chanted, putting our hands over his.

The mood was tense as we took our positions, and I kept a close eye on anything that might jeopardize our hopes or be cause for another riot. The hunger for blood, the thirst for payback, still lingered in the air.

The crowd, too, was restless, noisy and watchful. I looked at the officials on hand. Some observers had offered the opinion that in stopping the 400 meter final, they had responded to the mood of their audience, which was upset by seeing Halswelle outrun. Was that true? Would they do something like that here? There were no British runners in the race, we had beaten them in the qualifying heats by a good twenty-five yards. But I knew that even that might be grounds for a grudge.

Pál Simon of Hungary and Arthur Hoffman of Germany took their places with Billy Hamilton, who had drawn an outside position. I watched, chewing my lip.

The starter raised his pistol.

Marks.

Set.

Drive.

Hamilton leapt from his starting position with such force that within fifty yards, he had taken the inside lane—he was so far ahead no call of "foul" could possibly have stuck; Nate started his leg with a six yard lead on his opponents—Vilmos Rácz of Hungary and Hans Eicke of Germany. The crowd gave in to reckless abandon. Already on their feet, they shouted in a frenzy.

I wanted to shout, too, but I couldn't. I had to hold that fierceness in. Light a fire to it. Make it steam. I had to be ready to fly out of the blocks.

As the men made their way down the track, I could see that the other teams were no match for Nate's fury as he blazed his 200 meters, nearly scorching the ground as he ran.

My heart swelled in my breast with adrenaline and fierce pride. I bit my lip and fought the urge to yell.

No foul, Nate. No contest. Just run. Fill your sails with wind. A victory wind.

Hungary and Germany chased Nate desperately, but in vain. He bore down on me well ahead. I leapt away from him, beginning my 400 meters with an eight yard lead. Within the first two steps I had lost all sense of the world around me. I was borne forward on a hot wind of fierce desperation. It was sufficient. I did as Coach had asked—I gave it my all from the first step and the gap between me and my opponents—Otto Trieloff of Germany and József Nagy of Hungary—widened. Notwithstanding that I was running flat out from the start, I pulled away dramatically in the last 100 yards. The sounds of their labored breathing and fleeting steps fell away, faded, and were silenced. I was alone at the front, and hearing nothing but the wind of my own passage. I saw the crowds in the stands—all on their feet now—arms waving, mouths open in a wordless roar.

The Olympian: An American Triumph

I couldn't hear them. Couldn't feel them. Were they cheering me on or booing my progress?

I didn't care.

There was no strategy here, no careful pacing, no thought, just me and the wind and my desire. I ran what felt like the freest race of my life. *Free at last!*

I wanted to laugh out loud as I blazed a lonely trail down the track, but laughter required breath and I must give all of that to the race. Instead, I offered up one gigantic smile. I was the Black Eagle and I had come all this way to *fly*. I *was* flying.

I ran this race for the slaves who had never known freedom.

I ran this race for Mama and for Daddy.

I ran this race for Clinton, Hattie, William, and Mary Agnes.

I ran this race for the people of Philadelphia.

I ran this race for the great nation of America.

But most of all, I ran this race for me.

Fly, Black Eagle. Fly.

The officials clocked my time at 49.8 seconds, before I turned over the baton and a fifteen yard lead to Mel Sheppard. Mel, with the grace and dignity of a true Olympian, carried us home to Olympic gold with a twenty-five yard lead, just because he could.

We shouted in victory as Mel broke the finish tape. I leapt several feet off the ground. *Gold!*

We did it!

We did it!

A Novel by Craig T. Williams

We won!

With such a staggering performance, it hardly seemed as though it *was* a race at all. But it was a race—an official race—clean and beyond reproach. There were no accusations with which to contend, nor any questioning looks from the crowd of spectators. No one would call us cheaters, or dishonorable.

The crowd was still on its feet and applauding our ownership of Olympic gold when the Band of Grenadier Guards began to play "See the Conquering Hero Comes!" We were ushered across the grass to the corner of the arena where the drums and bugles of the Irish Guard played us to a spot before the royal box. There Coach Murphy received beautiful gold medals from Her Majesty Princess Alexandra, who was accompanied by Lord Desborough, members of the International Olympic Committee, and members of the British Olympic Council. We also accepted certificates from the marshals—each one made up with a sprig of oak leaves from Windsor Forest, tied up with the Union Jack.

If I had slept my whole life and dreamed every second, I could not have imagined such a scene. Words capable of conveying the experience to my family back home would be in short supply. Oh, no, there were none. All that I could think of, as I stood filled with pride was how to translate this experience and carry it over into every beat of my life, from this moment forward. To live *life every* day as a champion—that would be my mission.

I was a rich man now—filled to capacity with the spirit of the invincible athlete who knows nothing but glory.

31

Homecoming

August 31, 1908
Sagamore Hill
Oyster Bay, New York

"See the Conquering Hero Comes."

That pretty much describes our return to America. It was a theme song we carried in our souls as we debarked from the *Mauritania* with weary bodies and grateful hearts, thankful to be on dry, solid land. New York City was a welcome sight. It was good, good, good to be home. I'd gotten a bit of a cold (for which I blamed Bobbie Cloughen for coughing all over me the day he joined the games), and I was feeling a bit run down, though I was pleased the hernia seemed to have surrendered.

Our fellow Americans received us as if we were, indeed, conquering soldiers returning from battle. Surely a battle had been fought in Britain—both on the field and in the press—and we had prevailed; I wore the golden badge of honor around my neck as confirmation. It was the deepest honor to see thousands lining the streets in praise of our accomplishments.

The Olympian: An American Triumph

Two days later we boarded another, much smaller ship, the *Sagamore,* a boat owned by the Long Island Railroad, to honor a special request. We had been summoned to the "summer White House"—the home of President Theodore Roosevelt. The president had been unable to join the ten thousand that formed a parade in our honor, so he had requested our presence at his own home.

We approached the president's house from the ocean, steaming up the Atlantic coast toward Oyster Bay. It was there that our party was delayed three miles out, for our steamer was too large and the water too shallow for us to travel directly to the president's dock. This caused a delay in our expected arrival. A small fleet of rowboats appeared as rescuers to take us from our large boat to the shore, where we landed one hour after our appointed time.

One man began to whistle, and we all followed in a double line, marching up the hill and whistling "A Hot Time in the Old Town." Every man paused when we caught sight of Sagamore Hill. The large home appeared to stretch up into the sky and flow into the trees. The porch was wide and inviting and seemed the perfect place for a family to relax. I smiled at the thought of being in the company of Mr. Roosevelt again.

We approached the residence and paused at the steps, where the president of the United States and his wife stood in the doorway to greet us. They were like a family welcoming its sons home for a good meal, and that's how we were treated from that moment on, with great respect. The president and his wife created a reception line with our executive committee: James Sullivan, United States commissioner of the Olympic Games and an acquaintance of the Roosevelt's; P. J. Conway, president of the Irish-American Athletic Club; William McGloughlin, secretary of the Athletic Parade; and members of the Roosevelt family.

Each athlete proceeded to shake hands and receive congratulations before heading into the house. John Hayes, the marathon winner, entered first, followed by Mel Sheppard, now the greatest short-distance runner in the world, then sprinting champion James Rector, weight thrower John Flanagan, and myself.

I swelled with pride when President Roosevelt smiled big, gave me a warm greeting, and exclaimed, "I am very glad to see you. You did nobly."

I returned his firm handshake and said, my voice raspy from my cold, the prolonged sea journey, and much celebrating, "Thank you, sir. Your words mean very much to me."

James Sullivan began to introduce Coach Murphy to the president, but Mr. Roosevelt interrupted him, though not unkindly. "We don't have to be introduced. Coach Murphy is an American institution. I am mighty glad to see you," he said to Coach, who smiled at the words and turned a nice shade of red as he entered the house.

We gathered in the library, turning round and about, trying to take in all the deer heads, antlers, skins, guns, and trophies hanging on the walls. We swung toward the library door in unison when the president appeared there.

"Gentlemen," he said, "I want to say one word of greeting to you. I am sure you know that everyone in America is proud of you. I think it is the literal truth. The feat that this team has performed has never been duplicated in the history of athletics. I think it is the biggest victory by any team of any nation, and I congratulate all of you."

Well, with that, we burst into applause and someone requested a cheer for President Roosevelt, calling him the greatest president the country had ever had. We yelled so loudly in response we nearly shook the roof off the house.

"And you, sir," the president said to Mel Sheppard. "Two world records and three gold medals? I am impressed. Which are you proudest of, son?"

"Well, sir, winning the 1500 was the proudest moment of my life," Mel said humbly. "If I'd died at the finish, why, that would've been fine with me as long as I hit the tape first."

"I wish I could have been there," the president said. "It was the greatest race I've ever read about. Will you sit and tell me of it?"

The president seemed more boy than man just then, his eyes sparkling, his broad face pink. He moved to sit in a wing-back chair near the huge hearth over which hung the head of a majestic elk. Mel sat opposite him and took him through the 1500 meter race meter by meter. Then he did something that amazed me to the bone. He reached into his pocket and took out a Moroccan leather pouch, which he handed to President Roosevelt.

The President hesitated, then opened the pouch. An Olympic gold medal gleamed in the firelight.

"This is my prize for winning the event," Mel said. "I would be honored if you would keep it."

"But son," Roosevelt exclaimed, his eyes wide behind his spectacles, "this is–"

"I have two others, sir. I will not miss this one."

Teddy Roosevelt turned the medal in his hand, his eyes going from it to Mel. Mel grinned. The president of the United States grinned back.

"Like a schoolboy," Mel said after.

"This," the president said, in tones of awe, "will be one of my most treasured President Teddy Roosevelt possessions." He did not hand the medal off to one of his hovering aides, either. Instead, he put it in the pocket of his dinner jacket. I saw him patting that pocket throughout the evening.

As he had so many years ago, President Roosevelt ended the night with words that touched my heart. "Remember," he said, "that you're heroes for ten days, but when that time is up, drop the hero and go to work."

32

"A Life Well-Lived"

Wednesday, December 2, 1908

The past few months of life repeated in my dreams through flashes of light—the return home from Europe, a sweet kiss from Mary Agnes, the jovial faces of my parents as they met me at the railroad station, the letters from William and Clinton offering congratulations, and the special supper party given by Hattie and James. In between these remembered events I floated in glory of having won Olympic gold and a general warmth of festive celebration, making it difficult to separate it all from the reality of the here and now.

Now every time I opened my eyes I was caught in the sweetly hopeful gaze of Mary Agnes, her face suffused with love. We would touch in my brief periods of consciousness, which faded too swiftly to darkness. In those moments, we would just stare at each other, offering few if any words — for I had little breath with which to speak. We communicated in spite of that. It's in these times that hearts speak when words fall short of delivery.

Mary's tenderness would be supplemented by the touch of a cool cloth against my forehead, as Mama did her best to calm the fever that was wreaking havoc in my body, keeping me bedridden in my boyhood room, weak as a child.

Daddy stood by the foot of my bed, seemingly nailed to that same spot, while worry grew on him like moss. No father ever wants to see his child with one foot in the grave. He smiled, but I could see the anguish in his eyes. Hattie stood beside Daddy often, her normally smiling face filled with concern. Every time I opened my eyes, she would bow her head in silent prayer. Perhaps I should have had that lingering cough looked at immediately upon my return from Europe. Surely that would have been rational, but as I followed the words of Teddy Roosevelt once again, I chose to "go to work." For me this meant pouring myself into my veterinary practice, attending Boule meetings, and planning a wedding with Mary Agnes.

Certainly, a man of twenty-six can continue the business of life without succumbing to a summer cold, and so I had pressed on, living my life and refusing to be weakened by a hacking cough that grew worse with each passing week.

That sounded funny now, as I lay here with a dull pain in my chest, wishing I could turn back the hands of time and call upon Doc Foxworthy for healing. For it did seem that my condition, which had come upon me dramatically at the end of our sea voyage, was taking a turn for the worse. My eyes began to flutter, opening and closing, again and again. Suddenly, and for a time, I was standing on the dirt of Franklin Field as a familiar figure walked toward me out of a bright spring day.

I could not make out his face at first glance, but I was

able to see one hand in the air, waving to me in welcome. This man had appeared to me in dreams several times in the past few weeks, I realized, walking in my direction through a cloud that hung so low it seemed to be resting upon the ground.

As always I smiled, for I knew the man well, but I seemed unable to move my hands from my sides to return his wave. That was fine—I wanted to hold off his approach a bit, for I had come to understand in the past few days that seeing his face, welcoming him, would change my life, and I was not quite ready for that just yet. So I shook my head from side to side, telling him to wait for me a bit longer.

As always, I woke to find my beautiful mother resting on the bed next to mine. I cleared my throat to gain her attention. Mama gave one sweet smile in her slumber, as if she could hear me calling her name in my mind. Then she opened her eyes to me.

"My dream…" My voice was airless, fragile. It sounded so foreign to me.

Mama rose up and pulled her robe tight, rushing to my side. She placed her cool hand gently on my face and a tear escaped my eye. Mama nodded and a matching tear flowed down her cheek. She leaned down and kissed me.

"Hold on, John," she whispered.

I swallowed hard and blinked to answer. Mama bit her lip and walked out of the room, returning quickly with three sleepy and worried others. Daddy looked at me and paled to ash. Mary Agnes rushed to my side and dropped to her knees by my bed. Her hands gripped mine as if she might never let go.

A Novel by Craig T. Williams

Never let go.

Hattie clasped her hands in front of her chest, closed her eyes, and bowed her head.

Mama nodded at me to continue my words. I made attempts to clear my throat again, but could only muster the words "My dream…"

They each finished my sentence in their own way.

Mama smiled. "Yes, son, you *are* the dream."

"A champion!" Daddy declared.

"A fine doctor and a great man!" Mary Agnes cried.

"A man of honor," Hattie murmured.

It was not what I meant, but I appreciated their kind words and gave a weak smile to them all. My eyes began to feel heavy again, and the drowsiness in my body pulled me back into the dream.

I closed my eyes and was instantly back on the turf of Franklin Field, standing amid trailing clouds. I could make out the shadow of the man making his way toward me, one hand raised in greeting. I smiled and raised my hand cautiously in reply.

Within a second he was in front of me, and I smiled. Not in surprise—for I had known him all along—but in amazement at the look upon his face. He had been sixty-three years of age when he passed, but now he stood before me with the appearance of a man half that age. I recognized those keen, knowing eyes, though, and that warm smile.

"You have done well, John." He sounded like a proud daddy.

"I did my best."

"You know it's time?" he asked simply, searching my eyes for understanding.

Tears blurred my sight and my lips were reluctant to form words. "Aren't I too young, Pomp?" I said at last.

"It is not the years of life that matter, John. It is the life lived in the years." He tilted his head in that way of his. "Were you loved?"

"Yes."

"And did you love?"

"Oh, yes."

"Then yours was a life well-lived."

A life well-lived.

I had nothing more to say, for Pomp's words had soothed my soul. I nodded in understanding, took his hand, and began the journey through the clouds.

Epilogue

Glory

I did not fall apart at the official announcement of John's death. I walked upright with all the strength of my body and did not lose myself as the arrangements for his funeral were made. I did not even succumb to despair when I stood on the steps with Mr. and Mrs. Taylor, Hattie, Clinton, and William to greet the many well-wishers who graced the Taylor home with prayers, food, and loving thoughts of John.

Tears did not break from my eyes when John's trainer Mike Murphy performed the eulogy and described him as the "nicest man I had ever had to train."

Warm tears finally made their way down my face at the sight of the many carriages that stood in line behind the hearse awaiting the journey to Eden Cemetery. Still I did not fall down and pound the earth with fists and questions. "Why him?" and "Why now?"

I even smiled a little when, on the carriage ride to the church, I thought of John and horses. He loved horses, and I cherished the thought of those powerful animals carrying him to glory.

Even when William rose to read the letter Harry Porter, the acting president of the 1908 American Olympic Team and the gold medalist in the high jump, wrote to Mr. and

Mrs. Taylor, I did not crumble. William was a great orator, and he recited Mr. Porter's words with a pride-filled voice.

"It is far more as the man, than as an athlete, that John Taylor made his mark. Quite unostentatious, genial, kindly, the fleet-footed, far-famed Penn athlete was beloved wherever known… As a beacon light of his race, his example of achievement in athletics, scholarship, and manhood will never fade, if indeed it is not destined to form with that of Booker T. Washington."

Everyone in attendance smiled and nodded in agreement about the impact of John's life. Still, I managed to remain in the pew without falling apart.

Through it all I kept my composure and remembered my fiancé in a manner that would have made him proud. It was only when I was alone and sat on the edge of my bed with his scrapbook in my hands that I wavered. His parents had given me the book as a gift, and I had undertaken to read some of the articles in it. But the words blurred and became meaningless as tears obscured my eyes.

I rocked back and forth a bit to soothe myself and opened the journal to the last page. My heart jumped. Someone, probably Hattie, had taken the time to insert the last articles on John's life. I read the headline of the *New York Times* first.

NEGRO RUNNER DEAD:
John B. Taylor, Quarter-Miler, Victim of
Typhoid Pneumonia

A Novel by Craig T. Williams

The article described John as "the world's greatest negro runner" and went on to share the details of his service with the world: "Several thousand persons viewed the remains and, after the services at the house in which four clergymen, from as far away as Boston, officiated, fifty carriages followed the hearse to Eden Cemetery some four miles away. It was one of the greatest tributes ever paid a colored man in this city."

"Oh, John," I whispered as if he were in the room with me.

Grief suddenly seemed to have trapped itself in my body, and now it was seeking a way out. I breathed deeply and turned the pages, skimming over all the headlines.

"Red and Blue Athlete Runs His Last Race. John Baxter Taylor, the Former Colored Champion Quarter-Mile Runner of the Pennsylvania Track Team, Dies After Severe Attack of Illness." —*Philadelphia Inquirer*

"We can pay him no higher tribute—John Baxter Taylor: Pennsylvania man, athlete, and gentleman." — *Daily Pennsylvanian,* University of Pennsylvania

TAYLOR, CHAMPION SPRINTER, IS DEAD
STUDENTS MOURN COMRADE
GREAT RUNNER, TAYLOR DEAD

"We are proud of and can boast of having one of the greatest athletes the world has ever known." — (Class of 1908) University of Pennsylvania Veterinary School Yearbook

The Olympian: An American Triumph

Feeling overwhelmed and queasy, I turned the pages back, wanting to focus on his life instead of his death. That was when I found my page, titled simply: "Mary Agnes."

Here were pictures in grainy shades of gray, a copy of the poem he had given me as my first Christmas gift, a ticket stub from the Philadelphia Zoo.

The final item nearly broke my heart in two. It was the carefully written draft of his marriage vows, and I traced his handwriting with my fingertips and read the words John had written from his soul—words he had meant to say to me: "Even if I had no more nights and days to spend in your presence, I would always have the richest, deepest, and most profound love for you, which time and distance could never diminish."

It was then that I lost myself and fell to the floor, sobbing hysterically and clutching the scrapbook for dear life. My body convulsed and I cried until I had no tears left to give. I cried until my voice was hoarse and my mind had nowhere to go except back to the reality of my room.

When the storm had passed, leaving me weak and battered, I exhaled deeply and got to my feet, holding the scrapbook tightly to my breast. I went to the window and gazed up at the clouds where the winter sun struggled to break through, prying persistently at the wall of gray.

His life had affected mine greatly, not just as a memory or a regret or a dream that never was, but as an athlete, a champion, a man. The love of my life was the first black man to win gold at the Olympics and one of the first Americans to win an Olympic gold medal representing the United

States. He had become not only my personal champion, but a hero to our entire country.

As the sun burst through the clouds and streamed glory onto the earth, I smiled. I knew then that glory does not die. It simply transforms and is passed on to the next person willing to carry the torch in their heart.

Afterword from the Author

On December 26, 1908, just twenty-four days after the death of John Baxter Taylor, professional boxer Jack Johnson went on to become the first Negro heavyweight champion of the world.

Johnson held the title for six-and-a-half years. During his reign and for many years afterward he was the most famous African American on earth. A self-defined man who lived the essence of passion out loud and uncensored, Johnson was accused of being everything from a "dark menace" to one who posed a danger to the "natural order of things."

What he was able to demonstrate more than one hundred years ago remains a source of pure inspiration, even to those of this generation. This is a brief glimpse down the road to glory taken by one of greatest athletes who ever lived.

★★★★

Johnson was born into poverty in Galveston, Texas. His father was a school janitor and his mother, a laundress. As a youth, he was filled with many dreams and focused on life beyond the trials and tribulations of everyday living. He desperately wanted a way out of the plight of the common black man, a life riddled with hardship and struggle. With only five years of formal education, he took various odd jobs as a teenager, from carrying baggage for the local hotel to sweeping the neighborhood barbershop, but Johnson knew deep within his soul that ordinary living would never suit him. He was grander than the world into which he had been born. There was something burning within him, begging to live life full-throttle.

Growing up, Johnson was strong and fast and, on numerous occasions, engaged opponents outside the ring in battles royal. By the time he was eighteen, Johnson was sparring with veteran fighters and acquiring valuable skills. Within a few years, he emerged into the underground world of boxing, and took to the road in search of fighting contests.

He was best known for his particular boxing style, which was smooth and distinctive. Though he made the sport of boxing appear effortless during his fights, Johnson was precise and deliberate with his strategy. Oftentimes, the matches appeared more mental than physical, as he took a less aggressive approach and deliberately lay back—awaiting his opponents' critical mistakes, which ultimately ended up costing them the fight. When they faltered, he would pummel them.

Critical voices of the times suggested that Johnson exacted punishment from his white opponents and delivered much harsher beatings to them, as opposed to his black opponents— whom, it was suggested, he "took it easy on."

Johnson recalled his early fighting days as "rather difficult" as he traveled through Jim Crow's white America. And though boxing was one of the three biggest sports in the world, next to baseball and horse racing, it was still illegal in many states. However, despite the hardships, Johnson was earning between five and fifteen dollars per night, which translated into more income than his own father earned in an entire week.

Eventually, Johnson set his sights on becoming the heavyweight champion of the world, arguably a greater distinction in the public eye than being President of the United States. Despite all the title represented, however, there was no place in society for it to be captured by a black man.

Heavyweight Champion John Sullivan staunchly opposed the idea of a black man holding such an esteemed position and stated publicly that he would never fight a Negro for the prize. Yet, this was not a deterrent to Johnson, who was fixated on capturing the jewel. In pursuit of bigger purses and greater recognition, Johnson traveled from Memphis to Chicago, to Boston, and then to California. But though he was allowed to fight white boxers, he was not allowed to compete for the heavyweight championship. He persevered and continued to defeat white and black opponents alike, earning upward of a thousand dollars a night and winning purses all over the country.

In the spring of 1902, Johnson's first big break came at the age of twenty-four in Los Angeles, when he defeated Jack Jeffries, the younger brother of Jim Jeffries, who at the time held the world heavyweight championship title. Before the fight, Jack Jeffries was depicted by the *Los Angeles Times* as a "Greek god," whereas Johnson was painted as a "good- natured, black animal … a long, lean, bull-headed, flat-chested coon." Though the *L.A. Times* went on to predict a win for the "white man," the outcome was far from what was prophesied by sportswriters of the day. A headline for the *Times* captures the fight in a single line:

A Novel by Craig T. Williams

Johnson Knocks Out Jack Jeffries! The Colored Gentleman Put the Champion's Brother to Sleep in the Fifth!

After the knockout, Johnson graciously carried Jack Jeffries back to his corner, where he leaned over and said to the heavyweight champion of the world, "I can whip you, too!"

Although Jack Johnson had rightfully and honestly defeated the younger brother of the heavyweight champion of the world, Jim Jeffries refused to fight Johnson for the coveted title and offered this statement to the press: "When there are no more white men left to fight, I will quit the business." He went on to add, "The title will never go to a black man if I can help it."

In February 1903, Johnson defeated Denver boxer Ed Martin to garner the unofficial Negro Championship in Los Angeles. He then went on to defeat the top three African American boxers with his vision firmly focused on the world title.

After his October 1903 victory over Sam McVey of Oxnard, California, Johnson was placed in the position to legitimately compete for the heavyweight championship of the world. However, Jim Jeffries continued to reign as champion and stood by his decision to deny Johnson the opportunity for a match.

In October 1904, Jack Johnson ran into Jim Jeffries at a salon, whereupon Jeffries set $2,500 cash on the table and invited Johnson to a "private bout in the cellar." Jeffries said that if Johnson could walk back up the steps after the fight, he could keep the money. Highly offended, Johnson declared,

The Olympian: An American Triumph

"I ain't no cellar fighter!"

In September 1905, the *Police Gazette*, one of the premiere sports newspapers at that time, called upon Jim Jeffries to give Johnson a shot at the title. But again, Jeffries refused. Later that year, Jeffries retired undefeated, and professional boxer Marvin Hart succeeded him in claiming the title, which Hart held for two years before losing it to Canadian boxer Tommy Burns.

Through all of this, Johnson had not relinquished the dream and lay in wait for an opportunity to seize the championship. Interestingly, Burns took the same position as all other white boxers who came before him when it came to competing with blacks: *no deal*. Burns, too, refused to fight Jack Johnson for the title.

By this time, Johnson was obsessed with the idea of fighting for the championship. The dream of holding the esteemed title consumed him. Referred to by the media as "The Dinge," "The Big Smoke," and "The Ethiopian," Johnson was as celebrated as he was despised, and enjoyed wealth beyond what most Americans, black or white, would ever know in their lifetimes. Adorned with gold-plated teeth, finely tailored suits, diamond stickpins, furs, and automobiles, he was catapulted into an otherworldly stratosphere and lived a life unimaginable to most people of any era. Yet Johnson refused to back down on his relentless pursuit of a shot at the championship.

In 1906, Johnson took to the road again—this time, dogging the tracks of the new heavyweight champion, Tommy Burns. In his own words, "I chased Tommy Burns around the world in order to get him into the ring with me. It was a two-year job. I took on every potential contender between myself and the champion. I virtually had to mow my way to Burns, but he always made excuses."

Jack Johnson challenged Burns at every turn of the road, following him to San Francisco, New York, and as far as Paris, mocking him every step of the way. Burns stubbornly held to the position that "all coons are yellow" and continued to meet only white opponents. However, by the end of the second year of this game of cat and mouse, Johnson had begun to win public support, and everyone from the common man to royalty began to call for a match between the two boxers. King Edward VII, who was a devoted boxing fan, suggested that Canadian champion Tommy Burns was little more than a "bluffer."

With public pressure rising from every corner of the globe, Burns at last surrendered his position and said he would fight Jack Johnson for a purse of $30,000, which was so outlandish Burns thought no one would ever meet it. To his shock and dismay, the purse was met by Australian promoter Hugh "Huge Deal" McIntosh. Burns was paid $30,000 and Johnson was offered $5,000. What happened next was an unprecedented event in human history.

★★★★

December 26, 1908

On this historic day more than 20,000 white men from all over the world packed Sydney Stadium in Rushcutters Bay in

Australia. As Jack Johnson waited to be introduced, racial slurs and jeers rang throughout the stadium.

"The nigger's gonna lose!"

"All coons are yellow!"

"The white man is gonna kill the coon!"

The hostile air was only a reflection of what had already been set in motion just weeks before the big day.

"I'll beat this nigger," Burns had promised, "or my name isn't Tommy Burns!"

Johnson weighed in on the final verdict, offering this perspective from where he stood. "How does Burns want it? Fast and willing?" Johnson struck a pose. "I'm his man in that case. Or does he want it flatfooted? If he does, I'm his man again."

On the day of the fight, Johnson stood poised and graceful in the ring, flashing his signature gold-toothed smile. He bowed gracefully to the crowd in all directions, and even blew the spectators kisses. This may have only served to heighten tensions, as some interpreted such behavior as a mockery, but those who were familiar with Jack Johnson's style knew this was simply his way.

Still, with race relations at a critical point and given the high stakes, local authorities had been called and were on standby to come in and break up the fight just in case things got out of hand. With Hugh "Huge Deal" McIntosh serving as the referee, the bout was scheduled for twenty rounds with a designated three minutes for each round.

The first bell rang at 11:07 am.

Johnson charged boldly toward Burns. "Here I am, Tommy! Here I am!" he taunted.

A Novel by Craig T. Williams

"Come on, you yellow cur!" shouted Burns.

"Who told you I was yellow?"

"Come on and fight, nigger!" shouted Burns, rage painting his face. "Fight like a white man!"

Within seconds, Johnson, who had a five-and-a-half-inch height advantage over Burns, landed a deafening blow to Burns's unprotected jaw, and down he went with a thunderous collapse.

One.

Two.

Three.

Four.

Five.

Six.

Seven.

Eight ... and Burns rose to his feet.

Again Johnson knocked him down, and again he rose.

But, hold on—this was only round one, and by now the air of the stadium was thick with the brooding haze of racial tension. As subsequent rounds proceeded, and Johnson continued to perform, the fight seemed to take on the quality of a theatrical production.

"Hit here!" suggested Johnson, pointing to his sides. "Hit here!"

"Die, nigger!" shouted the fellows from Burns's corner. "Die!"

"Try hitting here, Tommy," teased Johnson, pointing to his stomach.

The mockery enraged the champion, but try as he

might, Burns could not land a solid blow on his adversary.

Johnson laughed.

Smiled.

And played with the crowd.

"Where did you learn to fight, Tommy?" he taunted with a grin, emasculating the Canadian boxer. "Did your mother teach you to how to punch?"

Swinging wildly, Burns could connect only with air. And when he swung, Johnson stepped in to exact a price.

It appeared to all who were witness to this bout that much more than a boxing match was taking place. In essence, this was the great "weigh-in"—but a weighing of human spirit and human worth, not merely of strength, brawn, or quickness.

Exhausted, Burns persevered—only to be met by glancing upper-cuts and slashing left and right hooks from Johnson. Several more times Burns would lose his balance, only to be supported by Johnson's embrace—a bizarre gesture in the world of boxing. Johnson seemed happy to prolong the fight—to let it play out till its completion—no matter the cost.

"Stop the fight!" spectators yelled from the crowd, once they came to realize that this was not a prizefight but a hopeless slaughter.

Johnson, though, was getting bored. Apparently losing interest in what was occurring in the ring, he turned his attention to bantering with those outside the ring.

He smiled.

Talked to spectators.

Taunted the fellows in Burns's corner.

Then smiled some more.

From the moment the first bell rang all the way up to the fourteenth and final round, the fight had been less a competition and more a descent into humiliation and embarrassment for the champion, Tommy Burns, and his fans. At the beginning of the fourteenth round, Johnson walked into the ring with a look of satisfaction. Never ceasing to smile, he seemed to anticipate his own victory. For Jack Johnson, the battle was already over and the war won.

Then came the most devastating series of blows that Johnson had yet to land during this fight, maybe his entire career—and all Burns could do was back up and try to protect what was left of his dignity. The crowd lost all composure as devastated spectators gave in to frenzy and police burst into the ring and stopped the fight, sparing Burns the further humiliation of an inevitable knockout.

"Stop the cameras from rolling!" police demanded.

"Stop the cameras!"

"Turn off the cameras!"

"Turn off *all* cameras!"

Moments later, Jack Johnson was announced the new heavyweight champion of the world.

Fiction writer Jack London, a boxing enthusiast wrote: "what ... [won] on Saturday was bigness, coolness, quickness, cleverness, and vast physical superiority... Because a white man wishes a white man to win, this should not prevent him from giving absolute credit to the best man, even when that best man was black. All hail to Johnson." Johnson was "superb. He was impregnable . . . as inaccessible as Mont Blanc."

The historical significance of this event is best summarized in the immortal words of Johnson himself: "I obtained my life's ambition and for the *second* time in history, a black man held one of the greatest honors in the field of sports and athletics."

★★★★

An immediate cry went up for the former champion, Jim Jeffries, to return to the ring to dethrone Jack Johnson, whose legitimacy was questioned, not only because he was black, but because he had defeated a man who had inherited rather than won the title. Tommy Burns was indeed not the "the man who beat the man," as Jeffries had retired undefeated. Jim Jeffries remained the one true champion, fans argued, therefore he must accept the responsibility to restore order.

"Jim Jeffries must now emerge from his Alfalfa farm and remove that golden smile from Jack Johnson's face ... Jeff, it's up to you. The White Man must be rescued."

— Jack London

The matter would be settled in Reno, Nevada on July 4, 1910.